FULL CIRCLE

To Gene

With appreciation

[illegible]

10 November 2022

FULL CIRCLE

DOBIE MCARTHUR

Full Circle

ISBN: 978-1-7111-6286-7

This book is dedicated to my family, without whom I would not be able to make it from day to day.

Special thanks to Tom Allen, whose persistent and gentle questions about the novel kept me moving forward, and whose willingness to serve as my sounding board kept me on track. It's fair to say that without him Full Circle *would have remained an unfinished project. I would also like to thank Danna Mathias for cover and interior design, and Constance Renfrow for copy-editing.*

THE CIVIL WAR SERIES

FULL CIRCLE

Full Circle is the first novel in the Civil War series, which explores the ongoing struggle to reshape the American value system. Set in the mid-2020s, *Full Circle* tells the story of Guy Pearle, the CEO of Innovative Applications Unlimited, a small East Coast company on the verge of an IPO. He is hounded by Lucinda Hornbuckle, the ambitious editor of Social Tech, who believes that publicly traded companies have an inherent responsibility to lead on social justice and climate change. In Lucinda's view, Guy is not sufficiently "woke" on either issue and must change his views or suffer the consequences.

Threatened by frivolous lawsuits from Lucinda, and battered by personal tragedy, Guy travels to Tarfaya, Morocco, home of the Africa Renaissance Project, where his newest green technology projects are being tested. When Lucinda nearly succeeds in taking control of IAU, Guy vows to return to the United States, but first must survive a deadly attack on the ARP compound.

Upon his return to the United States, Guy is determined to fight Lucinda and her powerful media allies for the right to run his company as he sees best. Along the way, he learns how to play the game Lucinda's way, and teaches her that actions do, in fact, have consequences.

OTHER NOVELS IN THE CIVIL WAR SERIES

Questionable Intent

Total Victory

American Insurrection

New Leadership

Old Ways

Unquestioned Authority

Normalcy Returns

CONTENTS

PROLOGUE

DO YOU EVER FEEL LIKE WE'RE ON THE VERGE OF a new Civil War? America's value system is no longer a unifying force. On many topics where Americans could once find common ground, partisans now hammer each other in pitched social media battles. While these fights might be worthwhile if they shaped a new consensus on the proper source of moral authority, more often than not, they are meant to punish, shame, and embarrass the other side for being "wrong"—whatever that might mean. Welcome to the new America, the land of morality by meme.

It may be tempting to ignore the ongoing struggle, to believe it won't have any meaningful impact on your own daily life. But think of the public figure whose views you find most objectionable. Now, imagine a scenario where that person has the authority to set the rules for all society—to define what is and what isn't socially and morally acceptable—for the next three to five generations. Still want to stay on the sidelines?

PART I - BATTLE

CHAPTER 1

GUY PEARLE STARED AT THE PRESERVATION LETter on his desk and thought, *Jesus! Is that bastard really going to sue me now? Why did he wait so long? It's been six months since we let him go, and he decided he's got an issue* now, *right before the IPO?*

He read the letter again. Most of it was boilerplate legal jargon about preserving company files and records, but one section practically jumped off the page:

> *. . . defrauding Mr. David Gordon of his property rights related to the Phishhook product by failing to disclose that the product was under development at the time Mr. Gordon's shares in Innovative Applications Unlimited were purchased back from him, and had been developed with funds provided by Mr. Gordon for the development and marketing of the Firebomb product.*

Guy leaned back in his brown leather executive chair, pushed away from his dark mahogany desk, and turned toward the large bank of floor-to-ceiling windows overlooking Washington

National Airport. His seventh-floor office in Crystal City was positioned so he could see most of the runway.

There was something refreshing and invigorating about watching the planes take off and land. When he was really stuck on defining a problem set or got trapped in an analytical do-loop, Guy found that watching the planes touch down on the runway helped to reboot the creative process. The landing sequence was reassuringly inexorable: emptiness, black dot, dot with wings, full-blown aircraft delivering passengers.

A glint of morning sunlight danced across the orange-and-blue body of a jetliner taking off, and for a moment, Guy wished he could be on that plane. He didn't know where it was headed, but wherever it was would surely be more pleasant than his office was about to be in just a few minutes, once Heather Alston from *Social Tech* magazine showed up for their interview.

They had met a couple of times on the Washington cocktail scene. Heather was young, in her early twenties, and so beautiful that it made him uncomfortable just to be in the same room with her. It wasn't a sexual thing. Guy and his wife, Janet, were happily married—and had been for more than twenty years—and if ever there had been a time when Guy could have been tempted to stray, it was long in the past. He chuckled to think that if he and Janet had ever had children, their oldest would be about Heather's age.

No, what made him uncomfortable around Heather was that her physical beauty was so overwhelming that he had a hard time seeing past it. He found it distracting, and that was embarrassing. As the founder and longtime CEO of IAU—Innovative Applications

Unlimited—he always tried to ensure that every one of his employees understood that their potential in the company was unlimited and based on their contributions and actions rather than on their physical appearance. That was why he'd put the word "Unlimited" in the company's name. He truly believed that everyone had unlimited potential, and he tried to live by that philosophy.

Except when it came to Heather Alston. Despite his best efforts, he knew that when she walked into the room, he would see her not as the strong, capable, competent young reporter he knew her to be, but as a blond bombshell whose face belonged on a fashion magazine cover. And he was mortified by that fact. Despite everything he believed and everything he'd accomplished; in her presence he was rendered a powerless schoolboy.

The intercom buzzed, and his receptionist announced that Ms. Alston had arrived for their scheduled nine o'clock interview. He checked his watch. She was ten minutes early. He considered asking his receptionist to show her in at 9 a.m. sharp, knowing he could put the extra ten minutes to good use reviewing the preservation letter. Instead, he simply said, "Please show her in."

Guy headed to his office's corner sitting area just as Heather entered. She stepped across the threshold onto the blue plush carpet, and glanced around, noting the bookshelves filled with framed articles about IAU, trinkets from Guy's worldwide travels, and other assorted memorabilia. He motioned for her to take a seat on the black leather couch and moved toward a chair with his back to the windows. He offered her tea, water, or coffee and, when she declined, he dismissed the receptionist, who closed the door behind her.

Guy was alone, for the first time ever, with Heather Alston, and he was petrified that he would do or say something that would betray his innermost thoughts. As he waited for her to sit, he pressed his hands nervously against the sides of his navy-blue suit coat, then took his seat and started to recline. Realizing this would seem too informal, he leaned forward again. He picked up a writing pad from the small table to his right and placed it atop his knees.

While he waited for her to begin, a dozen possible lines of inquiry flashed through his mind. *Social Tech* was the region's most closely followed online tech magazine, and this was supposed to be a puff piece. When Heather had called to set up the interview, she said the article was going to be about how IAU had risen so quickly to the top ranks of the rapidly growing DC tech sector. IAU was in the final stages of preparing its SEC filing to go public and would soon enter a "quiet period" in which the company was not allowed to make certain kinds of media or press statements.

The piece in *Social Tech* was likely to be the last publicity they got before the quiet period. In theory, at least, it should be a layup, but Guy was never one to take things for granted. His natural inclination was to prepare for the worst and enjoy being pleasantly surprised when things turned out better than expected.

He wasn't even sure if she was aware of the preservation letter, or that it represented a potential threat to the IPO. As it was, he had only learned of it minutes before, so there was no legitimate reason she would know about it. If she asked, he didn't quite know what he would tell her, but whatever it would be, he couldn't very well tell her what he really thought: If Megger, Mayberry, and Cassidy—David's law firm—had done even the slightest amount of due diligence, they would know that David's claims were totally bogus. If they filed a lawsuit and made the same claims about IAU publicly, it would undoubtedly have an adverse effect on the IPO, and IAU would have a counter claim for libel. Surely someone at Megger, Mayberry, and Cassidy was taking the necessary steps to avoid the disaster that would befall them if they filed such a frivolous lawsuit.

But Heather's first question wasn't about David Gordon, or the possible lawsuit, or any of the ten other things Guy most feared. She pulled out a small digital recording device and set it on the table, glancing at Guy for permission to record the interview. When he nodded, she asked, "So, have you picked your ticker symbol yet?"

Although it was an easy question to get the interview off to a smooth start, Guy instinctively straightened his dark red tie. "We're working on it. We're listing on the New York Stock Exchange rather than the NASDAQ, and someone else already has 'IAU,' which would have been the obvious choice. So, we've decided to hold a company-wide contest to see who can come up with the best three- or four-letter symbol. We're a company that thrives on our employees' ideas, so when we have a chance to create something new, we want to take advantage of the good idea factory we already have."

Heather barely noticed Guy's nervous gesture or the stilted cadence of his response. That was just how Washington worked: People came to work in suits and ties and behaved more formally than they would elsewhere. She had no inkling of his discomfort, in large part because he was reacting to her in the same way most men did. He, like at least half the men she interviewed, seemed fascinated by her widow's peak and constantly stared at it, regardless of whether they were speaking, or she was.

She continued, "Okay, let's follow that thread a little bit. I've done some homework on IAU, and your claim to fame is that you 'operationalize ideas.' What do you mean by that?"

"The best answer I can give is by way of example. This doesn't come from me—it comes from my chief technology officer, Carl Underhill, who told this story in a strategic planning session. He said, and I'm paraphrasing here, 'I spent most of my life thinking that everything useful had already been invented. Then one time while on a business trip, I stayed in a hotel with a curved shower curtain. I can't tell you the number of times when I'd showered in a hotel and just put up with the tiny space, crowded in by the curtain. That problem had existed for years, right before my eyes. More importantly, the opportunity to fix that problem had also existed, but I never saw it. Seeing that curved shower curtain opened my eyes to the idea that, even today, there are still areas where innovation is needed.'

"When Carl made that observation, I knew he was right, and it's been the driving idea behind the company ever since. At the time, I was jaded by all the gimmicks in the crappy little catalogs you find in airplane seatback pockets, and in the 'ten best gadgets' emails. The same was true for phone apps. There were literally hundreds of apps designed to do just about anything you can imagine, but it was clear that the motivation behind these gimmicks was to make enough sales to make a buck before the terrible reviews rolled in. I realized that the value proposition we wanted to have as a company was to make life better for our customers, not just to make a buck off them. When I put those glasses on, the world looked different. It helped me pick a new problem set. It also helped me find a different type of solution. We were able to find things that the big, billion-dollar companies overlooked. Phishhook was one of those ideas."

Heather stopped writing and looked up. "Before we get into Phishhook, will you please tell me a little about Firebomb? That was your first big success, wasn't it?"

"Yes, that's right."

"Please tell me a bit about that, at the ten-thousand-foot level. We're a tech magazine, but the features I do are more about the people and why they do what they do. Lucinda Hornbuckle, our founder and managing editor, whom I believe you know, does most of the really technical stories."

And there it was. Suddenly Guy knew where and how Heather had gotten most of her information about IAU. Yes, Guy knew Lucinda. They had both attended the University of Maryland some twenty-odd years ago, doing undergraduate degrees in marketing before moving into the MBA program.

At first, they knew each other from class. Then they became study partners and hung out at the coffee shop near campus. Eventually, they became romantically involved, but that ended badly. In Guy's mind, they had simply grown apart and quit seeing each other right about the time that Guy met Janet. After all, the Washington DC tech sector was small back then, and when

Guy and Lucinda inevitably bumped into each other now and then, they always grabbed a coffee to catch up. Guy was unsure whether Lucinda had the same impression about their parting, and he wondered how much non-public information Lucinda had shared with Heather about him.

"Right. So, I'll give you the elevator pitch for Firebomb. In the early days of the Internet, one of the easiest ways to attack a website was called a Distributed Denial of Service Attack, or DDOS. The way it worked was that the attacker would send a massive number of requests to the targeted website. Even in the early days, most websites had the ability to respond to multiple requests, but in a DDOS, the number of requests sent is massive and the website isn't able to respond. The net effect is that the website is unavailable to users because it gets overwhelmed with requests from the attacker."

"So how did Firebomb solve that problem?"

"As the name implies, our solution was to fight fire with fire. In essence, we threw a firebomb back at the attackers. We identified the IP addresses of the attacking computers and sent a massive number of requests back their way. That stops the attack."

"But doesn't that just slow down the Internet for everyone, with massive numbers of fake page-view requests going back and forth?"

"For someone who claims not to be very tech-savvy, you seem to have this pretty well figured out. You're exactly right. And that's why we needed venture capital to launch the Firebomb platform. If we had located all of our counterattack servers in one location, or even a few locations, all the counter-traffic would have had to pass through the key gateways, and that would have slowed down traffic for everyone. To make our approach practical, we had to distribute the counterattacking servers all across the world so we could generate the counterattacks from as close as possible to the original attacks. And that was no easy task. As often as not, the attacking computers were distributed all around the world, and quite often they were simply innocent computers that had been infected with a virus that allowed the attackers to take them over and use them for DDOS attacks. Using that approach, the attackers didn't even have to buy a lot of hardware. For us to counter that model, we needed a lot of infrastructure, and a lot of software development to create the application that managed all of the traffic. It also took a lot of work with various regulatory bodies to get permission to do the counterattacks, because what we were doing was essentially the same thing as what the bad guys were up to, just retaliatory."

"And that was extremely profitable?"

"No, not really. And it wasn't even a particularly elegant solution. It was eventually eclipsed by better approaches. But Firebomb put us on the map as the kind of small and nimble company that could take on hard problems and find innovative solutions—and not only could we find them, we could make them operational at a massive scale. We found it a lot easier, after the release of Firebomb, to get VC funding."

"So, as an Internet entrepreneur, were you disappointed that your first big success had to be one that prevented bad people from ruining the Internet for everyone else?"

"The Internet is clearly a benefit to society, but it has its negative aspects. The challenge of our time is to find a way to maintain the benefits while reducing the harm. Our generation will be judged on how well we do this."

"That's a pretty broad statement. Care to sharpen the focus a bit?"

"One of the greatest things about the Internet is that it allows everyone to have a voice and to share their views on the big issues in a way that has never been remotely possible before. It gives everyone a soapbox. That's really a very important thing, and, really, it has never been possible before. But there are a couple of interesting side effects. First, the power of the establishment media is substantially reduced in relative terms. The Internet gives everyone the opportunity to generate the same level of following for their ideas as the establishment media. That's a huge change, and it's generating debate about the importance of the media in setting the tone and the agenda for public discourse.

"The debate about the role of the press is not new. It's been going on for a long time. The creation of the Internet just gives that debate a new sense of urgency. For much of the past century, the intelligentsia insisted that publishers—who were seen as a part of the rich, white establishment—had a duty to promote ideas that would 'benefit' society. What was interesting is that those ideas were almost always liberal or progressive. So, many of the proposed reforms that we keep seeing—such as those championed by the Hutchins Commission on Freedom of the Press in the 1940s—are designed to move society in one direction, toward liberalism. Now that everyone can have their say, it is interesting that not all of the voices that are getting the most attention are the progressive ones, and there's a lot of discussion surrounding the need to find ways to control what ideas are allowed to be expressed.

"That leads to the second interesting effect of the Internet, which is that it gives a great deal of power to those who control the platforms, especially all those things that are lumped together into what is collectively called 'social media.' The idea that the Internet is this great democratizing force that allows everyone to have a say is currently being attacked by those who insist some opinions are dangerous. We have always had a debate about the limits of free expression, but what we're seeing now is something entirely different."

Heather finished writing, and then looked up from her notepad. She said, "You sound as if you think tech companies shouldn't play a role in deciding what is or is not acceptable speech."

"Look, I've known Lucinda Hornbuckle for a long time. I know she was very successful in the first dot-com wave of the late nineties and that she was an early participant in the first wave of what we now call social media. She has been consistent from day one in her belief that technology companies have a responsibility to promote the discussion of important social issues and, more significantly, to shape that debate. I mean, that's the reason she established *Social Tech*. And she has done a phenomenal job. So much so that if a tech company wants to go public, it's a lot easier to do so with favorable reviews from *Social Tech* in general, and from Lucinda in particular. But this is an area where she and I disagree."

"So, what is your view on the role of tech companies, then?"

"I think there are some areas where we're all in agreement and have been for a long time. For example, everyone agrees that it isn't acceptable to yell 'Fire!' in a crowded theater, to advocate for the overthrow of the government, or to threaten violence against others. There are slander and libel laws, and tortious interference laws that prevent people from saying and writing things with wanton disregard for the truth. But what we're seeing today is an effort to curtail speech in ways that go well beyond established norms."

"For example?"

"There are several topics that come immediately to mind. The first is climate change, or 'global warming,' if you're as old as I am. The second is gender. Gay marriage. Abortion and immigration. These are all topics where it used to be acceptable to have differing views, but now there's a herd mentality that tries to squelch any views that aren't considered politically correct."

"So, if you don't think social media platforms have a responsibility to regulate content, where *do* you stand?"

"Let's be very clear here. I am not saying that the Internet or social media platforms should be completely unregulated. The First Amendment prohibits the government from restricting free speech. Social media platforms are not the government and are therefore not restricted. They can, to a large extent, make their own rules and regulate content however they want. If I don't like the restrictions, I can cancel my account at any time."

"Have you ever done that?"

"I don't use social media anymore. I think, for the most part, it's a total waste of time. In fact, I can tell you the exact instant I decided social media wasn't for me."

"When was that?"

"When I saw a post from my brother-in-law that said, 'Mmmmm! Pizza for dinner!' And he posted a picture of a piece of pizza. I knew right then that social media was not for me. Just about every experience I've had since then has reinforced my view that social media is not a productive force in our society."

"So, if you don't use it, why do you care what happens on it?"

"I don't, actually. As I said before, the companies can do what they want, and if the users don't like their data being used in ways they don't understand or approve of, or if they get upset when the platform takes down their post, all they have to do is delete their account."

"Then what is it about what's happening in the current social environment that you disagree with?"

"My concern is that tech companies that are not social media platforms are being pressured to police their employees in the same way that social media platforms police content. I just don't think that is right or fair. As an employer, I have a responsibility to hire people who can do the job. There are certain other types of due diligence I'm responsible for performing, like making sure they are who they say they are, but so long as they treat their colleagues with respect, I don't believe I have an obligation to be the thought police. The workplace is not the proper place to define and enforce new value systems."

Heather smiled and said, "Well, if that's the way you feel, you're right—you and Lucinda don't see eye to eye at all. But rest assured, that's not why I'm here, and it's not why Lucinda asked me to do this interview. Lucinda doesn't mix politics and business."

Heather closed her notepad, reached down, and switched off the digital recorder. As she gathered her things and prepared to leave, she glanced around the office, taking in the plush carpet, the wood-paneled walls, and the built-in bookshelves. Guy relaxed, knowing that the on-the-record portion of the interview was over, and she hadn't hit him with anything he couldn't handle.

Heather turned back to him and said, "Nice digs. Seems pretty fancy for Crystal City."

"Yes, we were a little shocked when we first saw the place. Most of the space in this area is overflow for federal agencies or occupied by government contractors. We just happened to be looking for office space at exactly the right time. We took over the lease from a tech start-up that went bankrupt. It would have cost more to return the office to its original condition, so they just left it."

"Oh, before I go, I just have a couple more questions, off the record, if you don't mind. Mostly about the mechanics of the IPO process. Is that all right?"

"Sure, I don't mind at all."

He spent the next half hour walking her through the process that IAU had used to reach the decision to go public, then described the steps they had already completed and what they still had left. She wasn't taking notes but followed along and occasionally nodded. When he finished, she stood up and made her way to the large display case next to the main door. "You've got some really interesting artifacts. Do you travel a lot?"

"A fair amount. Work takes me to some interesting places."

"Anything interesting coming up?"

"Still off the record?"

"Of course."

"Then, yes, I'm going to Morocco next month for COPS32, the United Nations Climate Change Conference of 2026. IAU has been participating in a technology-focused project in Africa for several years. The theme of this year's conference is improving renewable energy technology to reduce the effects of climate change and improve employment prospects for those who have been affected by climate change."

"Interesting, but why is that something you need to keep off the record?"

"The fact that I am going to Marrakesh isn't sensitive. The fact that IAU is planning to make a major push into green technology—which is why I am going to COPS32—would be considered a forward-looking statement for the purposes of our IPO. As you know, we have to be careful about making statements that could influence investors."

Heather said, "When you do get ready to make that public, I want the story, okay?"

"Sure, not a problem," Guy said, as he walked her toward the door. Just before she reached the threshold, Heather paused and turned directly toward him. "One last question. When you submit your filing to the SEC, are you required to report on all of the potential risks?"

"Like what?" Guy replied reflexively, before it dawned on him where she was going.

"Like lawsuits from former board members."

Guy was flummoxed. There was no way she should know about the letter he had received by courier not half an hour before she arrived. He couldn't have hesitated more than a couple of seconds, but clearly it was long enough.

"That's okay," she said, "I'm pretty sure I already know the answer." She turned and walked swiftly out the door.

Guy stepped out of his office, with half a thought to chase after her and demand to know what else she knew, but before he could catch up to her, she stepped into the elevator. As the door slid closed, she reached into her purse and pulled out her cell phone. She pressed a number and brought the phone to her ear.

Brandon Leather, IAU's lead software developer and technical program manager, stood in the opposite corner of the elevator and did his best to ignore Heather's conversation. He pulled out his own cell phone and thumbed through one of his social media accounts, but he couldn't help overhearing when she said, "Yes, he knows we know."

When the elevator reached the ground floor, Brandon allowed Heather to exit first into the Crystal City underground, and he followed her for a short time, until he reached his favorite coffee shop, where he grabbed a bran muffin for a late breakfast.

CHAPTER 2

AFTER AN HOUR AND A HALF COMMUTE THAT should have been only forty-five minutes, Guy arrived home in Annapolis just before 8 p.m. and parked his SUV in the garage of the red-brick colonial he and Janet shared. He rolled the garbage cans down to the curb for tomorrow's collection before entering through the laundry room.

Janet was waiting for him in the kitchen. "Well, that was a pretty stupid thing to say."

Her harsh tone was completely out of character, and Guy struggled not to react defensively. "I'm sorry. What?"

"I read the interview you did with *Social Tech*."

Guy was surprised it was already online. Heather must have had some of it already written even before they sat down. "What about it?"

"If you don't think your company should take positions on social issues, then why on earth would you do just that? And not only that, you did it in an interview with the most socially progressive online magazine out there, with millions of subscribers—the very people you need to buy your stock and products."

"I didn't take any positions on social issues. I haven't seen the article yet, but if it says that I took a position on a social issue, then it's a complete misquote and I'm going to demand a retraction."

"There are no misquotes. Based on the way the article reads, I'm guessing she quoted you verbatim. The problem is that what you said doesn't actually mean what you think it does. By not taking a position, you are very much taking a position. On certain issues, there is no middle ground: You're either woke or you're not."

Realizing she was coming across much harsher than intended, she softened her tone and shifted to more neutral ground. "If you don't think business leaders should be out front shaping public opinion on social issues, then who do you think should be? Certainly not politicians, I hope. They're useless, and they're the last people we should listen to on social or moral issues."

Guy placed his keys on the corner table and loosened his tie. He welcomed the change in her disposition, and particularly in her voice. She was herself now, calm and helpful. From the very first time he met her; it was the sound of her voice that attracted him most to her. And when he traveled on business, hearing her voice on the other end of the line made him miss her even more. He grabbed two wine glasses from the cabinet and turned to her. "Malbec or Shiraz?"

"Depends."

"Depends on what?"

"On whether you want to fight or make up," she said, playfully.

"Well, I don't want to fight, but I don't know what there is to make up for, so you decide."

"Let's do Shiraz."

Guy poured two glasses of their favorite Australian Shiraz. He held them side by side to make sure they were roughly equal, though the one he kept for himself held just a tad more than the one he offered Janet. *I might need this.*

"Why didn't you tell me who was going to do the interview?"

Guy pulled a barstool out from the kitchen counter and placed his suit jacket on the back of it, then sat down, still trying to figure out what Janet was really getting at. "Who? Heather? Why does it matter?"

Janet leaned across the counter, took a sip of wine, and said, "Guy, I *know* you. I could have helped you prepare for that interview so you wouldn't be caught off guard. Do you think it was a coincidence that Lucinda sent *her* to interview you? Lucinda set you up, and you didn't even see it coming."

"I don't think I was set up at all. I thought it was a pretty good interview. I mean, I haven't *seen* it, but nothing happened during the interview that I couldn't handle."

"You are so naïve. You automatically trust everyone. You think that's one of your better qualities, but it's not. The reason you trust everyone is because you never really get to know anyone. What you have isn't really trust, it's just distance. You keep everyone—friends, enemies, business partners—at a distance, and that distance allows you to take them at face value. You need to learn how to figure out who you can—and who you can't—trust. And to be able to do that, you're going to have to learn to let people in, to open yourself up to the people who care about you. Once you learn to do that, you'll see the difference between people like me and people like Lucinda. How you could have dated her and then married me is beyond belief. Lucinda and I are polar opposites. I don't know what you ever saw in her. She is not your friend. You think she is, but she isn't. She's an evil, manipulative bitch."

"I don't know. You two have at least one thing in common."

"What's that?"

"You're both very liberal."

"That may be, but that's where the similarities end. Just because you don't see her agenda or can't figure out what it is, that doesn't mean she doesn't have one. And with her, I have no doubt that whatever she's got in mind is not going to help you. Based on the contents of that article, the negatives are clearly going to outweigh any potential positives.

"She sent a Heather to interview you—knowing that would put you off your guard—and got you to go on record about some of the most divisive social issues of our time. By naming those issues, you've created a laundry list of places where you are out of step with the mainstream. You might as well have put up a billboard in front of your office that says, 'We make great stuff, but we're still in the fifties on gay marriage and climate change!' I know that's not what you meant, because I know that's not what you believe, but you allowed yourself to be maneuvered into taking irresponsible positions. When it comes to Lucinda Hornbuckle, you just have a blind spot. You think she is aboveboard. She's not. She's evil, and she is out to get you. You need to wake up to that fact."

"Let's go sit down in the living room. This is a conversation that's going to take more than one glass of wine," Guy said, and led the way. He placed the bottle on the end table and picked up two coasters. He gave Janet the one that read: *Wine takes the bitch right out of me*. He kept the one that read: *Lord, give me coffee to change the things I can, and wine to accept the things I cannot*. Janet didn't seem to notice.

"Look," he said, "I agree that there is an important debate going on right now in our country. When I try to put it in the simplest terms, I would say that America needs a new value system. The one we have now is based on a moral code that originates mostly in Christianity. But it isn't working. More and more people are rejecting the faith-based value system. It was never universally supported—or even accepted—but so long as people of faith promoted the positive, widely accepted tenets of their faith and avoided getting all 'holier than thou,' the faithful and everyone else got along."

Janet countered, "But you can see as well as I can that religious institutions in America—and everywhere else, really—have been delegitimized by the very people who are supposed to guide us. When you mention religion now, people think of greedy Televangelists and pedophile priests. These scandals have undermined the authority of the church as an institution. For a lot of people, religion is no longer a moral beacon. And for some people, it isn't just that they no longer believe in religion, it's that they actively believe religion is evil."

"I agree, but there's more to it than that. When we first got married, we used to go to church regularly. Now we rarely go. Even though I consider myself conservative, I don't feel comfortable with where organized religion is right now. Truth be told, I think the Golden Rule is a pretty good rule to live by, and if everyone just followed it, we'd be a lot better off.

"But there are some issues, like abortion and gay marriage, where there doesn't appear to be any middle ground. I'd like to think that we, as a society, can find a way to reconcile differences of opinion on these issues, but when we no longer see faith or church as a source of moral authority on a particular topic, where can we—and where should we—go for guidance?"

Janet swirled the wine in her glass and took a sip. "Well, if you used social media, you'd know what America thinks."

"Oh, I know what America thinks. Just read the comments section on any article on any subject, and you'll find out what people think. About everything, in great, nauseating, profane detail. I know you brought that up because of what I said in the interview, but you're actually making my point for me. I don't think social media is helping us find a new moral compass. I think the absence of an agreed-upon value system is creating a real problem. There are a lot of issues where what we believed yesterday is no longer acceptable. We can agree on that, but we don't have a way to decide what we want to believe today. Social media is making the debate worse rather than better. It allows anyone with an Internet connection to rant and rave, and throw the F-word around, and call people morons and a lot worse. If this is how we're going to shape public opinion, we're screwed."

"And now you're making my point," Janet countered. "If you don't think we should look to the general public for guidance on divisive social issues, why shouldn't business leaders also be thought leaders?"

"For the same reason I think we shouldn't look to celebrities for moral advice. I mean, just because someone is a good actor or actress, and gets filthy rich playing characters on television or in the movies, why do they think we should listen to them on social and moral questions? It's interesting to me that much of what Hollywood puts out is full of the things they claim to be against, including gun violence, drug use, moral decadence—you name it and there's a movie full of it. And if I think we ought not to look to celebrities for moral guidance, why would I think that business leaders have any more moral authority? Throughout most of history, the family has been the primary source of moral values, and I don't see any reason for that to change now. I think everyone is entitled to their own opinion, but no one is really qualified to preach on some of these issues. If I want to know how to optimize my stock portfolio, I go to an investment advisor. I don't ask him how to get rid of a rash. He knows stocks, so that's what I ask him about."

"Or her." Janet pulled her leg up under her chin and wrapped both arms around her knee. Her wine glass dangled in her hand, and she stared into it, trying to decide how far she was willing to push this conversation, and how far her husband was willing to go. She decided to press on. "I know you think that just because I majored in women's studies, I never learned anything really important—"

"You know damn well that isn't what I think. What I've said in the past—and what I still believe—is that history may not tell us as much about our time as the people who study history like to think. I mean, if you look at the writings of the mid-nineteenth-century philosophers like Marx and Kant and Hegel, I think history has shown pretty well that they were just plain wrong. There has not been—and there isn't likely to be—a great uprising of the proletariat. They may have been completely accurate in their descriptions of the world they lived in, but I don't think those philosophers are relevant today. If we are going to solve today's problems, we need to try to understand the world as it exists today, not as it was more than 150 years ago."

"What about Nietzsche? I think it's interesting you left him out."

"What about Nietzsche?"

"I think Nietzsche's analysis is just as relevant today as it was in his time, perhaps even more so."

"It's been a long time since I read Nietzsche," Guy confessed. "So, help me out here and bring me up to speed."

"Well, there are five key concepts to Nietzsche. The first is that God is dead. The second is nihilism. The third is the transvaluation of values. Step number four is the will to power, and number five is superman."

"I disagree with the first one," Guy interjected. "And I have no idea what you mean by the other four."

Janet responded patiently, "You said yourself that religion is no longer a reliable source of moral authority. I think that's the same thing Nietzsche was saying. If science and secular values are at odds with the teachings of Christianity, eventually people will stop believing in Christianity. I don't think he literally meant that God is dead. His point was that if we no longer accept religious teachings as the basis of our moral code, then we need to find a new basis for the values we want to live by. I don't see a lot of difference between that and what you said not five minutes ago.

"And he's not advocating nihilism. His view was that nihilism—the belief that nothing has any inherent importance and that life itself is meaningless—was the natural next step once God is dead. In other words, if Christianity is the basis of society's value system and people abandon Christianity, there's no inherent basis for a value system."

"I'm not sure it *is* accurate to say people have abandoned Christianity in the United States," Guy countered.

"That's not the point I'm making. What I'm saying is that there was a time—I don't know how far back you have to go—but there was a time in the United States when the Judeo-Christian value system was accepted by a pretty sizable majority of the population. That is no longer the case, and the number of people who disagree with that value system is increasing, not decreasing. I'm not sure if they're in the majority yet, but they will be before too long."

"Okay, so I agree with you there, but Nietzsche's making my head hurt. So, help me understand how I can fix what I said today, and what I should do about the lawsuit."

"What lawsuit?"

"Oh, yeah. I was going to tell you about that, but you met me at the door with both barrels loaded."

Janet slid over to Guy and kissed him on the cheek. She rubbed her hands against his neatly trimmed beard, then tussled his dirty-blond curls. "I'm sorry. I didn't mean to unload on you, but I just wish you'd trust me sometimes about Lucinda. She's not a good person. And she not only understands where the public is headed on social issues, she knows how to use those issues against you. I'm not saying you have to get woke."

"You literally said, 'You're either woke or you're not.'"

"I'm trying to help you here, remember?"

"Okay, sorry."

"What I'm trying to tell you is that you're free to believe what you want to believe, but if you are going to be a public figure—and if the IPO is successful, IAU will be one of the largest technology companies on the East Coast, making you a very public figure—you need to understand how to navigate this new social landscape. First of all, you have to know what the key social issues are, and you have to understand where the majority viewpoint is on each of them. You can believe whatever you want, but when it comes to these really divisive social issues, if you're not properly aligned with the new majority, just don't even go there."

"That doesn't seem fair. If I'm in the minority on something, I have to keep my mouth shut?"

"First of all, life's not fair. You know better than that. Second, aren't you the one who said in an interview today that you don't think the leaders of tech companies should be taking on divisive social issues? What I'm telling you is to practice what you preach. Just never start a conversation about a social issue, and if the conversation does go there, learn how to steer it back to safety."

"So how much damage do you think I did today?"

"I don't know. Tell me about the lawsuit."

"You remember David Gordon, right?"

"Vaguely."

"He was one of our early investors. He put up a lot of money to help us develop Firebomb. He sent a preservation letter today claiming that IAU cheated him by releasing him from his position as a member of the board of directors. He said that we did it so he would lose rights to the profits from Phishhook, and that we used some of the money he invested for Firebomb to develop Phishhook. If that were true, he'd be in line for a lot of money after the IPO and after we launch Phishhook. But he already had a liquidity event where we settled up on his investment, and since he's no longer on the board, he won't benefit from the IPO."

"Is it true, what he claims?"

"Of course not."

"Then why did you fire him?"

"I don't know that I'd go so far as to say that we fired him, but we bought out his shares and moved him off the board."

"Sounds to me like you fired him."

"We didn't have a choice. We brought in an outside auditor to take a look at the books in preparation for going public. One of the staff accountants flagged a huge number of David's charge card purchases. He was using the company credit card on hookers and booze. In the last year that David was on the board, the ratio of inappropriate use to appropriate use was running about two-to-one. It was a potential disaster. The only good thing we could have said about it was that David appeared to be a very good tipper. Once all of those charges got flagged, we had no choice. We had to let him go, and he must know that his lawsuit will get tossed out, and he'll probably have to pay our court costs because it will be deemed a frivolous lawsuit."

"And yet he filed it anyway. Don't you find that a bit suspicious?"

"Well, first of all, he hasn't filed it *yet*. What we got today is a preservation letter. That's usually the step that comes before a lawsuit gets filed. But the timing is definitely unusual. All of this happened about six months ago, and I would have thought that if he had any kind of issue, he would have raised it earlier."

"So, what happens if it does get filed? What would be the impact on the IPO?"

"It depends a lot on the timing, but it could be catastrophic. If the lawsuit is filed before we lock down a company to run book on the IPO, we might not be able to get anyone to do it. In that case, we'd have to postpone, or maybe even cancel, and we've spent a lot of money on the IPO already. I doubt we could afford to do it again. It would be worse if the lawsuit came out right before the IPO. Once we're locked and cocked, the IPO is going to happen, and if that lawsuit gets filed at the wrong time, the whole IPO would be a bust. We wouldn't be able to raise the funds we need, and we'd start trading below our IPO price. That's the kiss of death."

"So, did it come up today in the interview?"

"Not on the record, but Heather made a comment right at the end that made it pretty clear she's aware that a potential lawsuit is out there somewhere. The way she said it was almost like a shot across the bow—like she wanted me to know that she knew. It was strange."

"Have you spoken to Nigel about this yet?"

"I haven't really had the chance yet. Since Nigel is the company's outside counsel, I would hope that he got a copy of the preservation letter at the same time I did, but I'm not sure. I'll talk to him about it tomorrow when I tell him about the interview."

"You mean he didn't know about the interview?"

"Why should he? It was an interview in a tech magazine—why would he need to know?"

"First of all, he's managing the legal part of your IPO, so I'd think he would want to let you know what you can and can't say publicly. Secondly, he might have recommended that you not do the interview at all."

Guy thought Janet was being a little over the top and wondered if she was motivated by her animus toward Lucinda. Janet sat silently for a moment, then asked, "Do you think she is behind it?"

"Who, Heather? No, I don't think so."

"Heather is barely out of college and can still manipulate men with her looks. She hasn't had time to learn how to really put the screws to someone. I'm talking about Lucinda. Not only does she know how to do it, she's good at it."

"But why would she? What's she got against me?"

"I don't know, but you'd damn well better find out."

CHAPTER 3

THE FOLLOWING MORNING GUY TOOK THE METRO to work rather than driving. He wanted time to organize his thoughts before the discussion with Lucinda Hornbuckle. The trip on the Orange Line from New Carrollton Station to Crystal City took an hour and fifteen minutes, including a line change downtown. As he made the ten-minute walk from the Metro stop to his office, he took in the sights and sounds of the underground. He found comfort in its stability—the soft lighting, how the temperature stayed constant whether it was hot outside or cold, the ever-present smell of coffee and bacon wafting from the half-dozen buffets that dotted the passageway.

As was his habit, he was at his desk working prior to 8 a.m., well before most of the staff, and he spent half an hour sketching out his thoughts on a notepad. He polished off two cups of coffee—the no-name brand, not the popular stuff—preparing for his discussion. He knew that everyone thought he was a cheapskate for buying the off-label stuff for the office. *Let 'em laugh.*

It's my little one-man rebellion, like an ant crawling up an elephant's trunk and threatening to knock him out. I may never succeed, but I can't let them just crush me underfoot. If they insist on getting into politics, they'll pay. Maybe not much, but if enough people agree with me, the coffee moguls will eventually learn that politics is bad for business.

Once he was comfortable with his plan, he dialed Lucinda's cell phone. As it rang, he flashed back to Janet's warnings, and tried to sort out if she had a legitimate concern or if she was just jealous of Guy's history with Lucinda. He couldn't be sure, but he was mulling over Joseph Heller's famous saying, *Just because you're paranoid doesn't mean they aren't after you*, when Lucinda answered.

Guy started to ask if she had a minute to talk, but she cut him off. "Hi, Guy! I know it's you because your college yearbook photo shows up on my caller ID, and I set 'Dueling Banjos' as your special ringtone."

"Oh, okay." *That's a little creepy.* "I'm just calling because I wanted to thank you for the piece in *Social Tech* yesterday. I thought Heather did a really good job of hitting the highlights, and I appreciate you getting it published so quickly so it didn't run into the quiet period."

"No need to thank us. We did the piece because the IAU IPO will be a major event in the tech space. We have an obligation to our readers to let them know what's happening, and your IPO is a big deal. But you know that, and that's not why you're really calling, so tell me what's on your mind."

Even after twenty years, Guy was still amazed by how direct she was. *This is the same woman who, when we were dating, would tell me when and how we were going to have sex, so I guess I shouldn't be surprised by her bluntness now. Subtlety was never her forte.* "Well, toward the end of the interview yesterday, after we went off the record, Heather mentioned something that surprised me, because I didn't think she should be in a position to know about it."

"You mean the preservation letter from David Gordon?"

"Yes. It shouldn't be a matter of public record yet since it's not on the docket anywhere, and if David is spreading this around before his law firm completes due diligence on his claims, he's opening himself—and anyone who repeats or publishes those claims—up to a lawsuit for slander or libel."

"So, you're calling to warn me not to run with David's claims that you misused funds provided for one project by using them on another project and cheated him out of his investment in the process. Is that it?"

"I see you're aware of the claims, but you should also know they're completely false. David doesn't have a case, and if he does file a lawsuit, it won't turn out well for him."

"You're operating under the assumption that David's goal is to win the lawsuit."

"Why else would he threaten one?"

"I can think of a couple of reasons. The first, and most likely, is that he's hoping you'll be motivated to settle. After all, he was one of your earliest investors and he stuck with you through some lean times. He might reasonably expect you to show him generosity now that he's fallen on hard times."

"I wasn't aware he had fallen on hard times," Guy said, sincerely.

"Well, when you let him go from the board, he didn't have much to fall back on. He made some big moves in the stock market and he took a beating. He's basically living hand-to-mouth as a consultant helping start-ups secure seed money."

"I'm sorry to hear that, but I'm not sure how that justifies a lawsuit. He knows as well as anyone that when you take risks for a living, you've got to set aside a nest egg and not roll the dice with everything you've got. In fact, he told me that the first time we met, when he was considering investing in IAU."

"It's interesting to hear you be so cautious, in principle, about not rolling the dice, when you're doing exactly the opposite in practice."

"I don't follow."

"You advise against rolling the dice, but that's exactly what you're doing by ignoring the risks from David's claims. You're rolling the dice on the future of IAU."

Guy had always believed that in every transaction someone was buying, and someone was selling. The key to success was figuring out early on who was doing which. Lucinda was making it very easy for him: She was selling salvation. All he had to do was receive her wisdom and he would be saved. What he didn't know yet was at what cost. "Let's suppose for a minute that you're right, and I need to take this potential lawsuit more seriously. What would a cautious person do about it?"

"Your best course of action would be to let a trusted intermediary—someone known to both parties—open a dialogue."

Guy took his own turn at bluntness. "Okay, so we open a dialogue. Based on what you've told me—and I assume you have it straight from David—what he wants is money. I have no philosophical objection to spreading the wealth around a bit with David, and I'm sure we could find a number that works for both sides. But what I really want to know is what the intermediary expects to gain from all of this. Should I say it that way, or should I just say, 'What do you want out of the deal?'"

"Either way is fine with me. It shouldn't surprise you that it concerns me to see someone like you abdicate your responsibility on social justice issues. I want you to be a leader."

"Aside from the fact that I went on record yesterday—in your publication, no less—saying that I didn't think it appropriate for business leaders to try to shape public opinion on social issues, I'm not sure you and I see eye to eye on many of the most divisive issues. Are you sure you really want me to take a stand?"

"I think you have a responsibility to take a stand, and to be on the right side of history. Society is changing, and it is moving in one direction, and one direction only. Just by being a public figure, you are thrust into the public eye at the front of the pack. You can either lead, or you can get run over."

"Look, Lucinda, you and I go way back. I admire your passion for what you believe in. And I admire what you've been able to accomplish. You're phenomenally talented—probably one of the most talented people I've ever met in my life. I *respect* you, but I don't think we have to agree on everything to get along. I think it would be better if we could find areas where we agree and work on those together."

"I'm listening."

"I believe that there are enough worthwhile goals for people to work toward that devoting one's talent to any one of them is sufficient. We don't have to work in lockstep toward the same agenda. If we can agree that doing something is good, we can work on that something together, even if we disagree on the underlying causes."

"For example?"

"You and I can agree that clean air is good, or that reducing the amount of plastic in the ocean is a worthwhile goal. But we don't have to agree on the larger issue of climate change or the exact nature of the recycling policies necessary to save the whales from plastic bags. Let's focus on the areas where we agree, not on punishing those who don't agree with us completely.

"Let's take the issue of famine. Everybody agrees that it's unfortunate when children starve. Nobody wants that to happen. But when you lump all starving children into a single problem, you ignore different causes and potential solutions. In some cases, children are starving because the society they live in is run by thugs who take everything for themselves. In other cases, there is a clear mismatch between the resources available and the resources needed to feed those children. If you treat those two problems with the same prescription, you're probably not going to like the results. No matter how many electric vehicles you put on the streets of San Francisco, the children in the Democratic Republic of the Congo are still going to starve if the country is run by corrupt politicians. No matter how strictly the government of China enforces a one-child policy, there will still be starving children in India unless something meaningful is done there. All I am saying is that we don't have to agree completely on the underlying cause of famine to work on it together."

"I should have known that a retrograde on social issues would also be a climate denier. It baffles me that someone who is as smart as you are about technology is a complete fool about climate science. There is no more room for debate. The science is settled."

It occurred to Guy that he had just found another area of agreement between Janet and Lucinda: that he was an idiot.

"You say the science is settled, but you're just being dogmatic. You don't want to listen to any other point of view."

"That's not true. I'm perfectly willing to debate the underlying causes of climate change because I have the facts on my side. Go ahead, give it your best shot."

"Well, first of all, if you're going to talk about climate change, you have a responsibility to define the baseline from which the changes are occurring. If you don't—and simply talk about climate change—then any day that is different from the previous day is proof of climate change; any year that's different from the previous year is proof of climate change, but that isn't good science. It's useless."

Lucinda came back hard. "What you're describing is the difference between weather and climate. Anyone who does even the slightest bit of reading knows this. You have an obligation to overcome your ignorance."

Guy knew it was a mistake to fight this battle on her turf. Climate change was one of her major issues, and she was extremely knowledgeable about it. She was a sought-after public speaker on the subject and covered the topic frequently in *Social Tech*. There was almost no chance that he could "out-fact" her on climate change, and zero chance that he could change her mind on anything. But he also knew that if he knuckled under without trying to make a case, Lucinda would despise him for such weakness, and his penance would be even harsher than if he fought and lost. He felt that the strongest arguments, or at least the ones she was least likely to overwhelm with barrages of data, were in the process arena, so he pushed gingerly into that territory and opened with a rhetorical gambit. "When it comes to climate change, why do we always assume that our old data is accurate?

As expected, Lucinda pounced. "We don't. We continually adjust historical data."

Bait taken.

"So, we were fallible then but have it right now? Exactly when did we figure it all out? When did we become infallible? When we set a new record for something like rainfall, why do we automatically assume the measurements we took when we established the record are correct? And why is it that once adjustments are made, they don't stay made? We keep adjusting the temperatures from the 1930s downward. If our climate scientists are so good now, why do they have to keep adjusting their adjustments?"

"You're just a fountain of bogus arguments. Do you have any idea how illogical that statement is?"

Guy pressed ahead, knowing that if she had a killer argument against his line of reasoning, she would have already delivered it.

"All I am saying is that environmentalists have been predicting doom and gloom for decades. When Earth Day was first celebrated in 1970, prominent environmental scientists were predicting that a Great Die-Off was imminent. According to those scientists, some four billion people were supposed to die of famine and hunger, including sixty-five million in the United States. That didn't happen, yet we're supposed to believe now that the end of the world is just around the corner? The fact that the people making these predictions also offer solutions which just so happen to give them a lot more control over everyone else leads to justifiable skepticism."

Before Lucinda could respond, Guy's office phone rang. He asked Lucinda to hold just a second and placed his cell phone against his chest to cover the microphone.

"Good morning, Guy, this is Nigel. We need to talk. Can you come see me?"

"I'm in the middle of something right now. How about later this morning?"

"That's fine, but make it quick. And whatever you do, don't do anything more about this article in *Social Tech* until you and I have had a chance to strategize."

"I'm on the other line with Lucinda right now."

"Guy, just hang up. Don't say another word to her. I know you don't see all this as a big deal, but if you're going to pay me a ton of money to give you legal advice, it might behoove you to—at least once in a while—take that advice. And my advice now is to just hang up the damn phone without saying another word to her."

"I'll be at your office within the hour."

Guy placed the office phone back in the cradle and returned to Lucinda. "I'm sorry, something's come up and I've got to run, but before I go, I want to make a larger point. We've spent the last few minutes fighting about climate change, and that has prevented us from discussing IAU's participation in an exciting new project in Africa that I'm absolutely positive you'd support 100 percent. All I want you to think about is this: We don't have to fight; we can disagree on some things, but we should be big enough to work together on the areas where we agree."

"This isn't over, Guy."

"What isn't over? Do we really need to finish a debate about climate change where neither one of us is really listening to the other and neither one of us is going to change our mind?"

"That's not what I'm talking about."

"Then what?"

"You need to get right with David. Do a quiet settlement with him and bring him back on the board. His departure isn't widely known and bringing him back won't be that big of a deal. More importantly, he can provide strong guidance to you and the company on critical social issues."

"I understand where you're coming from, but I can't commit to anything."

"Then go have your conversation with Nigel Winston, but understand that the longer you take to come around, the harder it's going to be."

Jesus, that woman is spooky.

CHAPTER 4

ON HIS WAY BACK THROUGH THE UNDERGROUND to the Metro, Guy didn't get the same vibe from his surroundings that he had felt three hours ago. The sights, sounds, and smells were the same, but the mood was different. Although there were no more people in the passageway now than there had been before, he felt crowded, confined, and tense. Like he was three steps behind Lucinda, and like Nigel Winston—a man he considered a mentor and a friend—was about to make a big deal out of something that would blow over on its own if left alone. He wondered why everyone seemed to be questioning his judgment. *If there really is something that needs to be sorted out, why is everyone else sitting around wringing their hands while I'm the one trying to find a solution?*

He hopped on the Blue Line and took it downtown to McPherson Square, walked the two blocks down Fifteenth Street to New York Avenue and entered the offices of Winston, Ingraham, and Noble. Two minutes later, he was in the reception area of Nigel's tenth-floor office, and thirty seconds after that, he was greeting one of the most famous lawyers in a town full of famous lawyers. "How are you, Nigel?"

"Another day on the right side of the pavement, and I got money in my pocket for beer. I'd say I'm doing pretty good."

Guy chuckled and felt the tension draining from his shoulders. With his Kentucky drawl and his funny way with words, Nigel had a knack for putting people at ease.

Nigel placed his hand on Guy's shoulder and steered him down the corridor. "Come on back to my office, my friend. Can I get you some coffee, or a bottle of water? There's someone waiting to see us."

Guy politely declined the coffee and water and was still processing the comment about another person when they reached Nigel's corner office. Stepping inside, he was shocked to see Janet sitting on the couch.

"What is this, an intervention?"

"Guy, relax. It's nothing like that," Janet said. "After our conversation last night, I reached out to Nigel and explained my concerns that Lucinda might be behind the preservation letter. I'm sorry if you feel like I'm getting into things that aren't my business, but I know you're hardly objective when it comes to Lucinda. I also know that you think I let my dislike of Lucinda color my views, so I've asked Nigel to weigh in."

Now it's two against one. And these two are supposed to be on my side!

Nigel took his cue. "We may not have any problem here, but we can't afford to be cavalier about it. So, let's review the bidding. I got a copy of the preservation letter this morning. My interpretation is that he's claiming you used money he gave you for one project to develop another one and then bought him out before the second one became a big success. In his view of the world, you owe him money."

"And you know as well as I do that those claims are totally false."

"Okay, okay, let's not get worked up here. We're all on the same side. Let's do the math on this. We can either take the letter at face value and prepare to fight the lawsuit, or we can interpret the letter as a ploy to force us into settlement talks to protect the IPO. Do you agree?"

"I think that pretty well sums it up, but I think we should consider Janet's point that Lucinda is behind this."

"Let's suppose for a minute that she is. What difference would that make in terms of how we respond to the letter? We can either settle or we can fight."

"I don't think it makes much difference if we decide to fight," Guy said. "We have a very clear case and David will lose."

"I'm not sure I agree," Janet countered. "If David is the only one we're fighting, he may fold when the facts get put on the table, but if Lucinda is behind it, she may be willing to keep fighting a lost battle just to inflict damage."

Nigel agreed. "One of the things I've learned about doing business in this town is that people can still hurt you long after they've lost the ability to help you. She may or may not be in a position to make the world love IAU and make the IPO successful, but if she digs in and decides to fight, she can still do some damage."

Guy stared blankly at Nigel. "That's interesting, but I'm not quite sure what you're recommending. Are you saying we should fight the lawsuit, or that we should seek a settlement?"

"I'm not saying either one, right now. I'm just trying to build a framework for our discussion. And I think we ought to step back a little bit to consider a third option."

"Like what?"

"Well, what is it that's driving the timing of the IPO? And, what I mean by that is, is there anything that prevents you from postponing the IPO or even not doing an IPO at all?"

"So, you're saying we should cave and just bail on the IPO?"

"That's not what I'm saying at all. What I really want to understand is where the IPO fits into the grand scheme of things. Is the IPO something we *have* to do, or is the IPO just something you want to do?"

Guy sat down next to Janet on the couch, while Nigel took a chair from the conference table and turned it around to face them. Nigel waited patiently as Guy mulled over the idea. It wasn't something he had considered before. Heretofore, he had supposed that the IPO was on a ballistic trajectory, and that it would proceed apace as soon as each item on the checklist was completed. Now, he was being asked to consider whether or not the IPO was even worth doing. He couldn't answer that without asking an even deeper question: *Why am I doing the IPO in the first place?*

The obvious answer was to raise funds for additional investments and acquisitions, to grow the company. Only Guy and a handful of people, including Nigel and Janet, knew that IAU was contemplating a major push into renewables and other green technologies. But was that really the reason for the IPO, or was it because *he* wanted to be the CEO of an up-and-coming, publicly traded tech company? Up to this moment, Guy had never really thought deeply about the potential negative consequences of going public; he had only focused on the positives. It was time to take stock. *I've got a great life now—a loving wife who is my friend and soul mate, an awesome job running IAU, and I love what I do. We're making a difference; we're doing things that matter. And, as Nigel likes to say, 'I've got money in my pocket for beer.' So why isn't that enough? Maybe it should be.*

"Okay," Guy said. "Let's suppose for a minute that we make it clear that we're not pressing ahead with the IPO. How does that help us to deal with the preservation letter?"

Nigel was quick to respond. "If Lucinda really is behind this, postponing the IPO will smoke her out. Her threat to the IPO is the only leverage she's got. If you take that away, she's got no power over you."

"We haven't even formally filed for the IPO, so wouldn't we look a little silly announcing that we're not doing an IPO we haven't even filed for yet?"

"You don't have to tell the world; you just have to persuade David and Lucinda that you're not going forward with it."

"And how am I supposed to do that?"

"I think the best way is to sit down with David Gordon. I don't think you have to be cutesy about it or anything. Just invite him to lunch and tell him you want to find a way to settle with him before he formally files a lawsuit against you. Put a big number on the table. If he's really doing it for the money, he'll take the offer. Get him to sign a non-disclosure agreement saying he renounces the claims in the preservation letter and that if he brings them up again, you're entitled to summary judgment and court costs, as well as punitive damages. I can have it drawn up for you by this afternoon."

Guy paused. He wasn't quite ready to go down that road. "But why should I give money to someone who was legitimately fired for misusing a company credit card? Aren't there any principles we're willing to fight for?"

Janet stepped in. "Guy, you've got to make a decision. Do you want to win a fight against Lucinda Hornbuckle, or do you want to get your way?"

CHAPTER 5

NOT SURPRISINGLY, DAVID GORDON READILY agreed to a lunch meeting. They arranged to meet at the Steakhaus restaurant on the top floor of the building opposite Guy's office. Guy, as usual, arrived several minutes ahead of schedule and requested a table where he could keep an eye on the door. David, also as usual, was running behind and sent a text message five minutes after the meeting was supposed to start, saying, *On my way*.

Just as well, Guy thought. *It might do me good to think about David's history with the company before we have our conversation. I need to generate some empathy for the guy if I'm going to agree to pay him a boatload of money.*

Guy recalled the first time he met David, nearly twenty years ago. David had been well known in the tech industry as well as in the venture capital community. He was in his early forties then, but had already launched several successful start-ups, primarily in the IT field. He was an odd duck whose physical appearance completely disagreed with his comportment. On the outside, he was a portly Korean–American fellow with rumpled hair and ill-fitting clothes. His father was American, and his mother was Korean. She had retained her Korean citizenship and never became proficient in English, except for the curse words. Taking after his mother, David cursed so often, and in so many inappropriate instances, that Guy had once asked why he wasn't more cautious about it. David then explained, without missing a beat, that American profanity had no meaning, so he wasn't bothered, but if he used Korean curse words then his lips would burn, and he would be embarrassed.

That was but one of David's idiosyncrasies. He was a glass-half-full kind of guy, but with him, it was always the top half that was full. He was so relentlessly optimistic about things that it was often difficult to separate fact from fiction in the stories he told. It was one thing to embellish. After all, artistic license frequently makes retellings more compelling. But David's stories varied from outlandish to fantastical. There was almost always a grain of truth in there somewhere, but it took some serious digging to find it.

The irony was that while David saw his style as an asset, most people felt sorry for him. Privately, they understood that this lack of trustworthiness was a liability that undercut his technical brilliance. To many, it was easier to deal with less capable people than to put up with David's drama.

Guy was one of those few who had made the conscious decision to wade through all of David's bullshit to get to the good stuff. And it had paid off. Handsomely. David had been one of the biggest proponents of Firebomb. Most of the technical people at IAU had initially scoffed at the idea of fighting fire with fire to deal with DDOS attacks. But David had fought hard to make the case that building a massive, distributed network would make this approach practical. And he had backed up his support for the concept with cash. It had taken years, and a lot of money, to implement Firebomb, and truth be told, though the idea worked, it never really turned a profit. But it had kept the doors open, and it had put IAU on the map. And there was probably some value in that beyond what David had been paid just over six months ago.

Guy's trip down memory lane came to an abrupt halt when David finally appeared. He was unshaven, more unkempt than usual, and smelled of a strange mix of kimchi and urine. His suit was wrinkled, and his untied tie dangled from both sides of his collar. In the middle of his shirt, just above pocket level, was a brown spot that was either old mustard or some sort of gravy.

David pulled up a chair and immediately grabbed the breadbasket, blurting out, "It's been a while, Guy. Good to see you."

"Hello, David. Thanks for coming. I spoke to Lucinda yesterday, and she suggested we have a chat."

David replied in his usual, unfiltered manner, "Yeah, she told me you were going to get in touch. I didn't believe her, but turns out she was right. She also told me that if I ask you for half a mil, you'll pay it and you'll put me back on the board."

"She did, did she? What else did she tell you?"

"She said that you'd probably pay the money, or something close to it, but you'd fight on the issue of putting me back on the board."

No one could accuse Lucinda of being indirect.

"Okay, before we get too far into discussing a deal, let's take a step back and look at how we got here. Why submit the preservation letter when you know you won't win?"

"Because Lucinda told me to."

Guy wondered if Lucinda had anticipated that David would be this direct. If not, perhaps there was a way to gain from David's candor. Guy couldn't see any immediate path to leverage, so he continued digging. "But why did you agree to do what she told you?"

David put down his butter knife and looked directly at Guy. "Mostly because I need the money. The VC business has slowed down for me in the past few years. I had some early success, but there are a lot more players now. When I first got into the business, my model was to invest in companies that had good ideas but were entering the valley of death—you know, the point where they have a proven product but are going to run out of money before it really takes off. That was my specialty, and I made a lot of money doing it—and I helped get a lot of cutting-edge technology into the market."

David picked up his butter knife and continued, "But with all the cheap money available, there are a lot of new people in the game, and a lot of the real big venture plays are happening out in California and in Texas. There's just not that much going on around here. So, I got into the stock market. I made some big moves. I took some short positions—big time—and lost almost everything. I made the same move as the big guys, but my timing was wrong. Two weeks after I had to liquidate my position, the bottom fell out of the stocks I shorted. If I'd had enough money to extend my position, I could have liquidated and gone short again, and it would have all paid off. Instead, I was wiped out and the guys with access to big easy money were able to hold on and clean up.

"You know, it's hard to climb up the mountain, but it's easy to fall off. And when you fall, sometimes there's nothing to stop you on the way down."

"I'm sorry to hear that, but why come after *me*?"

"Butler Bot."

"What? What about Butler Bot?"

"I don't know. I guess it just pissed me off, so to speak, that you created a miniature robot with artificial intelligence to clean up piss in public restrooms and made a killing off of it. My wife even bought one of the damn things for our house. It just bothered me that you got rich off an idea that anyone could have done."

"Yes, anyone could have done it, but they didn't. How many times have you gone into a public restroom and had to straddle the piss on the floor to keep it from getting all over your shoes? You had the exact same information I did about that problem. The difference between IAU and everyone else out there is that we were smart enough to see when enabling technologies had matured to a point where a solution became practical. When we looked around, we saw that cars could drive themselves across the country, and electric mowers could be taught to automatically mow the yard, and vacuum cleaners could be taught to clean a house, and we realized that the cost of that automation had come down enough to make it practical to put into the very specific application of cleaning up piss underneath a urinal or a toilet.

"And it isn't like we struck it rich instantly. The first model looked like a bathroom scale. We called it Tidy Bot, and we sold less than a thousand of them. Where we really took off was when one of the women on the design team had the idea of re-engineering the robot so it looked like a tiny butler in black slacks and a red coat. We added a sensor that could detect when someone was using the urinal and it would look up at them and shake its head before moving in to clean up after the guy. People thought it was hilarious, and the Butler Bots started flying off the shelves. We sold more than a million. We tapped into something.

"I can remember a time when there were restroom attendants. They would move in and clean up behind men who made a mess. But society decided that job was demeaning, so everyone just chose to live with piss on bathroom floors. We could have spent all our energy on a public relations campaign trying to persuade men not to piss on the floor, but there's no money in that. Our contribution, and the one we've been rewarded for, is getting on the right side of the value curve. Everyone hates the fact that there's always piss on the floor in public restrooms, but no one stepped up to solve that problem until we created the Tidy Bot. People are worried about robots taking people's jobs, but we found a job that people are happy to give to a robot.

"I can't say for sure because we didn't do any market analysis on it, but my impression is that Tidy Bot didn't see runaway success is because it was strictly functional. Butler Bot became a hit because it poked fun at America—American men—for making such a mess all the time. The bottom line is that we saw a challenge created by the changing values of American society, and we combined several enabling technologies to address the problem—and then we put a humorous twist on it. So how is that wrong?"

"I didn't say it was wrong. I said it pissed me off."

"I still don't see how that gives you the right to threaten me with a frivolous lawsuit."

"I don't know that I had a *right* to threaten you with a lawsuit, but I wanted to. Maybe I was a little jealous. You've got the lifestyle I've always wanted. Being a VC millionaire isn't all it's cracked up to be. First, your money is always at risk. On any given day, you can lose your entire investment in a company. If you're not good at what you do, you're out of business pretty quickly, but nobody ever says, 'This guy's been doing venture capital for twenty years, he must be pretty good at it.' Second, nobody ever appreciates the money men when good things happen. Somehow, it's always the tech people who get the credit."

"So that made you want to sue me?"

"No, it made me mad at you. Lucinda's the one who told me to sue you, and she paid me to do it."

David paused and looked down at his roll, realizing he'd slipped up. Before Guy could ask a follow-up question, David stood and bolted from the restaurant.

CHAPTER 6

THE EVENING AIR WAS SURPRISINGLY COOL FOR early November as Guy and Janet made their way to Dulles International Airport for the seven-and-a-half-hour flight to

Casablanca, Morocco. None of the issues surrounding the preservation letter had been settled, but in the week since their meeting, David had not yet filed a lawsuit. The threat had not vanished, but it didn't seem imminent. It appeared that Lucinda was taking a strategic pause in her battle against Guy and IAU. At the very least she was not making any overt moves.

Guy was grateful for the break, not only on the legal front, but also from the pressure of preparing for the IPO. It seemed as though he and Janet might actually be able to enjoy their trip to the UN Climate Change Conference in Marrakesh, also known as Conference of the Parties, or COPS32.

Guy had fallen in love with Marrakesh when he attended COPS22 back in 2016. He was especially taken by the town square, known locally as Jemaa el-Fnaa, and the city's famed La Mamounia Hotel. With its splendid gardens and magnificent views of the Atlas Mountains, the hotel was world famous, and reportedly had been the favorite of Winston Churchill. And the Jemaa el-Fnaa, with its snake charmers and dentists—who plied their trade on the spot without anesthesia and who displayed extracted teeth on trays as advertisement—made frequent appearances in movies. Marrakesh was a world apart from anything Guy had ever experienced, and he was eager to share it with Janet.

So when it had been announced that COPS32 would also be in Marrakesh and that Innovative Applications Unlimited would be allowed to attend as an observer representing the Africa Renaissance Project, Guy decided to make it a working vacation and paid for the trip himself so he could bring her along. Under company rules, Guy could have charged his travel expenses to

IAU. At the very least, he could have sought reimbursement for a coach-class ticket to and from the conference, as well as his own meals and hotel bills, but he liked the freedom gained from taking total ownership of the costs. And he wanted to rectify two mistakes he had made on his first and only trip to the African continent.

First, he opted to spring for business class. It cost him nearly all of his frequent-flyer miles, but last time, he'd found his aisle seat occupied by a corpulent Moroccan who pretended not to understand that he had stolen Guy's seat. After a couple of exchanges in halting French—the second language of Morocco and the only one the men had in common—Guy had finally given in and taken the middle seat. He consoled himself with the knowledge that even if he had gotten his aisle seat, the fat fellow's girth was such that Guy wouldn't have been much more comfortable anyway. He vowed not to subject Janet to such discomfort.

The second lesson he had learned the hard way ten years ago was that Casablanca was not all it was cracked up to be. He had broken up his trip to Marrakesh with an overnight in Casablanca so he could take in the sights and sounds of the city made famous to Americans by the 1942 film of the same name. What he learned was that, aside from one of the world's largest mosques and a knock-off of Rick's Café Americain from the movie, there wasn't a great deal to see in Casablanca. Although the city clearly showed the influence of French colonialism, it was pretty much like any other large industrial port city. For this trip, Guy and Janet would do only a brief layover in Casablanca, changing planes but not leaving the airport, before going on to Marrakesh.

As was common on west-to-east transatlantic flights, their aircraft departed at around ten in the evening and would arrive in Casablanca mid-morning of the following day. Janet used the time to read up on the top tourist attractions of Marrakesh, while Guy reviewed the agenda for the three-day conference on climate change.

This year's conference had two key objectives. The first was to highlight emerging technologies to fight climate change, with special emphasis on renewables. This was the primary reason Guy was attending, and the main reason IAU had decided to take up a substantial presence at the Africa Renaissance Project—the multi-national enclave in Tarfaya, Morocco, where dozens of companies and international research organizations were piloting cutting-edge technology demonstrations.

The second major objective of COPS32 was to find technologies that enhanced employment opportunities in developing countries. Guy rarely stumbled into debates on immigration, because it seemed that the only way to avoid being labeled as bigoted and xenophobic was to accept the notion of open borders. Immigration was another of those topics about which liberals had determined there was no more room for debate and only their opinion was legitimate. Guy decided he couldn't win debates, and, besides, it really didn't matter if he could. Nothing would change, because the politicians didn't want to solve the immigration problem; both sides just rattled off talking points about it on the campaign trail. To Guy, it was much more than that. He believed the best way to prevent the United States and other Western countries from being overwhelmed with migrants from poor and underdeveloped countries was to bring about the economic growth that made it more desirable for those would-be migrants to stay in their home countries. When the United States didn't look so much like the land of milk and honey compared to their own country, perhaps more of the migrants would stay home.

IAU had made a big investment in the Africa Renaissance Project, more commonly known as ARP. Guy had pushed the board quite aggressively to allocate nearly all of IAU's research and development budget to the half dozen or so initiatives he wanted to implement in ARP. He winced at the memory of the discussion with the board about why IAU should put so much money into addressing climate change. The conversation had turned surreal when several board members, who took a more alarmist view of climate change, pressed Guy about his personal views on climate science.

"For me," he had said, "fighting climate change is a goal, not a religion."

"What's the difference?" asked one of the senior members, who had been relatively quiet but now appeared willing to lend Guy a hand.

"A goal is a decision you make about how to live your own life. Religion is what people claim gives them the right to tell other people how to live."

He had prevailed, and the board had agreed, but it was a huge risk. If the projects failed, or if the ARP itself turned out to be just another pie-in-the-sky climate change white elephant, there would be no doubt that the blame would fall squarely on Guy.

It irritated him that Lucinda gave him no credit for taking such a huge risk on a project that clearly aligned with her goals. Being a fellow traveler was not sufficient; she demanded total conformity. Guy knew—or, at least, he hoped—that if IAU's participation in ARP turned out to be a big success, it would not only justify the board's faith in him, but also strengthen the argument he had made to Lucinda—that they didn't have to agree on everything to work on something together.

After checking in at La Mamounia, Guy and Janet took a quick nap and dressed for the conference's opening event, an evening social at the Palais de Congres. Guy wore a navy-blue business suit with a crimson tie, and Janet wore a full-length floral evening gown festooned with pink-and-orange blossoms. After picking up nametags at the check-in desk, the pair cautiously entered the grand hall. Neither was an extrovert, and this environment was especially intimidating. It was a smorgasbord of people and languages and countries and organizations, and neither Guy nor Janet had any inkling where or how to begin a conversation.

On her way back from grabbing a second glass of Shiraz, Janet's attention was drawn to a tall woman wearing a boldly colored Kaftan and matching scarf, and who was engaged in an intense conversation with a woman who appeared to be Chinese.

Janet waited a moment for an appropriate lull in the discussion, and said, "Excuse me, I'm sorry to interrupt, but I overheard the phrase 'debt-trap diplomacy' and I found that very interesting. Could you tell me a little about that?"

The tall woman turned to Janet. "Allow me to introduce myself. I am Ebiere Olani, Minister Consular of the Federal Republic of Nigeria. I was just explaining to my friend the concerns of my government about the practice of debt-trap diplomacy. This is when a country, like China, loans large amounts of money to smaller countries, such as Nigeria, for very large infrastructure projects. The Chinese do this knowing full well that the country will be unable to repay the loans, and when the loans come due and the country cannot pay, the lender takes over the asset that was put up as collateral.

"This is all part of China's One Belt One Road Initiative. The Chinese portray themselves as saviors of the poor. They specialize in infrastructure projects that countries can't afford on their own. According to the Chinese, these infrastructure projects are the missing link between the poor countries and economic prosperity. The Chinese get to put their excess construction capacity to good use, and the host country gets a new port, railroad, or road. They call it a win-win.

"Eventually—to hear the Chinese tell it—the country will become a strong trading partner with China. But they don't tell you that the main purpose of the port is so that the Chinese can haul away all of the country's raw materials and ship in all of the cheap manufactured goods China makes. These imports displace the already struggling local industry, which leads to the second thing the Chinese don't tell you about the One Belt One Road Initiative: The belt is for beating the people to whom they lend money."

The other woman, who either wasn't wearing a nametag, or else had it positioned so that Janet couldn't see it, didn't bother to introduce herself before launching a full-throated defense of the Chinese. "I'm sorry, Minister, but you know as well as I do that the Chinese have bent over backwards to restructure loans and forgive debt."

"Like they did in Sri Lanka, when they seized the port at Hambantota?" Ebiere shot back. Janet wasn't familiar with the reference, but there was no mistaking the contempt with which Ebiere put it out there. Before the Chinese woman could reply, Ebiere continued, "Do you really think that the world does not see through the debt forgiveness and loan restructuring? That's like saying an enforcer is being kind when he only kneecaps someone who owes him money. They're not doing it to be nice, they're doing it because dead men can't repay loans."

The Chinese woman didn't seem fazed. "Forgive me, Minister, but nothing that is happening in Nigeria now is remotely similar to what happened in Sri Lanka ten years ago. In the Hambantota case, the Chinese not only forgave more than a billion dollars in debt, they also invested an additional six hundred million to continue developing the port into a profitable operation.

"If your government is so concerned with the debt owed to the Chinese, then perhaps you can persuade the heads of your ministries not to take bribes and run up the price of these infrastructure projects. What is causing these defaults on Chinese loans is crony capitalism. Leaders in your country steer contracts to incompetent local companies who provide kickbacks to the politicians but can't do the work, and so naturally the projects end in failure. Then your country can't pay back the loan, and the Chinese have to take over the facility as collateral. You act as though the Chinese lose nothing in the process. These relationships are highly interdependent, and the Chinese have lost billions of dollars because they were taken advantage of by crooked politicians, including some in Nigeria."

Janet watched as the Nigerian woman grew more and more angry. She thought the two women might come to blows, but instead, the Nigerian Minister Consular turned on her heels and strode away, leaving Janet alone with the Chinese woman. Given the choice, Janet would have walked away, too, but that would have been even more awkward than staying, so she simply said, "Hi, we haven't been introduced. I'm Janet Pearle. I'm here with my husband who is a delegate to the convention. Are you with the Chinese government?"

"No, I'm a reporter with the *Washington Note*," the woman said, coldly. Janet wasn't sure if the woman was still riled up by the confrontation or if she was offended by the assumption. She decided to take a conciliatory approach, "Oh, I'm sorry. You were so knowledgeable about Chinese policies that I thought you might be from the embassy."

This seemed to ease the tension a bit, and the woman replied, "Forgive me. I do get worked up sometimes by people who should be in a position to know better, but I shouldn't take it out on you. Let's start over. My name is Arlene Tann, and I am a reporter for the *Washington Note*. I cover the science and climate beat, which is why I'm here."

"That must be fascinating. Are you based somewhere in Africa?"

"No, I'm actually based in DC. Until the 2024 elections, I was an investigative reporter for the *Note* covering politics, but after the change of administration, the *Note* scaled back substantially on investigative reporting. So, they assigned me to the climate beat. It's normally nowhere near as intense as that just was!"

Fresh off Guy's recent experience with Heather Alston, Janet wasn't keen to speak to a reporter, and spotting Guy not more than twenty feet away, she considered heading for him, until she realized that Guy was deep in conversation with a Chinese man. Fearing a reprise of the recent kerfuffle, Janet held fast. Nor could she think of a way to end the conversation in which she had found herself, so she pressed on in a neutral vein, "It must be very interesting, international finance and climate change and all of that."

"It is quite interesting. And don't get me wrong. I'm not saying that there are no concerns with the Chinese. They don't mess around on certain issues. I mean, for example, it's no coincidence that all of Africa has adopted the Chinese version of the 5G standard for cell phone data transmission. The American 5G technology was as good or better than the Chinese tech, but the Chinese had leverage and they used it. 5G will mean billions of dollars for the Chinese, and they won because they held so much sovereign debt.

"And you hear a lot of carping from Western countries, including the United States, about all of the loans the Chinese are providing, but in many cases, the African countries asked the West for development assistance—before they went to the Chinese—but it was refused. How is it that Westerners can get bent out of shape over loans for projects they themselves refused to finance? And it really just irritates the hell out of me to hear Africans screaming bloody murder about new colonialism on the part of the Chinese, when, in reality the loans are being made and the projects are being financed because the elite in the African countries are on the take. They want to blame the Chinese, but they should really look in the mirror. They're just as much to blame."

"Hypocrisy, unwillingness to take responsibility for their own actions . . . I guess your time on the political beat in Washington prepared you pretty well for this gig, after all," Janet quipped.

Out of the corner of her eye, Janet saw Guy step away from the Chinese fellow and begin speaking with a Middle Eastern man. She politely excused herself and walked over to join him.

"There you are!" Guy exclaimed. "Let me introduce you to Mr. Makram Abd Alsalam. He is the president of Sahara Freight Express, one of the leading import–export companies in Morocco, and he does quite a bit of work with the Africa Renaissance Project and the Noor Concentrated Solar Power Project at Ouarzazate. I've been very interested in that project because there's been some discussion of integrating the power plant facility with the rest of the Africa Renaissance Project, and Mr. Alsalam knows all about it."

Janet extended her hand and Makram shook it gently. He gave her only a slight glance before returning to his conversation with Guy. She couldn't tell whether he was dismissing her, or simply abiding by Muslim sensibilities. She didn't know much about Arab culture, but she knew that most Arabs were Muslims, and most Muslims considered it inappropriate for the sexes to mingle in social events such as this. For an American woman, who had grown up not only mingling with men, but interacting with them as equals, she was perplexed by her own reaction to his dismissive attitude. On the one hand, she was inclined to at least attempt to respect other cultures; at the same time, however, she wasn't about to kowtow to medieval beliefs about women. Fortunately, she noticed that her glass was nearly empty again and excused herself to search out another drink.

As she approached the bar, she couldn't help noticing a tall, stunning redhead who definitely looked American, both in the way she was dressed and the way she carried herself. Having had her fill of international experiences for the evening, Janet welcomed the idea of speaking with someone from back home. She angled toward the redhead and was delighted when she saw that the woman's nametag read *Kate Mulgrew, Public Affairs, ARP*.

"So, you're with ARP?"

"Yes, I'm the public affairs officer, and one of the delegates. ARP is participating in the conference as a nongovernmental organization this year."

"I know. My husband, Guy, is also one of the delegates from ARP."

"ARP was only allowed two spots, so I may meet him sometime during the conference. I can't be sure, though, because there are separate meetings for different groups. There is a special agenda for the public affairs group. What does your husband do?"

"His company does green tech, and they've got several projects operating at the Africa Renaissance Project. He's busy now talking to someone about export–import. It's all a bit much for me."

"What is?"

"I guess I'm surprised by the intensity of some people. I've only met three people tonight, not counting you, and they've all been intense. The first was a woman from Nigeria who was upset with the Chinese over debt. The second was an American reporter who said it was all the Africans' fault, and the third was a Moroccan who looked right through me like I wasn't even there. I couldn't tell if he was ignoring me because I was beneath him, or because he was offended that I was out in public uncovered."

"Well, if he's Moroccan, he was probably just ignoring you. This is a predominantly Muslim country, but the French had a lot of cultural influence here. They are strict, but not like in Saudi Arabia or Yemen. You can even go to topless beaches in Agadir, just a couple of hours from here. Morocco is very much a melting pot."

"So, do you live here in Morocco now?"

"Yes, there is an ARP facility—encampment, or whatever you want to call it—down at Tarfaya. It's at the very southern end of Morocco, very close to the disputed border with Western Sahara. I have been there about six months now. Most of the other people rotate through on shorter assignments, but I've signed on indefinitely."

"How do you like it?"

"It's interesting, but a lot more rustic than here. Marrakesh is a garden spot compared to Tarfaya. All we've got down there is open desert and twenty-mile-an-hour winds."

"My husband is very excited about what's happening down there. They're introducing a new technology that takes recycled plastic from the oceans and turns it into irrigation pipe and evaporation tanks for saltwater greenhouses."

"Yes, I recently wrote a press release on it. They use sonic welding to do the joints or something like that, don't they?"

"Yes, that's it. There are several other things they're working on. We thought about visiting the facility at Tarfaya, but we decided to spend those days vacationing here in Marrakesh instead."

"Well, I can tell you that you made the right choice. Marrakesh is a beautiful place, and if I had to choose between a couple of extra days here and going down to see the dust at Tarfaya, it's not even close."

CHAPTER 7

GUY'S ASSESSMENT THAT LUCINDA WAS TAKING A strategic pause was only partially correct. After his slip up at lunch, David had immediately informed her that the meeting had produced neither a monetary settlement offer nor a seat on the board for David. Lucinda was livid but knew she wouldn't be able to get anything more from David at this point. She decided to have Heather make another run at getting dirt on Guy or IAU.

When Heather entered Lucinda's office, as summoned, she was nervous. Lucinda's tone had been ominous. On top of that, there was something eerily hospital-like about Lucinda's spacious, all-white office on the seventh floor of the old Newseum building. The glass-topped desk, the double wall of windows—one facing the seven-story atrium and the other facing Pennsylvania Avenue—everything was intended to evoke the notion of transparency, but Heather knew better, and she had an inkling that this conversation would be anything but transparent.

"Have a seat." Lucinda pointed to one of the two sleek steel chairs facing her desk. "Let's talk about your article. It was a good start, but it didn't go far enough. We need to be more aggressive."

Heather was puzzled. In her thinking, she had accomplished everything she'd set out to do. Her piece on Guy Pearle and IAU had shown him to be out of step with current social norms, and she had telegraphed Lucinda's message about the preservation letter. "What's missing?"

"Do I have to spell it out for you? We need something that will give us real leverage over Guy."

"Like what?"

"I don't know. Figure it out, dammit. Do you want me to do your job for you?"

"I'm just not sure what you're expecting me to do, or what kind of information you're looking for."

"When you're a hunter, you've got to hunt. Use your tools and go get something."

Heather sensed that Lucinda was expecting her to do something either illegal or unethical, but so far, Lucinda had maintained complete deniability. If Heather were to get into trouble, there was nothing she could point to that would implicate Lucinda. Of course, that was exactly what Lucinda wanted. Heather decided to try one more time to get Lucinda to be more explicit. She played the flattery card. "I'm sure you've faced situations like this before?" she offered, hesitantly.

Lucinda adopted a mentoring tone. "You're young and you're beautiful enough that men treat you differently. You try to act like you don't realize that, but you're not fooling anyone except maybe yourself. Hell, you're hot enough that I'm sure you could work your magic with more than a few women, but I get the impression you don't really understand the full power of your sexuality.

"All women have an intrinsic understanding of the power of sex, but very few really understand what they can do with it. Even average-looking women have a lot more power than they realize. Looks are important, but they're less important than attitude.

"I'm going to let you in on a little secret. Here's what separates weak women from strong women: Weak women use sex for pleasure, strong women use sex to get what they want, and really strong women take pleasure from using sex to get what they want.

"The world is backwards right now. Men are in charge, but they're stupid. They think with their dicks. That is their key weakness, but there aren't enough women taking advantage of that weakness to set the balance of power right.

"Go out there and be strong, and maybe even try to be really strong."

Later that afternoon, Heather took the Yellow Line from the Archives to Crystal City, hoping to get an impromptu interview with Guy. As she ascended the escalator and made the left turn into the underground tunnel that radiated in the direction of the IAU office, she noticed Brandon Leather.

She quickened her pace enough to fall into step beside him, brushing slightly against his left shoulder. “Aren’t you the gentleman I saw last week in the IAU elevator?”

Brandon was amazed she remembered him. They’d been in the elevator for no more than thirty seconds, a minute at most. From his experience, women like Heather didn’t remember men like Brandon, but he silenced the warning bells in his head. *Maybe there really isn’t anything strange about this at all...* “Yes, that’s me. Name’s Brandon Leather, by the way.”

She extended her hand. “I’m Heather Alston.” They were walking in the same direction, so Brandon reached awkwardly across himself to grasp her hand. She held onto his for a few seconds longer than necessary, dipping her head slightly in a walking curtsy. “Oh my! We could never get married. Then I’d be Heather Leather!”

Brandon skipped past the “could never” part of her statement and drank in the “get married.” What started as a chuckle turned into a snort, and he pulled his hand away abruptly to cover his mouth. In his haste, he failed to release his grip pressure and he pulled her hand nearly to shoulder height before letting go.

Heather didn’t miss a beat. Although she wasn’t really thrown off balance, she steadied herself by placing her hand on his shoulder. She kept it there for a good ten seconds, long enough for Brandon to meet her gaze, look away, and look back again.

“Do you know if Mr. Pearle is in the office today?” she asked.

“No.”

“No, he’s not in the office, or no, you don’t know?”

"Sorry, what I should have said is that he and his wife are in Morocco for a few days. They're at some big climate change conference, and he won't be back for maybe another week or so."

Heather stopped dead in her tracks and dropped both arms to her sides, lowering her gaze to the reddish-brown tiled floor. Brandon stopped walking. "Is something wrong?"

"Sort of. When I was here last week, I was doing a story on Mr. Pearle and IAU. He told me about some of your products like Firebomb, and he mentioned Phishhook, but I was so busy taking notes that I forgot to get answers to a couple of follow-up questions. My boss is all over me to get info for an update to the story, and I'm on a deadline. I've got to get the info by tomorrow."

"I'm not sure if it's helpful, but I was the lead software engineer on both of those products, so I know the technical information pretty well. Those two products are how I got promoted to IAU's lead project manager. If you've got a few minutes I can try to answer your questions."

"Would you really? That would be such a big help. I can't thank you enough." She grabbed his wrist and squeezed it. She would have held on longer for effect, but they reached the elevator and he pulled his arm away to press the call button.

They didn't speak again until he had signed her in as a guest and escorted her back to his cubicle. There was only one chair in the small, cluttered workspace, so Heather leaned on the desk. Brandon sat down, realizing that if he pulled his chair forward to access his keyboard, he would be only three or four inches from her. As tempting as that was, he was simultaneously petrified at the thought, so he pushed his chair as far away from her as he could get and stared up at her. Her hot-pink suit jacket and matching skirt radiated heat into the confined space, and her perfume wafted across the short distance between them. He was mesmerized.

"Before we get into Firebomb and Phishhook, have you seen our Digital Authentication System? It's pretty cool, and I designed most of it."

"What does it do?"

"It defeats deep-fake videos by embedding a blockchain on the bitstream. It's tied to the device that makes the original recording, and it creates an authentication signature that is a combination of the device's serial number and the time, date, and location. That makes it possible to compare a deep-fake to the original to show the real content and identify any manipulation. High-profile organizations are the key customer set. Think White House, members of Congress, political parties, the Department of Defense, and the like.

"There is a process that will also convert existing video to include the blockchain data. It requires a key from the person doing the conversion or else it doesn't work. That proves who did the conversion and when and where. The key innovation that makes it practical is the use of time, geography, and device as the encoding elements. These can be broken out by a proof service.

"We're not the first, but we developed a toolkit that made inserting the blockchain information practical. The first goal was to extract data that existed and embed that via software in the media storage device. That protected the forward path. Then we created an app that did the same with cameras on phones. Then we created another app that allowed you to upload legacy digital data and protect it.

"Our Digital Authentication System was a big deal in the 2024 presidential election. Both political parties were targeted by deep-fake hoaxes, and we gave them the tools to prove the hoaxes were not real. I mean, that was a game changer."

He spun to his left and pointed at two framed thank-you letters, one from the current occupant of the Oval Office. "Pretty cool, right?"

He expected her to agree that a thank-you letter from a sitting president was, indeed, pretty cool. He hoped that she might even be a little impressed. Her response, though, was something he would never have dreamed of.

"You like me, right?" she cooed.

"I don't really know you, but you seem nice enough."

"And pretty?"

Before he could answer, she leaned in and whispered, "Look, Brandon, you're one of the smartest men I think I've ever met. I know you don't owe me anything, and whatever happens to me won't change your life one bit. But I'm really in a bind here. I need something significant I can take back to my boss, something that will give me a big story. Is there anything you can tell me that would make a good story? I can keep you out of it. I just need something so I don't get fired."

Brandon lowered his gaze. He knew he was blushing. He considered getting into the technical details of how Firebomb and Phishhook worked, but everything he could tell her was already public in the user's notes published on their website. "There is one thing that's not widely known. I mean it's not huge, but it puts the whole Firebomb thing in a different light."

"What's that?" she asked, grabbing the arm of his chair and spinning it so that he had to face her directly.

"Well. It was pretty much a commercial failure. On the technical side, it worked, but only marginally. And everyone knew it wasn't a long-term solution. The black hats could always use onion routing to defeat traffic analysis, which is something we had to do to target the counterattacks. But once we had the capability in place, we got the attention of Cyber Command."

"How so?"

"We won a big contract to conduct offensive operations. It's not classified or anything, and we haven't done much with it, but it's pretty interesting because it allows the government to do things without getting their hands dirty."

"That is really interesting. I'm not sure if it is quite enough to save my job, but it is helpful." She shifted directly next to him, her hips within inches of his face. Brandon had been to strip joints where even beautiful and completely naked women didn't have this effect on him. He stared straight ahead.

"There's one more thing," he stammered. He knew he was about to blab something he shouldn't, but he was being driven by forces beyond his control.

Heather leaned back against the desk, and over the next few minutes Brandon described a cyber incident that had taken the company's servers offline for two days. One of the company's outside lawyers had forwarded a crude, politically incorrect joke to Guy Pearle. Unfortunately, the joke carried a sophisticated

Trojan horse that was designed to activate only when Guy Pearle opened the email. Guy read the email, activating the virus, which then shut down the servers.

Brandon still had a copy of the offending email on his desk, and he pointed to it. Heather saw the name of the original sender: Nigel Winston.

CHAPTER 8

ARLENE TANN ARRIVED AT THE RESTAURANT ON the corner of Tenth and Pennsylvania about twenty minutes early. She wanted to scope out the place and review her notes before Lucinda Hornbuckle arrived. Arlene was doing a profile on the influence of tech money in politics and Lucinda provided an interesting angle. She was not a tech billionaire and was not pouring tons of money into political campaigns, but she was just as influential as some of the bigger players. Malcolm Rutherford, the billionaire owner of the *Washington Note*—who'd made a fortune in the social media start-up wave of the twenty-teens and currently held a majority position in three of the largest social networking platforms—was intrigued by Lucinda and had asked Arlene to do the profile. It was outside her current beat, but it wasn't so long ago that Arlene had covered politics, so she was a good fit for the assignment.

The objective was twofold. The obvious goal was to tell the world about this brilliant woman who was reshaping the online news industry. *Social Tech* was a new kind of online magazine, with a completely new business model. Print media had primarily been driven by ad revenue, but that model fell apart when media went mostly online. Nearly all online ad revenue had been concentrated in the hands of a few big players, and traditional print and small online papers got choked out. Some, like the *Washington Note*, were ultimately acquired by the same tech giants who had put them out of business. Many of these were now vanity projects to push the views of the new owners. They never made a profit, but that wasn't the goal. They existed to describe the world not necessarily as it was, but as the owner wanted everyone to see it.

Arlene had initially chafed at the intrusion of the owner's editorial views into the newsroom, but she assuaged her discomfort with the thought that the new model wasn't really that much different than the old one. The biggest difference was that the newsroom now only had to deal with the idiosyncrasies of the owner, rather than trying to stumble through the minefield of the major advertisers' hidden red lines. Moreover, Malcolm—like most of the new tech billionaires—was liberal to the extreme, so his idiosyncrasies weren't all that idiosyncratic, at least not from Arlene's perspective.

But Lucinda Hornbuckle had created a completely new model of funding the news, and it depended on two things. First and foremost, Lucinda had built a reputation as a technical expert on a broad range of topics. She could talk climate change from atmospheric CO2 models down to molecular chemistry. She understood venture capital and could cite the rules for going public—on any of the exchanges—backward and forward. She understood not just renewable energy sources, but the entire spectrum of energy options, and could cite the pros and cons of each with remarkable detail. She was also a champion for social justice issues ranging from LGBTQ+ equality to racial justice and reparations for slavery. You name it, and she could make the case for why things were the way they were, why that was bad, and why things needed to change. Some suspected she had a photographic memory. Others believed she never slept and read all the time. But the one thing everyone agreed upon was that Lucinda Hornbuckle was a force to be reckoned with, and someone you didn't want to cross.

And that was the second element of her business model. Hers was a simple proposition: Agree with me or be destroyed. And by "agree with me," she meant not only "support the things I support," but also, "give me money." In the late nineties and early two-thousands, she had been a tech innovator, getting in on the ground floor of a half-dozen or so of the biggest IPOs in the tech space. She'd made a ton of money, but not the kind that allowed her to buy or build her own publishing empire. For the media organization she wanted, she still needed an ongoing source of revenue, and that could only come from sponsors. But the old-fashioned way of getting a small fee for each page view or larger blocks for advertising in special issues was insufficient. She wanted big money, and she wanted it fast.

Few people really knew the details because the contracts were shielded by a non-disclosure agreement viciously enforced by teams of high-dollar cutthroat lawyers, but a few of the companies she had dealt with later went out of business, meaning they had no assets for the lawyers to threaten, so the principals were willing to talk off the record. To hear those survivors tell it, Lucinda was remarkably candid in her approach. She asked for a meeting, telling the owners that she wanted to do a profile on the company. The sit-down occurred, and she made clear her philosophy that business leaders had a responsibility to stand up in the fight for social justice and against climate change. The way they could do that, she said, was to drop a boatload of cash on *Social Tech*. They weren't even going to get ads in her magazine for their money. All they were going to get was the good feeling of being on the right side of history, fighting the good fight and all that crap. Oh, and yeah, she would tell them at the end of the interview, if they did this, *Social Tech* wouldn't come after them.

She had started small, practicing on companies that were seeking venture capital. Most of them were ideologically aligned with her, so it wasn't a philosophical disagreement that caused them to balk at her demand for allegiance. And quite often it wasn't even the money. In the venture world, big bets were placed every day, and a few hundred thousand dollars here or there wasn't going to make or break a company. Those who bought in, with both money and philosophical allegiance, often did quite well—she knew how to pick winners, and she knew how to influence the moneyed elite. There were a few who stood up to her, but she came through on her threat to destroy them, so pretty soon it became a self-fulfilling prophecy. The only thing worse for a tech start-up on the East Coast than not getting Lucinda Hornbuckle's attention, was getting her attention and not doing what she wanted.

Critics might call it graymail, but that was exactly what made her most interesting, and possibly useful to Malcolm Rutherford. He knew she was a master in the ways of Washington and that she knew just how far each of the rules could be bent without breaking. This was something Malcolm lacked. He was a Brit who had come to the US in the 1990s because the tech world was moving much faster in America. He focused on getting rich and became a US citizen not because he identified with the country but because it was useful for business. What he had learned, however, was that while being rich bought a certain amount of power, it was not as much as one might think. He saw Lucinda Hornbuckle as someone who could teach him how to wield true Washington power. The second part of his mandate to Arlene was to explore whether Lucinda and *Social Tech* might be willing to collaborate on some special projects Malcolm had in mind.

When Lucinda arrived, she blew through the door like a whirlwind, her raincoat swirling around her as she scanned the restaurant for Arlene, whom she knew only from the picture attached to her byline. She spotted Arlene at a table for two along the windows that fronted onto Pennsylvania Avenue, and made her way over.

"I liked this place a lot better when it was Ten Penh, but the food is still pretty good. How are you doing?"

"I'm fine, thanks. And thanks for coming. I know you're busy."

"I'm never too busy for a dinner date with a reporter from the *Washington Note*. And, besides, I need something from you."

Wow, that was fast. This lady does not mess around! "Oh, really?" Arlene opened the door.

"I hear you've just come back from the COPS32 conference in Morocco. My latest target, Guy Pearle, was a delegate there. I'm hoping you met him. I need to get his attention, and so far, I'm not having much luck. He's a significant threat, and if I don't get him turned around soon, he can do a lot of damage."

"I didn't meet Guy, but I met his wife. She seemed a little out of place in the diplomatic scene, but nice enough."

"Oh, Janet, yeah, she's a sweetheart, and she's got the right worldview, but she's not willing to take on her husband."

"From what Janet was telling me, it seems like Guy is doing all the right things. His company is heavily invested in green tech, and I hear they're planning to make an even bigger push in that direction once they go public. I don't see how that makes him a threat."

"Oh, he's doing all the right things, but for the wrong reasons. And that's what makes him a threat. If he does the Stations of the Cross, but rejects the orthodoxy, then he normalizes nonconforming behavior. There is nothing more dangerous to our movement than someone who supports green tech but rejects the larger implications for government policy. And he is a Neanderthal on social justice issues.

"I was hoping you might have seen something that would give me a little leverage over him. You know how men are when they travel. There's a strong correlation between opportunity to be unfaithful and the actuality of being unfaithful, and there are a lot more opportunities when men are far from home. Show me a man who's never strayed, and I'll show you a man who just hasn't been tempted by the right bait. But I wasn't aware Janet went with him, so I imagine he was on his best behavior."

"Like I said, I didn't meet him."

"That's okay, I've got my best asset on him, a young reporter named Heather Alston. Tall, blond, and very good-looking. You should see the rack on her. I can't decide whether I am jealous or turned on. Maybe a little of both."

Arlene was not surprised by the hypocrisy of an ardent feminist speaking in such demeaning terms about a female subordinate. Hypocrisy was common in Washington. Hell, it was the norm. But the comment about Lucinda being turned on by a young woman was intriguing. Maybe there was more to the pixie haircut than just a fashion statement. She wondered if Lucinda was aware that Arlene was gay and was flirting, or if she was just being flippant. She never considered, not for a second, the actual truth: Lucinda knew Arlene was gay, and though she had no sexual interest in her at all, she was willing to exploit any attraction that Arlene might feel for her.

"So, now that we know there's nothing to be done about Guy Pearle, let's fix the rest of the world."

"Where should we start?"

Lucinda got focused and serious. "Here's how I see the world," she said. For the next half hour, Lucinda laid out her vision of the way things were, and the way things should be. She began by making the point, with which Arlene could not disagree, that the key remaining battleground in the ideological wars was the workplace. The battle for schoolyards and academia had been won long ago. These days, there were hardly even any skirmishes of note on those fronts. Schools, colleges, and universities were dominated by liberals, and they were doing a great job of conditioning children and young people to be the same. Children came into the classroom with a plethora of views their parents had imprinted upon them, but by the time they graduated, they were well indoctrinated in the absolute truths of climate change and social justice.

Arlene was mildly surprised at these blunt terms. Words like "conditioning" and "indoctrination" were usually hurled by conservatives criticizing the American school system, but Lucinda adopted them as if they were perfectly value neutral.

As Lucinda described it, the workplace was where things were falling apart. There had been a time when churches had served as a bulwark against liberal orthodoxy, but even that was changing. The Pope, of all people, had come on board with gay marriage. And once he had become a champion of the fight against climate change, the battle against the churches was over. It wasn't that the Pope carried all that much weight and had brought the faithful over to the light. In fact, the Pope's push into liberal causes had had the exact opposite effect—it had destroyed the Catholic Church as a touchstone on moral issues. There were some who still believed, but they either believed what the Pope was putting out, which fit perfectly with the message of the Left, or they just quit fighting altogether.

But the workplace was much harder to crack. There were too many businesses that employed people and affected daily lives. It would be impossible to go after them one by one. Instead, Lucinda suggested, it might be possible to pressure publicly traded companies to take on social justice and climate change goals. If they were successful there, the norms would flow down to smaller companies.

"You know, the Chinese already do that," Arlene offered.

"I've read about that, but not enough to be an authority. Tell me what I should know about how the Chinese do it."

"They put a Communist Party cell in every company to make sure the company conducts business according to acceptable practices."

"Wow, it's too bad we can't do something like that here. That would be awesome."

"Actually, there is an organization that's doing something along those lines. It's called Chinese–American Green. They go by 'CAG,' and they have adopted a model that looks a lot like the Chinese social credit scoring system. All of the employees in the company sign an agreement stipulating that they will support the CAG value system. They're mostly focused on climate change, but they're pretty forward-thinking on social issues, too. For example, the employees all have to give CAG access to their social media feeds, and employees can be fired for posting or promoting racial hatred, bias against gay marriage, or climate denial propaganda.

"I met some of the leaders of CAG at the conference in Morocco. They're trying to get all of the companies and organizations in the Africa Renaissance Project to become members of CAG and accept a social media monitor. I can introduce you to them if you'd like."

"That's brilliant," Lucinda said, abruptly standing up. "Turns out you've got something even better than what I was originally looking for." She positioned herself so her thighs and hips were close to Arlene's shoulder and, when Arlene turned to look up at Lucinda, her face.

"Let's do this again sometime, without the notebook," Lucinda said, as she bent over and kissed Arlene on the cheek. Before Arlene could recover, Lucinda was out the door.

CHAPTER 9

"YEAH, I SEE YOUR POINT," NIGEL WINSTON SAID, drawing it out to emphasize that he was merely acknowledging Guy's point, not agreeing with it. "If we made that offer to David Gordon, and if he accepted both the half a mil and the seat on the board, there would be no reason for him to pursue the lawsuit. But there are a couple of other things that we need to consider. First of all, the report from the outside accounting firm—the one that discovered David has a taste for the ladies—will be filed with the Securities and Exchange Commission when we file for the IPO, as will a record of a $500,000 payment to a guy we just fired and then brought back. It won't take a lot of digging for someone to find that and start asking questions. I'm already hearing rumors that there's talk of going beyond the greenshoe and possibly even doing a naked short."

Guy had received an email earlier in the day from Advanced Capital Placement on that very subject, and Nigel's name had been on the copy line. It was more than just a rumor, and they both knew that. What Guy couldn't understand was why Nigel was linking them together. "What does that have to do with this?"

"Well, the greenshoe allows the book runner to provide some price support if the stock comes out weak at the IPO."

"I know that," Guy shot back, "and a naked short allows them to try to cover for a busted IPO by selling shares short. If the IPO goes poorly, they can still make money by buying shares after the price goes down and delivering before the three-day closing period. It's only legal for the book runner, and it only happens if they are concerned that the IPO might flop. I was in the same briefings that you were, but what I'm trying to understand is why you're linking the possibility of a naked short with the threat of a lawsuit from David Gordon. I just don't see any connection between the two."

"There may not be a link. But when we first had the conversation about the lawsuit, you weren't convinced that Lucinda was a part of it. Now you know that not only is she involved, she's the one responsible for the whole thing."

Guy took a detour, implicitly agreeing with Nigel but not going so far as to admit it. "But why is she insisting that I become an advocate for the issues she cares about? There are some areas where we agree and some where we disagree. Why does she need me? She's got her own online platform to push her views. Why can't she just leave me alone?"

"Because you have more credibility than she does, and when you become a tech titan—and make no mistake about it, that's where you're headed—you will be a threat to her. She is trying to take you out. Do you put it past her, or think she's incapable of orchestrating a naked short, just for the purpose of inflicting harm upon you?"

"I think you give her way too much credit. She's powerful, and she's smart, but she's not the Antichrist."

"I don't want to make her out to be worse than she is, but I do think we have to be careful here. I've made the mistake more than once of thinking that because a woman is beautiful, she can't also be smart."

"Oh, I know what she's like. Don't forget, Nigel, I dated her. And I know you were burned by your ex-wife, but I'm not sure that's relevant here."

"Not just one ex-wife—both of them. *And* their lawyers. They were pretty and they were sweet, but every one of them carried a six-inch knife in their four-inch stilettos. When we got into settlement, they used that knife to gut me, financially and emotionally. And the whole time they were doing it, all I could think of was, 'Wow, aren't they pretty?' If it weren't for those mistakes, I would have retired back to Kentucky a long time ago."

"Well, I'm glad you didn't. You've been a good friend to me, and a good mentor. I don't think we—and I mean myself and IAU—would have come this far without your guidance and counsel. But this is a big step. If we file a countersuit, we're effectively declaring war on Lucinda. I've already talked with the team at IAU, and they're ready to support us no matter which way we go. But I'd like to have one more conversation with Janet. Can you give me half an hour or so?"

"Sure, I'll be here for another couple of hours. Call me when you're ready."

Guy ended the call and turned to Janet, who had been listening to his side of the conversation. She didn't need a lot of background on where things stood or what was at stake. She just needed the answer to one question.

"Guy, what is most important to you? And don't say that it's me. That's not what I mean. I'm talking about what is important to you when it comes to the IPO. Why are you doing it?"

"It *is* you, for the record, even in terms of what happens to IAU and the IPO. The reason I'm doing all of this, the reason behind everything I've done for the past twenty years, is to make you proud of me. I married you because of what you made me want to be. I want to be someone that you admire, and that desire to make you proud is what gets me out of bed every morning. It's what gets me through the bad days, and it makes the good days even better. And that's what I want here. I want to be successful, to make a dent in the universe."

"And you can, but you have to do it on the universe's terms. You don't get to pick the era into which you're born. Think of what Einstein might have been able to do if he'd had access to a computer. But he didn't. He still made amazing contributions to the world, even though he didn't have as much access to knowledge or the computing power that we all carry around in our cell phones. He did that because he knew he was onto something and he never gave up. Your greatest attribute, and the thing that I have always admired most about you, is that you are fearless."

"But why this? Why do I have to get involved in trench warfare on social justice issues when all I want to do is create things that make life better for people?"

Janet stepped closer and wrapped her arms around Guy. She leaned back and brought her eyes to his. "You've heard the saying by Edmund Burke, 'The only thing necessary for the triumph of evil is for good men to do nothing.' Well, you're the good man in this situation, and you've got to do something."

"Do what?"

"Fight! Fight that bitch and put her in her place."

Guy knew that Janet was lumping together the specific fight with Lucinda and the larger fight against the social justice warriors. Maybe they were one and the same to Janet and to everyone else, but to Guy, they were completely different. There was a history there, something that he feared Janet would not understand.

In high school, Guy had never gotten past "hands over the shirt" pawing. He'd been nerdy, and while he'd been on a few dates, they never led to much in the way of romance. He hadn't felt left out, left behind, or cheated. He just thought that was the way it was.

All that changed when he got to college and met Lucinda. He was initiated into the magical world of sex. And, with Lucinda, what a world it was. In her college days, she was a master magician: round in all the right places, firm and flat where she should be, and soft in ways that drove men crazy.

On top of that, she was the most uninhibited person Guy had ever encountered, sometimes taking him to the edge of his comfort zone and beyond. He wasn't sure whether the vivid images of their encounters were memories or psychic scars, but he knew they were indelible.

Lucinda seemed little affected by their passion and would roll out of bed after their trysts as if nothing remarkable had happened. Not so for Guy. Her nonchalance was impossible for him.

He was intoxicated by the specter of what she showed him, and terrified that he might fall so deeply in love with her—and with what she made him feel—that he might never recover.

Everyone who learned about their relationship supposed Guy had a soft spot for an old flame. Nothing could be further from the truth. His feelings were a mixture of repulsion at the cravings that she had drawn out of him and fear that she might find a way to rekindle that want. Every encounter with her was another chance to awaken the monster. That was why he was afraid of her.

How could he explain this to Janet? Dare he even try? What good would it do to open that door into his past? The danger was clear. Janet was prim and proper and would find the whole thing disgusting. And she would undoubtedly think less of Guy, even as she protested that she wouldn't. But how could he explain to Janet what was going on in his head if he left that out?

She would always have doubts, but it was better for her to have doubts based on suspicions than for her to know the truth. Knowing Janet, her suspicions were undoubtedly much tamer than the reality. It could do no good to rip away the veil that cloaked this dark part of his past. He would not tell her; he could not. He must simply believe that she would trust him if he did the right thing.

He pulled Janet close to him and kissed her forehead. The smell of her perfume and her shampoo, the warmth of her body pressed against him, gave him the strength he needed. He wrapped his arms more tightly around her and whispered in her ear, "Thanksgiving is coming up next week. It's my favorite holiday. No presents, no pressure. Just good food and football. I am so lucky to have you."

The decision he had to make was clear. When Nigel Winston answered his phone, Guy said, "It's time to poke the bear."

CHAPTER 10

BRENDA BULLOCK WAS EXCITED WHEN THE IN-tercom buzzed and Lucinda Hornbuckle asked her to come in. She'd only been at *Social Tech* a few weeks, but already she had been assigned tasks that were far more interesting than she'd ever dreamed possible.

Brenda was only three years out of high school, having made a conscious decision to forgo college. She had read too many blog posts about young people who were successful at work but who could never attain financial independence because they had taken on crushing amounts of debt to get a degree that was meaningful to them, but otherwise useless.

For most of her life, Brenda had been an outsider. Blowing off college was just another gemstone in her tiara of uniqueness, right alongside her blue, spiked hair, her nose ring, eyebrow piercings, and double rows of stud earrings. Some could handle the body mods, or at least the ones they could see, but had a hard time dealing with her intense and vocal support for LGBTQ+ rights. And, although they never admitted it, she knew that more than one of her exes had broken up with her because she was, as one of them had so subtly put it, Rubenesque.

But at *Social Tech*, Brenda felt like she had found her calling. The research she was doing, combined with the things she was learning from Lucinda, made her feel that her efforts were significant. She thought Lucinda accepted her for who she was, body mods and all. Which was true, but not in the way Brenda supposed. Lucinda could spot a broken child a mile away, and knew that Brenda's quest to stand out masked a craving for approval that would make her easy to manipulate.

Brenda grabbed her notepad and bounded down the hall toward Lucinda's office, meeting up with and matching stride with Heather Alston, who was headed in the same direction.

"Ladies, where do we stand? Give me an update, please," Lucinda asked when both of them had taken a seat.

Brenda looked deferentially toward Heather, assuming the briefings would be done in order of seniority, but Heather nodded her assent for Brenda to speak first.

"I've learned quite a bit about the Chinese–American Green group. They're headquartered in Beijing but have an office here in Washington, DC. They call themselves 'CAG' and are very focused on social justice and combating climate change. Their values align very well with ours here at *Social Tech*."

Brenda's report came across like a high-school term paper, which was not unexpected. Although Brenda didn't pick up on it, the corners of Lucinda's mouth pursed slightly, but not enough to affect her calm, reassuring tone. "Yep, got it, thanks. Keep up the good work. Heather, what have you got for me?"

Heather looked down at her notes and ran through the highlights. For Brenda's benefit, she covered some of the things she'd already discussed with Lucinda, including the virus that had infected IAU's servers and the politically incorrect email.

Lucinda leaned back in her chair and said, pensively, "Well, the server problems are interesting, but I don't see much that we can do with that. There's probably not a company in the country that doesn't have problems with funny cat videos and diet secrets. There's just no leverage there. But did I hear you right? Did you say that they traced the virus back to a specific email?"

"Yes, it was a joke forwarded by IAU's outside counsel, a man named Nigel Winston. As dirty jokes go, it was pretty weak, some sexist crap about a restaurant that names entrees after famous politicians. There was a four-piece chicken dinner named after a female senator that included two left wings and two small breasts. It was juvenile, not even funny, really. But it does say something about Guy Pearle, and about the law firm that he's using, if an email like that is all it takes to trick them into downloading a virus."

"Did your source mention anything about keylogging software?"

"No, why?"

"No reason in particular, just curious. It's not uncommon for an attack of the type you described to serve as a cover for the insertion of a keylogging program. Sometimes the victim is so focused on getting their servers back up and running that they don't notice the attacker implanted a malicious script in the boot file. If there is a keylogger, the attacker can see everything that gets typed on the system, including passwords, so they can take complete control. Sometimes it happens, sometimes it doesn't. I was curious."

"I'll go back to my sources to see what I can find."

"No, that's not necessary. I think we're going to have to move straight to Plan B anyway since Plan A doesn't seem to be moving fast enough. The naked short play isn't working, and David Gordon is acting like an arrogant prick, which risks screwing up everything, so we're going to have to get more aggressive."

Brenda was puzzled. "Naked short?"

Lucinda's patience was tested, but she knew that she had to give approval before she could withhold it. She knew that Brenda looked up to her like a teacher, so she played the role. "You can and should look it up on the Internet, but here's the high-level version. I've got a source who is telling me that the company running book for their IPO is asking IAU to consider letting them do a naked short. That is only done when there is a lot of short interest in the stock, meaning that more people think it is going to decrease than think it will increase in value."

"But," Heather interjected, "I thought you wanted them to do a naked short."

"I do, or I did, but it didn't have the desired effect. I wanted IAU to agree to a settlement with David Gordon and to give him a seat on the board in exchange for David agreeing to drop the lawsuit. That was the whole reason for pushing the naked short. If that happened, we wouldn't have been in the driver's seat, but we would have had one hand on the steering wheel. David would have given us a lot of control over what they did.

"But Guy and his lawyers weren't fazed. They seem to think that the greenshoe will cover all the short selling and, in a worst-case scenario, they can do a small short beyond that to keep the

IPO on track. Because they are the company running the IPO, that's legal for them, but it wouldn't be legal for me or any of my allies to really get aggressive in shorting the stock—at least, not to the level that would be necessary to damage the IPO.

"The basic problem is that we didn't create enough short interest. I tried to push it up, but most of the people I was talking to were either afraid of having the SEC come after them for illegal short selling or were hoping to buy before the pop and make a fast buck when the stock goes up after the IPO. There's a lot of positive buzz about IAU, and it's difficult to create short interest in the face of that.

"And on top of that, David Gordon has flaked on us. He's getting greedy and wants to increase his settlement to a million bucks. I told him I'd see if that's even possible, but that was just to buy time. I'm going to leave him hanging and keep the threat of the lawsuit in place, but I'm not optimistic it's going to produce anything.

"Bottom line, we tried, but it didn't work. Now we have to step it up a notch.

"Brenda, I need to send you to the CAG headquarters in Beijing. You've got to get a really good understanding of how they do what they do. Once you're an expert, I will work to get you inserted into IAU. I don't have a plan for that yet, but I'm working on it.

"Thanksgiving is just around the corner, and I don't see a window to get you to Beijing between Thanksgiving and Christmas. I think it'll take you at least a month to gain the level of expertise you'll need, and I don't want to ask you to be away from your family during the holidays, so, realistically, we're looking for a spot right after the first of the year."

Brenda had no idea what she was supposed to do when she eventually got "inserted into IAU," or even what that meant, but she trusted that Lucinda would provide the necessary guidance. She could tell that this was important to Lucinda and missing a holiday or two was a small price to pay to demonstrate her loyalty. She chuckled and said, "You've obviously never met my family. They're a complete freak show, and I never spend holidays with them. It's waaay too depressing. So, I'm good on that front. And, as far as I can tell, the Chinese don't celebrate Thanksgiving. I mean, they observe Christmas, but not like we do here, so I can go as soon as I'm able to make the travel arrangements.

"I'm going to get a kick out of telling my mom that I won't be available this year for the annual group photo because I'll be in *China*!" She made an exaggerated fist-pumping motion, and neither Heather nor Lucinda could tell whether she was excited about going to China or about being handed a trump card she could play to avoid the annual family gathering.

"All right, then," Lucinda said, trying to keep Brenda from high-fiving her. "I appreciate your enthusiasm. Make sure you take a company laptop that has video-conferencing software on it. I'm not paying for cell phone charges from China."

Brenda practically raced out of the room to start planning her trip, leaving Heather and Lucinda alone.

"What do you want me to do?" Heather asked.

"It's not a question of what I want you to do. It's a question of what you're willing to do. I want you to get me some useful dirt on Guy Pearle. It seems like the only really damaging thing in this town is for a married man to get caught sleeping with a younger woman. Everything else just gets ignored. That's the kind of leverage I need, and I need it soon.

"He's about to become the latest tech billionaire, or at least a multimillionaire, and one of the few on the East Coast. In case you haven't noticed, we're in the nation's political center of power. If he manages to go public before we can get him thinking right on social issues and climate change, he will do serious damage to everything we're fighting for."

Heather was just as woke as Lucinda, but she wasn't willing to sleep with a source to get information or material for blackmail. In Heather's view of the world, being woke was more than just pushing a certain viewpoint; it also required being dignified and treating others with respect. Sleeping around for the cause was not woke.

And it wasn't lost on her that Lucinda had expressed concern about the fact that IAU had identified a specific email that carried the virus. As a reporter, Heather got paid to connect the dots, usually as they related to the subjects of the stories that she wrote. Connecting dots wasn't a habit that one could just turn on and off; it was on all the time. Heather was seeing some pretty big dots.

Her sense of decency told her that she needed to get as far away as she could from Lucinda Hornbuckle and *Social Tech*, and fast. But the timing was wrong. The lines connecting Lucinda to potentially illegal hacking were blurry. If she was going to expose Lucinda's wrongdoing, she would need more direct proof, and she could only obtain that from the inside. As distasteful as it was going to be, Heather realized she needed to stay at *Social Tech* and stay close to Lucinda. More importantly, she needed to ensure that Lucinda didn't suspect she was being maneuvered into incriminating herself. Manipulating a master manipulator wasn't going to be easy, but Heather had learned from the best.

She leaned down to pick up her purse, while also deftly unbuttoning the top two buttons of her blouse. Now was not the time for half measures. She stood up and crossed to Lucinda's desk, where she placed her purse and notepad. Then she leaned far enough over to give Lucinda an eyeful.

Lucinda was taken aback. "Where's that been? That's what I'm talking about!"

Heather grinned, knowing full well that Lucinda believed she was practicing the moves she would use on Guy. Heather licked her lips and turned her head coyly to one side. "Well, let me just say that you've been an inspiration to me. Thanks to you, I know exactly what I need to do."

CHAPTER 11

JANET PEARLE WAS RUNNING LATE. AFTER A LATE lunch with Guy at Union Station, she had taken the MARC Train back to where she'd parked at New Carrollton station. Normally, they traveled together whenever possible to reduce their carbon footprint, but today they had taken separate cars, as Janet needed to hurry home to prepare for tomorrow's Thanksgiving dinner.

She considered taking the elevator to the top floor of the seven-story parking garage but decided to get her steps in instead. It wasn't enough to cover an extra piece of pumpkin pie, but it was a good start. As she approached her car, she saw Guy's SUV in the spot next to hers and remembered that she needed to stop at the grocery store to pick up some celery for the stuffing. She wasn't a huge fan of celery in stuffing, but it was Guy's favorite and he'd been under so much pressure lately; she wanted to do something nice for him.

She paid for parking and headed east on Route 50 toward Annapolis. On most days when she crested the hill just past Enterprise Road in Mitchellville, Janet could see the two-lane bridge that crossed over Route 50 just east of Freeway Airport. Today, though, she saw a cloud of smoke where the bridge should be. A small Cessna trying to land had clipped the radome on final approach, and the plane cartwheeled onto the grass between the runway and the highway and caught fire. The fire quickly spread along the south side of the highway, and a dense blanket of gray smoke was floating into the eastbound lanes. Some motorists were pulling over to see if they could help, while others were trying to clear the area as quickly as possible, before the inevitable traffic jam. The situation quickly became chaotic, resulting in three or four fender-benders that jammed all three lanes.

In the far-left lane, Janet considered stopping to see if she could lend a hand but realized that maneuvering across traffic would only add to the chaos. She couldn't be sure how long it would take for traffic to clear, but she knew it was going to be long enough that she would have to choose between stopping to get celery and cooking tonight's dinner. She decided to prioritize Thanksgiving and called Guy to let him know.

When Janet's call came in, Guy was on his office phone talking to the lead IPO specialist at Advanced Capital Placement. There was some concern that the greenshoe might not be enough to cover the short interest, and the specialist was walking Guy through the mechanics and risks of a naked short. Guy saw Janet's picture pop up on his cell phone, and he made a mental note to call her back when he could. For now, though, he pressed a button that automatically sent a text message saying, *Sorry, I can't take your call right now*.

When the call rang through to voicemail, Janet said, "Hi, honey, it's me. I'm on my way home, but there's been some kind of accident near Freeway Airport and traffic is a mess. Since tomorrow is Thanksgiving and I need to stop at the store for celery, I won't have time to thaw the pork chops I had planned to cook this evening. Why don't you just grab something there before you head home? Love you, bye."

When Guy finished the phone call about the IPO, he grabbed his cell phone to check Janet's message before calling her back. He smiled when she mentioned picking up celery. *What a sweetheart. She's going out of her way just for me.*

Then he heard the crash.

Janet had been just about to hang up when it occurred. An eighteen-wheeler, fully loaded with Sheetrock, slammed into the stopped Volvo at more than sixty miles an hour. The young truck driver was pouring a cup of coffee from a thermos to help him stay awake and alert, and wasn't focused on the road in front of him as he crested the hill.

The first indication the truck driver had that there was a problem was when the huge red Peterbilt rammed into the rear of the Volvo. Instinctively, he slammed on the brakes, but it was far too late. The massive truck devoured the Volvo like a shark attacking its prey. By the time the truck finally came to a stop, it was resting on top of the Volvo, which had been reduced to less than half its normal height. The station wagon's two rear wheels had been blown out by the force of the impact and the weight of the truck.

At first, Guy didn't comprehend. He heard the violent clash of metal on metal and breaking glass, but his mind didn't want to hear what he thought he was hearing. Maybe a vehicle close to Janet's had just been demolished, and her phone had picked up the sound. Janet was okay. *She had to be okay.*

He tried to call her back, but his call went to voicemail. He tried twice more with the same result. He played Janet's voicemail again. As he listened to the call for the second time it dawned on him that he wasn't hearing someone else's car—it was Janet's car being obliterated. In that instant, he realized that everything he cared about in life had just been destroyed.

Suddenly, Guy found himself thrust beyond the safety of his workaday existence into a realm he had known to exist but had never given any serious consideration. He didn't know how to feel. For a time, he couldn't feel anything. Like electrical circuits subjected to a hundred times their rated current, Guy's emotional pathways had just been overloaded, blown, fried. The first internal circuit to come back online was the one carrying pain. As suddenly as it had tripped off, it came back on. And when it did, Guy wished he could turn it off again.

After the accident, the next few days were a blur. Guy had always assumed he would be the first to pass and that Janet would have everything put in place for an orderly goodbye. That was the way nature intended it. Men didn't bury their wives—women buried their husbands. That was just the way it was. But even that wasn't supposed to happen until they were older, much older. The notion of Janet dying first—and in her forties—just wasn't something they had ever contemplated.

Both he and Janet had grown up Catholic, attending mass regularly, but had stopped going shortly after their wedding. Janet, in particular, had found it difficult to reconcile her views on abortion with those of the church. Apart from the occasional wedding, baptism, or funeral, they'd barely set foot in a church over the past twenty years.

Many of their friends were members of the local Methodist church, and someone recommended it for the funeral. Guy asked, and the church was able to accommodate the request. The people he dealt with at the church were kind and supportive in a "neighbor from three doors down" kind of way. Some of them, especially the older ladies, seemed to be at ease with a ritual they had been through many times. Many clearly sensed that there would only be a few more of these rituals before they themselves were the ones being honored, and they showed Janet the utmost respect—perhaps hoping for the same when it was to be their turn.

During the memorial service Guy couldn't help noticing that the words of the Apostles' Creed seemed different than what he remembered from his childhood. Out of habit, he formulated a question for Janet, his best friend, but before he could finish, he realized that the time for asking her questions was past. Now, he would have to find the answers on his own.

The last song of the memorial service was "Amazing Grace," one of Janet's favorites, and as the first verse started, a wave of grief washed over him, reminding him again that this was real. He could not catch his breath through the sobs that tore through him, and he weakly mouthed the words. But he knew that Janet would expect him to sing, because, as terrible as he was, she still liked to hear him sing. So, he steeled himself and pushed through the last verse, mercifully drowned out by everyone else.

When the ensuing reception was over, all of the guests filed out of the hall. The ladies and gentlemen who acted as ushers remained for a respectful amount of time, watching the pictures of Janet cycle through on the monitors at the front of the room. They, too, eventually filed out, leaving Guy alone.

For reasons that he couldn't quite comprehend, Guy felt compelled to gather up the remaining programs from the service, as if leaving them there would somehow be abandoning Janet. He was in the midst of stacking them when the pastor, Reverend Walker, came up and placed his hand on Guy's shoulder. "That's okay, Guy, we'll take care of that."

Guy dropped his arms to his sides and stared plaintively at the reverend.

Reverend Walker said, "I won't try to tell you that I know what you're feeling, because I don't. I could tell you that I lost my wife several years ago to cancer, or that I've officiated at dozens, if not hundreds, of memorial services and funerals. Those things are true, but they don't give me a right to claim that I know your pain. Every loss is different. But I will tell you this: God has a plan for your life. You may not be able to understand it right now, but it's important for you to try to learn what that plan is."

Guy made no effort to mask the bitterness he felt. "And what about my wife?" he asked. "Did God have a plan for her, too? Was it part of His plan for Janet to be crushed by some moronic truck driver? Or maybe that was all part of His plan for the truck driver, and my wife just had a supporting role."

The reverend took a deep breath, clasped his hands together behind his back, and said, "I won't tell you not to be angry, but I will tell you that it won't serve any purpose to be angry with God. There are things that seem to defy explanation, and life is filled with pain, but you may find some consolation in knowing that Janet is in Heaven now. If nothing else, I hope you can find some comfort in that."

"I wish I could believe that," Guy said coldly. "But I can't. The idea that Heaven is a wonderful place where people go when they die may be the only thing I can hang on to—the only way I can come to grips with the loss of my wife—and I'm not going to reject it, but I can't help noticing that the concepts of Heaven and Hell just happen to be about the best way a man could think of to control other men. What happens if there really is no Heaven or Hell, and it's all just a scheme concocted by the church to control those who can be duped into believing?"

"Faith is never easy, Guy, but what is the alternative?"

"I don't know, Reverend. What is the alternative?"

"Well, when faced with a crisis like this, some try alcohol. I've seen others turn their pain and anger onto themselves, as if they were somehow to blame. And I have seen some turn to faith. The church doesn't always have answers, but it always has people who care, people who honestly want to help you."

"Well, thank you, Reverend. I appreciate your kindness, and I'm sorry for being rude. I didn't mean to take it out on you."

"Think nothing of it. God bless you. Come see me or call me anytime if you want to talk."

Although he made all the arrangements for the burial, Guy could barely focus on the details. The one thing that stayed with him was the difficulty of picking a cemetery. He and Janet had never really discussed the issue. Janet was an only child whose divorced and remarried parents had already passed on and were buried in different states, so there was no natural choice based on family ties. The only thing he knew for sure was that Janet didn't want to be buried in the cemetery near the roundabout on West Street in Annapolis. It was a remark she'd made nearly every time they passed by it. Beyond that, he was on his own.

Eventually, he discovered that the same Methodist church had cemetery plots available. He picked two spaces next to each other, choosing to place Janet on the left so they could lie throughout eternity as they had lain each night.

The search for a cemetery had pushed into the week before Christmas, and Guy knew that Janet would not want to impose on the joy of others. He organized a small graveside service that wasn't even at the graveside—it was in a covered area near the section of the cemetery where Janet was to be laid to rest. Her gravesite would not be ready for another few days.

When the gravesite was ready, Janet was lowered into her final resting place, attended only by the two men whose job it was to do such things. Guy was grateful that he didn't have to watch her being lowered into the ground.

When everything was completed, he went to her grave with a floral array, a mix of her favorite flowers. The florist nearest their home had known Janet quite well and had been kind enough to help Guy select a beautiful arrangement.

By the time he visited the grave, he had no more tears to cry. He laid the bouquet next to her headstone and stared at it for a few minutes. The air was cold and dry, but a single snowflake drifted down and landed on his cheek, Janet's final kiss goodbye.

CHAPTER 12

THANKSGIVING. CHRISTMAS. NEW YEAR'S. JANET'S memorial service and funeral. Her birthday and what would have been their twenty-first anniversary. All of these came and went during a jumbled six-week period where each day was just like the one before. Guy was numb and alone, engulfed in a deeper loneliness than anything he had ever experienced. There were a few days, scattered here and there, when the pain seemed slightly less intolerable than the day before. But those days only made him feel guilty, because he couldn't stand the thought of actually learning to bear the pain. In his head he knew that the pain would eventually lessen, but in his heart, he couldn't escape the sensation that the absence of pain was a betrayal of Janet's memory.

Finally, in the second week of January, Guy started to re-engage. He knew that as CEO of IAU, he couldn't just disappear. There were decisions to be made.

He called Nigel Winston. "Nigel, I just can't do it anymore. I can't fight with Lucinda, but I don't know what to do. If we don't fight, she will win. You said a few weeks ago that we could postpone the IPO. Is that still an option? Can we do that without doing too much damage?"

"I can make that happen. There will be some fallout, but it will be manageable. I'll take care of it, if that's what you want."

"Okay, thank you. I'm going away for a bit. I've appointed Carl Underhill as interim CEO. He's been with the company since the beginning. He's very capable and has my full trust and authority. Please work with him until I get back."

Nigel was about to offer his sympathy for Janet's passing when the line went dead.

. . . .

IT WAS JUST AFTER THE MARTIN LUTHER KING holiday when Heather Alston phoned Brandon Leather to see if she could schedule a follow-up meeting. She wanted to dig a little deeper into the story about the virus that had shut down

IAU's servers, and to find out if there really had been a keylogging program buried in the boot file. She never got the words out, though, because within seconds of taking her call, Brandon told her that Guy was still out on leave and wouldn't be back for at least for another week or two, and that emotions at IAU were still pretty raw after Janet's death.

Heather went immediately to Lucinda's office to inform her of Janet's passing, hoping this sad turn of events would, if nothing else, get Lucinda to drop her crusade against Guy Pearle.

"Well, that's a shame," Lucinda said, staring out the window onto Pennsylvania Avenue.

Heather said, "Yes, I feel sorry for him. She was so young, and now he's all alone."

"Oh, her. That's not what I meant."

"What did you mean, then?"

"What I meant is that I thought you were ready to get into the game. I knew that if you went at him with what you showed me a few weeks ago, there would be no way he could resist. Now, what's the point? He won't be in the mood to sleep with you for a while, and even if he does, he's a widower, so it won't matter. There's no scandal in a grieving widower banging a hot young blond. It's just pathetic."

Heather was too stunned to reply and just walked out of the room. She stopped at the door and turned to glance at Lucinda, simply amazed at the callousness of this disgusting woman she had once admired.

PART II – EXILE

CHAPTER 1

THE FIFTY-THREE NEW ARRIVALS TO THE AFRICA Renaissance Project sat restlessly in the bleachers of the gymnasium. They had arrived in small groups at the Hassan I Airport in Laayoune, in neighboring Western Sahara, over the course of the morning. By noon, everyone except a pair of twin sisters from Kansas was present and accounted for. The sisters had missed a connecting flight from Casablanca and would be coming in the next day. All those who had made it to Laayoune on time were shuffled onto two yellow school busses, along with their suitcases and gear, for the two-hour drive to the ARP compound in Tarfaya, on the Moroccan coast. Although hardly anyone on the busses noticed, they were escorted by two armored Suburbans, each carrying four heavily armed security personnel.

Upon arriving inside the ARP compound, the newcomers were given a five-minute bathroom break and then ushered onto the gymnasium bleachers with no explanation or instructions. They were hungry, tired, and jet-lagged, and their patience was running thin.

For the first ten minutes, they sat silently, expecting someone to come greet them. Then a few people began to chat. Ten minutes later, almost everyone in the group was busy getting to know their new colleagues. The noise level rose from a quiet hum to a steady din.

Few noticed the man in khaki trousers and a light-blue polo shirt stride into the gymnasium and take a spot front and center on the bleachers. He walked quietly, unobtrusively and without fanfare. He held his clipboard against his thigh, pushed up his silver, wire-rimmed glasses, and said, "May I have your attention, please?"

The conversations continued. After waiting a spell, he raised his voice slightly. "May I have your attention, please?"

The crowd chatted away, engrossed in their conversations.

"*Silence!*"

The shout came from deep within the khaki-clad man's chest and rang through the gym like a thunderclap, bringing all talk to a halt.

A young black man in the second row, wearing blue cargo pants and a white tee shirt yelled, "Who the fuck are you?" Several others catcalled and whistled.

The man with the clipboard pointed to a twenty-something male in the first row and ordered him to start doing push-ups. Although he was not the one who had shouted—that man was seated directly behind him—he nevertheless complied.

Everyone in the bleachers stared. After thirty seconds or so of silence, the man in the khaki trousers motioned for the young man to retake his seat. "People are brave, willing to run their mouths when they think they are anonymous, but they lose their nerve when they see the consequences. Only a coward would remain silent and let someone else be punished for their own actions.

"Why did you mouth off?" he asked, looking straight at Sam Fischel, the one who had shouted the vulgar question.

Sam rose to his feet to show that he wasn't going to be intimidated by this puny white guy. He looked around, gathering nods that implicitly made him the spokesman for the group, "Who the fuck are you to tell us what to do? You see a gay black man and all of a sudden you go on some kind of power trip, calling me a coward and shit. What's up with that? You better step off before I come down these bleachers and teach you a thing or two."

Max ignored the accusations that he was racist and homophobic. He said, "Oh, okay, hold that thought. Let's dig a little deeper into what you just said. I am intrigued by your choice of words. Your willingness to address me in such a vulgar manner tells me that you don't respect me. I get it. You're a millennial. I have to earn your respect. No problem.

"Let me start by introducing myself. My name is Maxwell Burke, but you can call me Max. I am the security chief here at ARP. It's my job to keep you alive so you can go back home to Mommy in one piece when you finish here.

"So, why should you respect me? It might matter to you that I did two tours as a Marine infantryman in Iraq and two tours in Afghanistan. Some people who find themselves in a new environment where terrorist attacks against civilians are on the rise, might find those four combat tours to be useful qualifications for a chief of security. But that isn't why you should respect me. In fact, I'm going to agree with you. I don't think you should respect me until I've taught you something useful.

"But a lack of respect for me doesn't free you from the obligation to act like a civilized human being. I asked the room politely for their attention, but everyone decided to just keep jacking their jaws. Then you decided to run your mouth like some tough guy, but when I made this young man do push-ups, you didn't own up to what you said, and you certainly didn't stand up for him.

"That might be how it's done back home, but it won't work here. Our survival depends upon each one of us knowing certain things and acting in certain ways. We must treat each other with respect and act in a disciplined manner, not like a bunch of assholes who don't give a damn about anything beyond getting something exciting to post on social media.

"This is a difficult and complicated environment. It may look safe, but the threat is real, and it is increasing. There is a group operating in Western Africa called Terrorists and African Nationalists, or TAN for short, that has been trying to sabotage this project almost from the start. They seem to think that giving the people of Africa tools to build a better life is going to decrease the power of Islam. They would like nothing better than to catch a few of you outside the compound and get famous by videoing themselves cutting off your head. That doesn't make any sense to me, but I'm not here to change their minds. I'm here to educate you about the threat and to keep you safe. And to do that, I need all of you to pay attention. I trust that I have your attention now and that if I ask you to be quiet, you will do so.

"My goal today is to teach you two things. First, I want everyone to understand the concept of a rally point. That's the place you go to when your primary location is untenable. For us—and this is something I want you to memorize—the primary rally point is Tarfaya City Hall. If you were paying attention, you saw it shortly before you entered the compound. It's a three-story building with a red tin roof, about a quarter of a mile west of the main gate. If you didn't see it, you should make a point to locate it as soon as you can."

The young Brit who had been doing push-ups raised his hand and asked, "Why is that the rally point? Why wouldn't we just come back here?"

"Good question. Please, stand up, introduce yourself, and tell everyone what you do."

The young man stood, clasped his hands together in front of him, bent his head down slightly, and said, meekly, "My name is Nigel Franklin."

"Speak up, young man, no one can hear you. When it's your turn to be heard, make sure that you *are* heard," Max said, his voice booming across the gym.

The young man raised his chin and looked directly at Max, his voice stronger and more confident. "I am Nigel Franklin. I am a program specialist in the United Kingdom's Department for International Development. I came here to ARP to work on the new seawater greenhouse project."

"Thanks, Nigel. Well done. I can see that you know how to take instruction. That's great. Have a seat. And thanks for being a good sport about the push-ups.

"So, back to your question. Why is City Hall the rally point? It's the tallest building within twenty miles of here, so it's visible from nearly everywhere you will need to go outside the compound.

"If the terrorists attack us, they will probably target the compound first. Your instincts are going to tell you to come back here. You'll think, 'It's safe; it's where my friends are. That's where I need to go.' But if we're in the middle of a firefight, coming back one or two at a time isn't going to do anyone any good. There's also a chance you might get shot if someone sees you running into the compound by yourself, and they don't recognize you. We have about four hundred people working here, with fifty or sixty newcomers each week and the same number departing. Chances are that you won't be able to get to know everyone here by sight. As you can tell from looking around, we're a pretty diverse group, and you won't be able to tell the good guys from the bad based on appearances alone. Bottom line, it's not safe to come back to the compound if it's under attack. Gather at the rally point.

"If those inside the compound are able to defend it, hang out at the rally point until you get word that it's safe to come back. If the fight to defend the compound isn't going well, organizing a counterattack from the rally point is the best option, because City Hall has an armory where we've been allowed to store extra weapons and ammunition. If you happen to forget your weapon, you'll be able to pick one up at the rally point along with plenty of ammo. Make sense?"

Nigel and several others in the group nodded.

"Okay," Max continued. "The second thing I'm going to teach you today is how to use an AK-47. And when I say 'use an AK-47' I mean that I want you to know how to load it and fire it, how to find a good fighting position, and how to kill the guy who is shooting at you before he kills you.

"If you're wondering why you're being issued an AK-47 rather than an M-16, that's a fair question. It's because the AK-47 is the most widely used weapon on the planet. It's cheap, it's simple to operate, and it's what we have. If you learn how to use it properly, it will do everything you need it to."

For the next half hour, Max taught the new arrivals how to load their weapons with dummy bullets and to dry fire. He taught them how to assume a good firing position by having some take positions behind the bleachers while others critiqued them. He demonstrated the two most common mistakes novices make—sticking the barrel of the weapon too far out of the window, and exposing one's forehead over the top of the windowsill—and taught them what to do instead.

Guy Pearle sat alone in an unused corner of the bleachers, watching and wondering if he had made a mistake in coming here. In the eight weeks since Janet's death, he had been on the long downward slope of an emotional roller coaster. He had come to Africa in the hope that a change of scenery—a place where every street and restaurant he passed didn't remind him of Janet—might give him a chance to start the long climb back up the other side. So far, though, he had his doubts.

After the training session, Guy made his way through the in-processing line. He was given a welcome package containing a map of the ARP compound, including directions to his assigned quarters, and general information about the facilities, such as the location and hours of the dining hall, medical center, and the recreation center. He received his badge and a lanyard and instructions that he was to wear the badge at all times when inside the compound. Then he got his ration card and a small slip of paper with the Wi-Fi password. The last items he received were an AK-47 with six thirty-round magazines and nine boxes of ammunition with twenty rounds per box. He placed the magazines and ammo in his backpack and slung the AK-47 over his other shoulder.

Guy followed the highlighted path on the map from the gymnasium to his assigned quarters, which proved to be a small trailer, ten feet deep and thirty feet wide. Four of the trailers were grouped together behind a concrete T-wall perimeter that stood twelve feet tall, providing ample protection from small arms fire. There was a telephone pole at each corner, from which wire mesh and canvas netting were suspended over the trailers to protect against mortar rounds. The canopy wasn't thick enough to shield the occupants of the trailers from an explosion but was designed to make the mortar detonate in the air above the trailers, rather than inside one. Each trailer had been placed on a cinder block foundation, with three steps leading up to the door.

When Guy entered his trailer, he saw that a small bathroom stood straight ahead, and a door on the right featured a large, round insignia depicting an Eagle, Globe, and Anchor capped by a banner that read, *Semper Fidelis*. Guy recognized it as the emblem of the Marine Corps and wondered how many Marines there were at ARP. He hoped there were others besides Max.

He entered the room that was his quarters and saw a metal-framed bed boasting a three-inch thick mattress, a green wool blanket, and a pillow in an off-white pillowcase. There was also a wall locker, a desk with a chair, and a small table supporting an older model flat-screen TV. Everything looked like it came straight out of a military surplus catalog. A small air-conditioner protruded from the wall at the rear of the room. Guy turned it on and started to unpack.

Halfway through unpacking, Guy sat down on the bed, buried his head in his hands, and fought back tears, trying to understand why God was so angry with him. What could he have done that was so heinous that God's punishment was to take away Janet? Everything else was in shambles, too. The postponement of the IPO might become permanent if he couldn't find a way to outmaneuver Lucinda Hornbuckle. And now, here in Africa, nothing was turning out like he'd expected. He thought ARP would be a place where he could find peace of mind and immerse himself in meaningful work. Instead, he was a conscript in a ragtag bunch of do-gooders who might be attacked at any moment by armed terrorists.

He thought back to Reverend Walker's words. He knew that the reverend would remind him that punishment and reward for one's actions come in the afterlife, not in this life, but if it wasn't a punishment, Guy could not comprehend how a merciful God could do such things. He tried his hardest to see some sign of God's hand, but he could not.

Then he heard the door creak and looked up to see a small pug-Chihuahua mix with a wagging tail and hopeful eyes making a beeline for Guy. Instinctively, he reached out to pet her, and she flopped down on her side, exposing her belly in invitation.

Guy was rubbing her belly when he heard footsteps and looked up to see Max Burke. "I see you've met Peanut."

"I thought the welcome package said we weren't allowed to keep pets."

"Well, she's not a pet, per se. She's kind of the compound mascot. She likes everybody and I don't know of anyone who doesn't like her. Don't go thinking that she's partial to you just because she lets you rub her belly. That's her signature move. She does it for everyone."

Guy stood up and assessed Max. He was not the sort you'd pick out of a crowd as being a Marine. He was of medium height and build, with gray-blue eyes and a deep tan but no scars or tattoos, and the style of his glasses made him look more academic than macho. The only thing that really screamed Marine was his short hair.

"I'm sorry, we haven't been introduced. I'm Guy Pearle. I'm with Innovative Applications Unlimited and we have several ongoing projects here. I'm here to check on our projects and to make decisions about possibly expanding our footprint here. Is it really as dangerous as you said, or was it just a show to get our attention?"

"There may have been some theatrics, but the threat is real. My problem is that I can't—*we* can't—afford to be unprepared. When this threat hits, it comes quickly, and I won't have time to get people trained and focused. I have to get them thinking about the threat from day one.

"I know it's a little rough, and I'm sorry for that. I'm aware this isn't the Marine Corps and people didn't sign up for boot camp. But the Marine Corps is what I know, and when it comes to preparing people for challenges, the Marine Corps is not a bad place to start.

"I remember when I went to boot camp in San Diego. They pick everyone up at the airport for the bus ride to the training depot, very much like we do here. Our ride is a good bit longer, which is kind of a pain in the ass, but the welcome is a lot friendlier here. When you get to the recruit depot in San Diego, they start yelling at you to get off the bus and fall in on the yellow footprints painted on the sidewalk. They're screaming and yelling and no matter what you do, it isn't right. You feel helpless and small. The whole point of that orientation, and for a lot of what happens in the first few weeks of boot camp, is to break down the individual to get him ready to be a part of the team. I can't do all of that, and I wouldn't even if I could, but I need to get people to understand that they can't afford to be complacent, and we all have to be a part of the same team."

"Well, it's a good thing you didn't tell me to get down and do push-ups. I wouldn't have done it. You'd have looked pretty foolish then."

"Why do you think I didn't pick you? To do my job, I have to be able to read people. I knew a couple of things about you just from the way you sat in the bleachers and looked at me when I came in."

"Like what?"

"You're not a conformist, you're comfortable in your own skin, and you don't feel a need for anyone else's approval. You see yourself as a leader, and there's nothing wrong with that. But you've also got something else on your mind, something that's eating at you. I don't know what it is, and I'm not asking, but you need to sort it out quickly or you'll end up like the last person who had this room."

"What happened to him?"

"He could never adjust to this place. Like you, he refused to participate in the initial training. He never made any friends, and just sulked around, sticking to himself."

"So, he left?"

"No, he committed suicide."

CHAPTER 2

THE NEXT MORNING GUY MADE HIS WAY TO THE dining facility. He showed his badge and ration card to the local guard, and as he stood in line for runny eggs and overcooked bacon, he glanced around, hoping to see a familiar face. He thought if he could find someone who'd been on the flight from Dulles, the bus ride from Laayoune, or even the training session, at least they'd have something in common to talk about.

When he turned away from the serving line toward the dozen rows of tables, he noticed the young man who had been so vocal yesterday. Guy stopped by the coffee station and the pastry table, then made his way to where the young man was sitting alone.

"May I join you?"

"Sure, man, whatever."

"Thanks. My name is Guy Pearle. I think we were in the same in-processing group yesterday."

"Yeah, maybe."

"Is it just me, or is this place a bit strange? It's not quite what I was expecting."

"Tell me about it. If it's as bad as that dude was saying yesterday, they shouldn't bring us in until the Marines are done, know what I mean?

"Yeah, I hear you."

"I mean, like, I'm in IT. I came over here to put in some new hardware for a fucked-up little company called IAU or some shit. I don't do guns, and I didn't come here to fight terrorists. And this food sucks, man. As soon as I can find the dude I need to talk to about getting these new servers installed, I'm going to get it done and get the hell out of here."

"Well, I think I'm your man. These wouldn't happen to be a couple of Dell PowerEdge R1020 rack-mounted servers would it?"

"Aw, man, I'm sorry. I called it a little fucked-up company. I didn't mean it, I was just . . ."

"Don't worry about it," Guy said. "What's your name, by the way?"

"I'm Sam Fischel."

"Where are you from, Sam?"

"I was born and raised in Washington, DC, the last plantation in America where black folks can't vote. I used to do IT work as an independent contractor for the Department of Health and Human Services, you know, like a 1099-type dude, but I got restless and decided to try something new. I saw the posting for this gig and thought it might be nice to travel a bit, check out my roots. This is my first time in Africa."

Sam looked around the dining facility and dropped his napkin onto his tray. "So far, I ain't loving it. But, hey, man, I'll catch you later. I've got to find shipping and receiving to see if those servers got here yet."

Guy finished his breakfast and set out to find the workspace module labeled 4A. The workspaces, like the living quarters, were made from ten-foot by thirty-foot trailer units. The number of trailers fastened together determined the size of the workspace. The ten-person module allocated to IAU consisted of three trailers that were nearly identical to the residential units with a few minor exceptions: a double door for the main entrance; and two doors into each room, one from the central corridor and one into the adjoining room. The biggest difference was the center section. Rather than the shower, toilet, and sink found in the residential quarters, the workspace units had two small restrooms side by side, each with only a toilet and a sink. The workspaces were furnished with the same tables, desks, and chairs found in the residential units.

As he entered the office area of the compound, Guy passed through a checkpoint and waived his badge at the local guard. He walked down the central alley to the fourth gap on the right in the T-wall barriers, ascended the stairs and entered the office.

When he entered the trailer, Guy looked first in the rooms on the right and didn't see anyone. Then he walked into the first room on the left and saw a woman in her mid-thirties with auburn hair, talking on her cell phone. She had her back to him, so he retreated into the central corridor, but even there, he could hear every word she said.

When she hung up, Guy stepped back inside, and she turned to greet him. She was above average height, almost as tall as Guy and had striking green eyes. "Hi, I'm Kate Mulgrew," she said. "I'm the Public Affairs Officer for ARP. I hope you don't mind my being here. They put me in this space last week because the company that is assigned to it only has a couple of people."

"No problem. Yeah, for now it's just me and one IT guy. Strangely enough, I ran into him at breakfast this morning. He'll be here before long, I expect. He's trying to track down some servers that we ordered. By the way, I'm Guy Pearle. You look vaguely familiar. Have we met somewhere before?"

"I don't think you and I have met, but I do believe I met your wife a couple of months ago at COPS32 in Marrakesh. How is she?"

From the look that crossed Guy's face, Kate could tell she had touched a nerve. Instinctively, she said, "Oh, I'm sorry," without knowing why.

"No, that's all right," Guy said. "You had no way of knowing. She passed away right before Thanksgiving. Car accident."

"Oh, I'm so sorry," Kate repeated. She turned back to her desk, and Guy was about to search out an office space he could claim as his own when Sam Fischel opened the main door and stepped into the module.

"There you are, man. I'll tell you one thing; this place is fucked-up. They won't release the servers to me unless you're there to sign for them. Like I'm going to steal them or something, just 'cause I'm black? This is Africa, everybody's black. What they pickin' on me for?"

"I'm sure it's not a race thing, Sam. I'll come with you and we'll figure it out."

When Guy stepped toward the door, Sam saw Kate for the first time. "Oh, I didn't see you. You fine, mama! My name's Sam, Sam Fischel, IT specialist extraordinaire. You work here in this office?"

While Kate was trying to think of a polite way to brush Sam off, Guy said, "Okay, Sam, let's go see if we can get those servers. We got work to do."

"I'll tell you what, man. It's like we just imported the whole fucking bureaucracy into Africa. You wanna beat the terrorists? Give those motherfuckers a taste of bureaucracy, that'll slow 'em down. Gotta sign in triplicate to get your bullets and bombs."

When they were out of the trailer, Guy stopped before exiting the T-wall barrier and said, "Sam, we're going to have to work together. I respect you and your talent, but I'd like to ask you to do two things. First, please cut down on the profanity. If you don't want to be stereotyped, then don't act like one. I know you're smart. You couldn't have obtained your IT certificates if you weren't. That's hard stuff. I don't know if the profanity is an act, if you're just trying not to look like a geek, but it's inappropriate. And I'd like you to stop.

"Second, take it east with Kate. We're going to be working in the same office for eight weeks. If you want a love life, I've got no objections to that, but keep it away from the office.

"Tell you what, if you do those two things for me, I'll double your pay. When IAU put out the requisition for this gig, we had no idea that you'd be working in conditions like this. The pay is too low for someone with your skills, so I'm willing to double it, but only if you act like a gentleman. Deal?"

Sam thought for a moment of pointing out that he was gay, and that he had simply been complimenting Kate, but he didn't want to risk having the offer rescinded, so he simply said, "Deal."

CHAPTER 3

FOR THE NEXT FEW DAYS, GUY AND SAM PREpared for the arrival of the remaining IAU staff, who would operate the three projects IAU had chosen to bring directly to ARP. For the previous six months, IAU had been working through subcontractors who represented the company in the scientific forums present at ARP. Based on the subcontractors' reports, conditions at ARP were ideal for each of the three projects.

The first, and most ambitious, was the Solar Powered Plastic Processing project, or SP3 as it was known to the staff. Since 2020, IAU had been successfully operating an SP3 installation in the Great Pacific Garbage Patch—or, more specifically, the Eastern Garbage Patch located between California and Hawaii. At least a dozen teams had previously tried and failed to develop a method for recovering plastic waste from the ocean, but IAU had finally managed it. Carl Underhill, IAU's chief technology officer, had served as the lead engineer for the project and received the Gold Medal Award for Engineering from the American Society of Naval Engineers.

At first glance, the SP3 appeared quite simple. It was a massive barge, just over thirty feet wide and a hundred feet long, covered with solar panels. The barge drifted through the garbage patch and, using three different processing techniques, collected large, medium, and microscopic pieces of plastic.

But the simplicity masked an incredibly complex web of engineering innovations. The collection and filtering processes had been among the most difficult to develop. There were easier methods available, but those processes were more likely to harm marine life. The IAU engineers had worked through several versions of collection and filtering processes to make the SP3 harmless to sea life.

After the plastic was collected, it was passed into the central section of the barge, where it was then melted and formed into small pellets, which were stored in a hopper. When enough plastic pellets were available and the barge's batteries were fully charged, the final step in the process was to form the plastic into a bale. For that step, the IAU engineers designed a device that resembled a 3D printer. The plastic pellets were melted and forced through a flexible hose with compressed air. A computer controlled the hose and adjusted the nozzle on the end to create a half-inch layer of plastic on top of a special trap door, the surface of which was designed to prevent bonding with the hot plastic. The printer added layer after layer of plastic, building up the bale.

About halfway through the forming process, another computer-controlled device embedded a wire rope through the middle of the bale that connected each bale to the one before and after it in the manufacturing process. After the wire rope was inserted, the forming machine kept adding solid half-inch-thick layers of plastic until it reached the upper third of the bale. When that point was reached, the machine began to incorporate air pockets into the bale to provide for positive buoyancy.

The processed bales of plastic measured ten feet wide, twenty feet long, and six feet high, and they weighed just over one ton. As each one was completed, the trap door underneath the bale swung open and rollers pushed the bale downward until it was completely clear of the barge. As the barge moved forward, the bale rose up from underneath and it floated—connected to the bale behind it and the barge by a wire rope—until it was ready to be retrieved by an ocean-going tug and towed into port.

The entire process was automated, from selecting the best path to collect the most plastic, to forming the bales and sending a notice via satellite link that a string of bales was ready to be retrieved. The SP3 operated continuously, limited only by the available sunlight. It was not a fast process. The solar panels were relatively small, and the amount of plastic in the Great Garbage Patch was not that dense—less than a hundred kilograms per square kilometer in most places. But the SP3 was patient. It was fully automated, powered by solar energy, and the small amount of maintenance that was required every six months was provided by the crew of the ocean-going tug when it came to retrieve the plastic bales.

SP3 was not a commercial project. With market prices of fifty to seventy-five dollars per ton of recycled plastic and a production rate of only two bales per month, the amount of plastic processed by the SP3 was enough to cover operational costs, but not capital costs. But it was not designed as a profit-making venture. It had been designed in response to requests from the US government and several other international environmental organizations. Not everything was about making money. Sometimes it was necessary to undo the harm that had been inflicted upon the environment by previous generations.

What made SP3 potentially viable for ARP was the presence of the South Atlantic Gyre, which contained its own garbage patch, and a thermal gradient off the coast of Africa that was high enough to permit ocean thermal energy conversion, or OTEC. The Japanese had been the original developers of OTEC, in large part because of their easy access to waters with some of the largest thermal gradients between the deep waters and the surface temperatures. But there was a stretch of ocean between Africa and South America with temperature gradients that averaged between twenty-two and twenty-four degrees centigrade, a difference that was large enough to support OTEC.

IAU had licensed open-cycle OTEC technology from the Japanese to minimize the risks associated with the refrigerants necessary for a closed-cycle system. They combined the OTEC technology with their own advanced battery charging and ocean-going autonomous vehicles to create an additional power source for the SP3, which had the potential to double output to four tons per month. Marrying the technologies solved one of the challenges that prevented the widespread use of OTEC—the fact that the power was generated in the middle of the ocean and had to be transported back to shore to be useful. Undersea cables had proved impractical but storing the power in batteries, which were transferred to SP3 by autonomous vehicles, made it possible to consume the power locally.

The pilot project IAU had done in the Pacific had been successful, if strangely reminiscent of science fiction movies where robots roamed about non-stop. But there was still one problem that remained to be solved before SP3 could support the other IAU projects at ARP: The plastic bales still had to be recovered from the water and transported to the compound for use in the sonic welding experiment and the sand plasticizing project.

Guy thought he had found a solution and hoped to get it resolved within the next two weeks. He had reached out earlier in the week to Makram Abd Alsalam of Sahara Freight Express, whom he had met and received a card from at the COPS32 event in Marrakesh. Makram had driven down from Agadir the day before and was coming to the IAU office this morning to discuss the logistics of recovering the bales of plastic from the port at Tarfaya, getting them processed through Moroccan customs, and delivering them to the IAU warehouse within ARP.

Kate had been kind enough to help with arranging the visit. She had purchased a traditional Moroccan tea set with a silver alloy teapot, a dozen glasses in assorted colors, a folding tray table made of Atlas cedar and carved with Moorish designs, and a brass tray. The teapot was unlike American or British teapots, with their full round bodies and short snouts. Rather, it was tall, with a medium-sized base and a very long and thin spout. She had also purchased an electric hot plate to boil the water, mint leaves to make the tea, dates, and an assortment of pastries.

She had arranged all the chairs in the room, as well as a few borrowed from next door, in a circle around the tea table, with the dates and pastries on one of the main desks and positioned herself next to it.

When Guy arrived, he was surprised to see such elaborate preparations, and mentioned that he had just come from the dining hall. He noted that their guest was also likely to have just eaten before his arrival, since their meeting was scheduled for 8 a.m.

Kate explained that the American style of doing business would not work in Morocco. She was careful to note that she was not an expert but had done quite a bit of reading about Moroccan culture to prepare for her role at ARP. "Americans go to meetings and jump straight into business, but that's not the norm here in Morocco. Things are different, and slower, here. The culture of Morocco was deeply influenced by the Arab Conquest of North Africa as well as Spanish and French colonialism. The indigenous Berber and Sahrawi peoples also injected customs and traditions into what now makes up Moroccan culture. The result is a delicate mix of ancient and modern traditions. These may seem quaint and time-consuming to Westerners, especially to people who are accustomed to the fast pace of the DC area, but you need to slow down a bit."

"Okay, I'm game for learning something new," Guy replied, but he wasn't sure their guest was going to be big on tradition. He had read Makram's profile online and noted that Makram had been educated in England. He also recalled from their meeting at COPS32 that Makram spoke English with a perfect British accent. From what he had observed, he was pretty sure that Makram was quite Westernized, but he saw no reason to make a fuss about it.

When Makram arrived, he quickly proved Guy's point. "Ah, tea!" Makram said. "Thanks. I appreciate the thought, but it's not necessary. If you come to my office in Casablanca, we serve tea with every meeting, but I can do without it. I was born in Casablanca but raised in the UK. I prefer Earl Grey to Moroccan mint tea, but please, go ahead, don't let me stop you."

He took a seat in the chair nearest the door and said, "I'll tell you what, I'll show you how to pour tea in the authentic Moroccan way."

Makram took the teakettle from the burner and raised it almost two feet above the tea glasses on the brass serving tray. He deftly tilted the kettle and a stream of steaming tea poured into each glass without a single drop spilled. When he finished pouring, he left the first two glasses on the tray and handed the third one to Kate, then one each to Guy and Sam. Finally, he took one for himself and raised it slightly, as if making a toast to the group, then took a small sip and placed it back on the serving tray.

"It's customary to start with a little small talk," Makram continued, "but we can dispense with that. It was a seven-hour drive down here from Agadir yesterday and I've had more than my fair share of small talk. Let's get to business."

Guy had a sense that he and Makram were going to get along just fine. He placed his tea glass on the serving tray and invited Makram to see the inner workings of the projects IAU was bringing to ARP.

"Do you know the history of this area?" Makram asked as they walked to the warehouse where the sonic welding and sand plasticizing equipment were stored. Guy, Kate, and Sam indicated that they had limited knowledge of the area, other than the fact that it was just north of the border between Morocco and Western Sahara—a disputed region that had broken off from Morocco after the Spanish relinquished control in the mid-1970s.

For the next several minutes, Makram regaled his hosts with the most interesting historical points about Morocco in general, and the Tarfaya area in particular. He explained that most of North Africa speaks Arabic because of the Arab Conquest in the mid-seventh century, and that the Arabs pushed into Spain in the early eighth century. He noted that the capital of Morocco, Rabat, took its name from the Arabic word used to describe the fortresses at the frontier between Muslim lands and those of the nonbelievers.

"Even this area, sometimes known as Cape Juby, has a very interesting history. In the late nineteenth century, a Scottish engineer whose name escapes me at the moment, proposed the creation of the Sahara Sea by cutting a canal from just north of Tarfaya to El Djouf, a vast plain a few hundred kilometers southeast of here. The idea was to turn the desert green by flooding El Djouf with seawater. He thought this would cause rainclouds to form over the desert, eventually allowing agriculture to flourish in this part of Africa. As it turned out, he was incorrect in thinking that El Djouf was below sea level, so no canal was ever dug.

"You may also have heard the story of *The Little Prince.* The Frenchman who wrote that novella in the early 1940s spent nearly two years here in Tarfaya in the late 1920s. He was a pilot for Aeropostale. The plane crash that serves as the basis for the story occurred on the other side of the continent, between Libya and Egypt, but it is believed that much of the desert scenery described in the book is from this area. So, you see, you are not the first to come to Tarfaya with dreams of conquering the desert."

By the time Makram finished his history lesson the group had reached the warehouse containing the sonic welding and sand plasticizing equipment. Guy took over the conversation and explained the purpose and operation of the sand plasticizing equipment.

"As you can see, we have two primary ingredients: plastic and sand. The sand is sourced locally; the plastic is shipped in. We heat the plastic into liquid form, mix in the sand with some proprietary hardeners, and extrude the mixture into blocks and planks of varying lengths. The resulting material is extremely rugged and holds up quite well under the desert conditions. Depending on the shape, the material can be used to build housing, to line ponds to prevent water from seeping into the ground, and—this is one of our most exciting applications—for road construction.

"We are very fortunate to have this facility located so close to the Tarfaya Wind Farm. That facility produces more than three hundred megawatts of energy, and we use a lot of electricity in making plasticized sand. But the potential is remarkable. There was a time when the plastic recycling market essentially died out. The Chinese had been the largest purchaser of plastic waste, but they eventually had their fill and the bottom fell out of the market. The amount of effort required to recycle plastic made it more expensive than buying new plastic products.

"If we are successful here, we will revitalize the market for recycled plastic. People will have an incentive to recycle, knowing that it will go into a highway or an affordable housing unit rather than into a landfill or into the ocean."

Guy didn't seem to notice the grimace that crossed Makram's face at the notion of Morocco receiving tons of recycled plastic and taking up the title of king of plastic waste, but Sam spotted it.

Guy was so excited about the possibilities he was describing he simply swept the group along to where the sonic welding equipment was set up. "This," he said pointing to a large contraption that looked like a welding machine with a robotic arm, "is the enabling technology that makes it all possible—the sonic welder. It is tuned to the appropriate frequency for each kind of plastic and when the pieces are held together in a jig, it can make a permanent joint that is just as strong as the core material. We can assemble a half-acre pond in less than a day, and a single-story affordable home in two."

He picked up a sample from a workbench and showed how the pieces were formed with a tongue-and-groove feature that easily locked them into place while the sonic welder permanently fastened them together. "This stuff is lighter than wood, almost as strong as aluminum, and it has an R-value of six, which is comparable to polyurethane board. We can make three-inch thick walls for homes, and those walls have both structural and insulating properties. For the roofs, we need to increase the thickness to ten inches, but we have a special extrusion machine that forms roofing pieces in a honeycomb fashion that is both lightweight and structurally strong. We bring the home to the site as a kit in a single truckload. More than 80 percent of the contents of the home will be made from this plasticized sand. We use standard windows and doors, and we need electrical wiring and plumbing, of course. Based on our tests, we're confident that it would be safe to use our recycled plastic products for plumbing, but we're not looking to fight that battle.

"When the truck arrives at the site, all we have to do is level it out, set the utilities, and snap the pieces together. Once the pieces are in place, the sonic welder is programmed to fuse all the joints. Like I said, a well-trained crew can do it in less than two days. These houses are not luxury condos, but they are incredibly affordable, and they make great use of recycled materials."

Makram listened with interest, but clearly remained unconvinced. "How do you keep it cool? Here in Tarfaya, the temperature is relatively stable and doesn't get too hot, but if you go north and inland, like to Ouarzazate, the temperature gets up to almost forty degrees centigrade. That's over a hundred degrees Fahrenheit. That house will become an oven. Nobody will want to live in it."

"That is a legitimate issue, and we're working on it. First and foremost, the house is designed with solar panels on the roof that drive a sophisticated cooling system. The solar panels also reduce the amount of sunlight that falls directly on the house."

"Anytime you use the word 'sophisticated' to describe something that is designed to work in the desert, you're asking for trouble. The heat and the sand destroy everything."

"I understand that this is a harsher environment than what we're accustomed to dealing with, but, interestingly enough, we think that might be a solution rather than a problem. There are literally millions of tons of plastic waste generated each year. Much of that can't be recycled because it contains organic waste, mostly food waste. We're working on a process that involves burying the waste, organic material and all. The heat and dust that you're talking about will help us to clean the plastic. All of the organic matter will be absorbed into the soil, which will help the soil to hold moisture and will provide nutrients for plants. When we 'mine' the plastic from the soil after the desert has cleaned it of organic material, we'll be able to separate the plastic from the soil quite easily and use the enriched soil in seawater greenhouses to grow crops.

"Right now, to be honest, I believe our biggest problem is going to be getting enough recycled plastic to meet the demand for this product."

"Your enthusiasm is commendable, but I am not the one who needs to be persuaded. The desert will prove soon enough whether you are right or whether you're just another fool. I'm here to help you get your recycled plastic from the port and into this warehouse. Let's go take a look at the port."

CHAPTER 4

MAKRAM ABD ALSALAM TOOK A FLIGHT FROM Laayoune back to Casablanca after the meetings at the Africa Renaissance Project, leaving his driver to make the twelve-hour drive up the coast. He had much to think about. His original intent had been to conduct a detailed reconnaissance on the ARP compound to identify potential security weaknesses that could be exploited by the Casablanca cell of the Popular Front for the Liberation of Saguia el-Hamra and Rio de Oro, known locally as the Polisario.

Makram's grandfather had been among the founding members of the Polisario in the early 1970s. The organization began as a group of young idealists who wanted to bring socialism to the Sahara. Accounts varied as to what had actually happened, but Makram's view—which mirrored that of his grandfather—was that the Spanish had simply tired of being colonialists, the United Nations and other organizations with a mission to protect the local population had failed to do their job, and Morocco had taken advantage of the situation to become the administrative power in Western Sahara by fiat. With the exception of iron ore in nearby Zouérat, the region didn't hold enough economic potential for anyone to pay attention.

As Makram's grandfather told the story, the world sat idly by as more than three hundred thousand Moroccans, escorted by thousands of Moroccan troops, gathered at Tarfaya in November of 1975. They stormed across the border with no resistance from the Spanish troops stationed there. The wishes of the local population, who overwhelmingly favored independence, were well known, but no one was willing to stand up for them.

Over the next twenty-odd years, the Moroccans had withstood the guerilla war the Polisario waged. The first step in holding off the guerilla attacks was to build a massive wall along the southern border of the disputed area. The wall was more than two meters high, with a trench behind it on the Moroccan side, and combat outposts every few kilometers. It was not impenetrable, but it was sufficient to keep the Polisario from regaining the territory.

The first wall secured an area known as the "useful triangle" with Laayoune in the center and Smara and the phosphate mines at Bou Craa defining the southern edge. When the initial wall proved successful, the Moroccans continued to extend the wall deeper and deeper into Western Sahara. By the late 1980s, the Moroccans had built six walls, the last of which extended all the way south to Bir Gandouz and Guerguerat, encompassing nearly all of the disputed territory.

In the early 1990s, the Polisario effectively merged with the leadership of the Sahrawi Arab Democratic Republic, or SADR, and the joint organization was given control of the portion of the former Western Sahara territory outside of the Moroccan walls. With fewer than one hundred thousand citizens and virtually no economic resources within the territory assigned to SADR, the Polisario was beyond impotent—it was irrelevant. Although several dozen countries had initially recognized SADR and established diplomatic relations with the country, many of those subsequently withdrew their recognition. Of all the conflicts in the world, the fight for control of Western Sahara was perhaps the most forgotten. With each passing day, it was becoming more apparent that Morocco's annexation of Western Sahara was final.

But there were those like Makram Abd Alsalam, who fully intended to undo the Moroccans' land grab and return the Sahrawi Arab Democratic Republic to its rightful boundaries, and to perhaps make up for the decades of oppression by taking control of the southern portion of Morocco, as far north as Tan-Tan and potentially all the way to Sidi Ifni on the coast. For nearly a year, Makram and the other members of his group had stockpiled weapons at Tindouf, the southern Algerian city that had once served as headquarters for the government-in-exile of the SADR.

The primary problem was that the Polisario, by itself, lacked the men and resources to carry out such an attack on southern Morocco. Of necessity, they had aligned themselves with practically every group they could find that was willing and able to put men into the fight. It was for this reason that the group was given the pejorative name of Terrorists and African Nationalists by many Westerners. Makram not only resented the name, he vowed he would shape the rebels into an effective fighting force and drive the Moroccans and their allies from Western Sahara, and thereby prove the Westerners wrong. As the leader of the rebellion, he expected a prominent place in the expanded government, perhaps as Minister of State.

But to achieve that goal, he would first have to persuade the Islamists and the nationalists within his group that laying waste to everything within the disputed territories would ultimately be unproductive. And now, more than a dozen of them—mostly leaders from other cells scattered throughout the region—were gathered in his offices in Casablanca to receive his report on the security weaknesses at ARP, and to outline a strategy for seizing the compound.

"It is my opinion," Makram began, "that a force of a hundred men can take control of the ARP compound. They have weapons, but only a few trained security personnel. Most of the people who work there are civilians who stay for only a few weeks, or a handful of months at most. Most are like the Peace Corps volunteers we have all met. They are there because they believe in the mission, but they are not likely to fight to defend the compound if we can make it clear that our victory is inevitable and that we won't harm them if they surrender without a fight."

One of the cell leaders, a hardline Islamist from Algeria, disagreed. Hakim al-Wahid argued, "We should not show weakness. This will be our first and largest strike against the infidels. We must show the world that we are powerful. The best way to do that is to destroy everything within the compound, and to kill every Westerner we find.

"You are forgetting that this is not simply a fight for you and your friends to regain control of the Western Sahara. For most of us, and nearly all of those who will be doing the actual fighting, this is jihad. Your purpose may be to gain power, but our purpose is to rid Africa of infidels. In the time of the Prophet—peace be upon him—the glory of Islam was spread far and wide by the mujahideen. We must follow their example, and God willing, we will control all of Africa before our grandchildren reach adulthood."

Makram wanted to point out that Hakim was remarkably willing to shed the blood of others when he himself would be staying safe in Tindouf but opted for a scholarly approach instead. "Yes, there were many mujahideen who martyred themselves in service to the Prophet—peace be upon him—but would it not be better to convert these Westerners to Islam than to kill them?"

"Brother, that is not jihad. The Quran commands that we attack and defeat them. We cannot allow them to continue to exist.

And we cannot wait much longer. If the Chinese become strong here as they have in east Africa, they will bring their value system, which is stronger than that of America. They will be much more difficult to defeat than the Americans and other Westerners.

"And the Americans must pay for the thousands of innocent women and children they have killed throughout the Muslim world with their drone attacks. Do not speak to me of innocence. They claim to have a representative democracy and to choose their leaders, so when they do nothing when their leaders carry out these drone attacks, they are every bit as guilty and should suffer the same fate."

Makram could tell by the facial expressions of those around the table that the argument was swinging against him, but he offered one last plea for a peaceful approach. "You have seen it yourself. The American system does not provide for majority rule. In many cases, the person with the most votes has not become the president. The young among the Americans do not hold the beliefs of their fathers, and they do not support their government. They worship crystals and stars, and do yoga, and hold protests against the fascists who are in charge.

"They have abandoned Christianity and are searching for truth and strength. Why should we waste valuable time and resources killing these people who already hate Christianity? Their beliefs are born of ignorance. They hunger for guidance. Do you believe for one minute that they will hold to their silly beliefs when presented with the truth of Islam?"

Although he did not fully embrace this argument, Makram felt that it was acceptable to dissemble slightly to support his case, and it seemed to work. The other cell leaders murmured in agreement. It would not do any harm to take the ARP compound with as little bloodshed as possible. There was likely to be enough combat for even the most ardent jihadists in taking Tan-Tan and Sidi Ifni, the two cities along the coast north of Tarfaya that offered the best blocking positions for counterattacks by the Moroccan armed forces. If the world had stood by while the Green March took Western Sahara fifty years before, perhaps they would not intervene this time, either—especially if the conquest did not result in too many casualties.

Makram had one last argument in reserve: He was impressed with what he had seen at ARP. They might have been foolish, and they may have been infidels, but he sensed that they were genuinely interested in developing technology that could tame the desert and bring a better life to the Sahrawis. If the people at ARP could be persuaded to see the wisdom of adopting Islam as their faith, that might just bring a return to the glorious days that had given the world such prominent Islamic scholars as Omar Khayyam and Ibn Khaldun.

Making that argument would be risky. He might appear too bookish and unwilling to carry out the jihad. Fortunately, he did not have to make it. Hakim had sensed he was not winning, and rather than risking a definitive loss in the dispute—which would be accompanied by a loss of standing—he agreed to take a more moderate course of action. For the time being, the group would plan to send a smaller force to capture the ARP compound, while the majority of the forces would deploy against Tan-Tan. Since it would be at least three or four months before the rebels had sufficient weapons for that attack, there was no need to make a firm decision on how to deal with the ARP compound yet. That could come later.

CHAPTER 5

WHEN BRENDA BULLOCK HAD FIRST LEARNED that she was going to China she was over the moon. She had never set foot outside of the United States and didn't even have a passport. She didn't speak a word of Chinese and knew virtually nothing about the country except that it was the largest Communist country in the world. From her perspective, that was all she needed to know. If there was another system of government that was different than what she saw in America, it must be worth trying. The American system was rigged against people like her, and the idea of a place where everyone was treated equally held great appeal.

Her frustration with the American government was intensified by the rigmarole she had to go through just to obtain a passport. Fortunately, she had been able to cite pending international travel plans to reduce the processing time from eight weeks to two.

She put the time to good use, downloading a couple of phone apps that allowed her to learn a few phrases of Mandarin. She was stunned by the complexity of the Chinese characters and the difficulty of the tonal system but was grateful that someone had developed the pinyin system, which spelled out the sounds of Chinese characters using the English alphabet. By the time she was ready to travel, she had learned enough phrases that she felt confident people would understand she was trying to absorb everything she could about China and its people. She made a lot of progress in learning about China, but she was nonetheless delighted to receive an email telling her that the Chinese–American Green group would send an English speaker not only to collect her from the airport but also to be her constant companion and host throughout her six-week training period.

Soon, after a fourteen-hour Air China flight from Dulles to Beijing Capital International Airport, she arrived in Terminal 3, where she looked for the young woman who would be her host, Li Ming. During her research, Brenda had been surprised to learn that more than 85 percent of the families in China were represented by the top one hundred surnames. More startling still was the fact that three surnames, Wang, Li, and Zhang, accounted for more than 20 percent of the population. With nearly 1.5 billion people, somewhere around three hundred million of them shared one of three family names. Brenda, who searched online for her own name now and then and had been frustrated to learn how many other Brenda Bullocks there were in the world, could only imagine what it must be like for Chinese people with one of the most common surnames.

From her research, Brenda understood that Chinese names were traditionally presented in the format of family name, or "*xing*," followed by given name, which was known as "*ming*." She also knew that referring to someone by their given name only, as was common in the United States, would be considered impolite. She had practiced the phrase for "hello" over and over, hoping her tone was correct. As she exited the customs Hall, she saw the woman she recognized from several Skype conversations and greeted her host. "Ni Hao! Li Ming! It's so nice to meet you. Thank you for coming all the way to the airport to meet me. I appreciate it so much."

Although she was only slightly above average height for an American woman, Brenda was at least six inches taller than her host. As Brenda leaned forward to embrace her new friend, Li Ming stood stock still, as if bracing for a punishment. Li Ming closed her eyes, waiting for it to be over and hoping that her discomfort was not obvious.

Li Ming came from a generation that was accustomed to Western traditions. She had chosen English as her foreign language on the National College Entrance Exam, the Gaokao. And she had concentrated in the social sciences, with a particular emphasis on modern American culture and politics. She spoke American English with almost no discernable accent, due in large part to the countless hours spent singing along with American pop tunes and watching American movies. But meeting Brenda was still a bit overwhelming—a true test of what happens when theory meets practice.

Li Ming put on her happiest expression. "Hi Brenda. Welcome to Beijing." She looked at the two large roller bags Brenda was pulling and immediately doubted the wisdom of traveling from the airport to downtown via the Capitol Airport Express, also known as the Airport Beijing City rail, or ABC. However, it was too late now, so she pressed ahead. "Here, let me take one of those."

As Terminal 3 receded into the distance, Brenda could not help thinking that it looked like an upside-down bowl, or maybe a turtle shell. She, too, was feeling overwhelmed—by the magnitude of the city and everything in it. Although the subway system was well signed, and in English, there were more than four hundred stations. That was more than four times the number of stations in the DC Metro system. And the million passengers that rode the DC Metro each day paled in comparison to the twenty million who used Beijing's.

After the hour-long subway ride to the apartment complex where Brenda and Li Ming were to share a two-bedroom flat, the two had a late dinner. Although it was nearly 10 p.m., Brenda was still adjusting from DC time, which was twelve hours behind.

Brenda had timed her arrival so she would have the weekend to shake off jet lag and perhaps to do a bit of sightseeing. Li Ming had laid out an itinerary that would cover several of the largest tourist attractions in the city, starting with Tiananmen Square and Qianmen Street. Brenda paced the vast expanse of the square, which measured more than half a mile in length and nearly a third of a mile wide, simply awed that this square had existed for more than six hundred years. Nothing in America was that old, and she was delighted to see this tiny part of Chinese history. She was unaware of the square's more recent history, including the 1989 massacre during which hundreds had been killed and thousands had been injured. While doing research on China, she had seen a link to a story about the massacre but had opted to focus on only the positive aspects of the country.

Li Ming was about the same age as Brenda and had never been more than a hundred miles from Beijing. She also had no knowledge of the Tiananmen Square Massacre, because it had happened well before she was born and all mention of it had been scrubbed from the Chinese Internet. Li Ming had been told that the American might ask strange questions that implied horrible things had happened at the square, and in this case, she was simply to say that it was all exaggeration—Western propaganda that was not to be believed. Fortunately, Brenda was not the sort to ask probing questions; she just wanted to drink it all in, and the subject of the Tiananmen Square Massacre never came up.

Li Ming worked hard to be an excellent tour guide, showing Brenda around the square and the more famous tourist attractions it contained, including the Monument to the People's Heroes, the Great Hall of the People, the National Museum of China, and the Mausoleum of Mao Zedong.

Brenda spent the weekend absorbing everything she could. She, too, was working hard—to be a good guest and to only ask questions from a positive point of view. She was surprised that the iconography was so similar to what she had seen in the United States, but she made no mention of it. The Monument to the People's Heroes, with its eight bas-relief scenes of recent military triumphs would blend in well with any of the monuments located on the National Mall in Washington, DC. The architectural style of the Great Hall of the People and the National Museum of China reminded her oddly of the Pentagon. And the Mausoleum of Mao Zedong looked remarkably like the Lincoln Memorial, right down to the twelve columns that stretched across the front. The biggest difference, as far as Brenda could tell, was that the Mao Zedong Mausoleum—like everything else in Beijing—was covered in a layer of soot or grime that gave it a grayish tinge, and she made a mental connection between the smog that blanketed the city and the discoloration of all its buildings but decided not to mention it. The takeaway for Brenda was that national pride, however expressed, seemed to contain recurring themes.

Qianmen Street, just south of Tiananmen Square, reminded her even more of DC. The half-mile-long street was forbidden to vehicles and numbered among the most frequently visited tourist sites. Two things jumped out at Brenda. The first was the number of American fast-food restaurants. She knew the Chinese welcomed other cultures, but of all the things to import from America, why fast food? Studies had shown, and her own experience confirmed, that fast food was the quickest path to obesity, and she wondered why the Chinese would want to emulate that part of American culture. The second thing that surprised her, even though she knew to expect it, was the lack of personal space. The crowds on this street were so thick that she was bumped or jostled constantly, and she found it unnerving.

After covering the top attractions in the central core of Beijing, Li Ming took Brenda to see the Olympic Park and its two most famous sites: The Bird's Nest and the Water Cube. Brenda had little appreciation for the architecture, but her host seemed to be proud of the buildings, so Brenda praised them. She recalled from her crash course on the country that China had poured more concrete in one three-year period than the United

States had poured in all of the twentieth century, and it occurred to her now that what she was seeing in Beijing might not be an ideal model for rebuilding Africa. The cookie-cutter skyscraper apartment buildings, the massive influx of people from rural to urban areas, and the persistent air pollution—these were not the things that could revitalize Africa. But Brenda did not question it. She was sure that others new better, and her role was to learn what she could for later implementation.

After a weekend of hitting the top tourism attractions in the city, Brenda was ready to knuckle down and learn how the Chinese–American Green group would push environmental stewardship to the forefront around the world. She was sure that if the top two economies in the world could be reshaped to put the environment first, the rest of the world would have to follow. And she knew that CAG had at least a dozen ongoing projects harnessing cutting-edge technology to improve the lives of the locals.

By prior arrangement, she and Li Ming focused most of their energy on the CAG plan to take over the Africa Renaissance Project at Tarfaya. Although the Chinese didn't use the words "take over," and instead used the euphemism "join," it was clear to anyone who reviewed the plan that the intent was to take over ARP. That fit perfectly with the goals that Lucinda had laid out, so Brenda didn't balk at the idea, even when she learned things that directly contradicted the stated purpose of simply helping all the existing ARP partners to maximize the impact of their research.

When she learned that the Chinese were planning to replace the security force at ARP with four hundred soldiers of their own, her first thought was surprise that there was a need for soldiers at all. In her next weekly briefing with Lucinda, she made sure to ask why so many soldiers were being sent to protect a green project, but Lucinda explained that it was only a precaution and nothing Brenda needed to worry about.

With Lucinda, Brenda focused carefully on the positive. In doing so, she was sometimes forced to say things that contradicted her own observations. She was particularly disappointed with the way the men at CAG treated Li Ming. Nearly everyone in the group spoke English, but a few of the older men would frequently switch to Chinese, and even without understanding a word they were saying, Brenda could tell they were belittling Li Ming. And, sometimes, when the discussion turned to the United States or Africa, the men would make comments to each other in Chinese and laugh raucously while Li Ming just sat with her hands in her lap. Brenda suspected, but didn't dare ask, that the men were making off-color comments about Americans and Africans—and maybe about Brenda herself.

As her six-week training period drew to a close, Brenda remained optimistic. She was able to block out the negative experiences and was eager for the next phase of her grand adventure. Most of her training had focused on promoting the Chinese Belt and Road Initiative, or BRI. The plan, which had been unveiled more than a dozen years before, aimed to build massive infrastructure projects in some of the poorest areas of the world, especially Africa. Brenda was given the title of BRI Ambassador, with a mandate to extol the virtues of the infrastructure projects the Chinese were bringing to Africa. She never thought to question why an American would be called upon to promote the BRI. She and Li Ming were to function as a team, with Brenda focusing on promoting a positive image for the BRI, while Li Ming was to report all feedback—positive or negative—to the CAG. The team would make their debut at a conference in Dakar, Senegal, where the CAG would be announcing a major investment in the ARP.

CHAPTER 6

AS THE DAKAR SUMMIT DREW NEAR, KATE Mulgrew was busy preparing promotional literature about the Africa Renaissance Project. The Chinese were rumored to be sending a large delegation, and that they planned to invest up to $2 billion in ARP. That would be a game-changer, and she wanted to make a good impression.

Kate wanted to make sure that the history and purpose of ARP was spelled out clearly to differentiate it from several other organizations and movements that bore similar names. Some were shady, others were simply unsuccessful, and she worried that any confusion on the part of the investors could only do more harm than good. She developed a white paper to distinguish their ARP from the 1940s African Renaissance Movement, which had attempted to revitalize the continent after the sordid legacy of colonialism. She believed that ARP—unlike the Movement, which had once been prominent but ultimately faded away—would bring lasting peace and prosperity to the people of Africa. Most people, she thought, should easily be able to make the distinction, but she was leaving nothing to chance.

Given that the summit was being held in Dakar, home of the notorious African Renaissance Monument—which had been designed by a Romanian and built by a North Korean company with very little input from local workers—she also wanted to make sure that everyone understood what made ARP different. The monument, she learned to her dismay, had been commissioned by a former president who—until his passing—had tried to claim royalties from entrance fees to the monument. That was the same president who had run for office on an anti-corruption platform that he immediately abandoned upon entering office. Kate had heard from a friend in the State Department about a conversation between the newly elected president and a visiting delegation of US senators who had asked the president why he had reneged on his promise to rid the government of corrupt officials. According to that story, the president had said, "When I ran for office, I truly intended to rid the government of corruption. But when I took office, I realized that if I got rid of everyone who was corrupt, I would have no one left to run the government."

That story, in Kate's eyes, explained much of the misfortune that had befallen Africa. Even those who rose to leadership positions—what would be deemed positions of great power elsewhere—soon found that what they really wanted was wealth, and there simply wasn't enough of that to go around. Of the fifty-four countries in Africa, only a handful had enough resources to meet the needs of more than a thin slice of the population. Although Thomas Hobbes had lived in England and published *Leviathan* in the mid-seventeenth century, Kate could not help but notice that the world Hobbes described must be all too familiar to those born in Africa in the early twenty-first century. Perhaps more than anywhere else in the world, life on the African continent was, in Hobbes's words, "nasty, brutish, and short."

But Kate Mulgrew was an activist and an optimist. She believed that there was no problem that could not be overcome, and she believed that ARP was the key to overcoming Africa's problems. The Dakar Summit, which was intended to take the ARP from a hodgepodge of independently funded and resourced programs into a global initiative—with major funding from at least half a dozen international organizations and countries—was the event that would change ARP's future for the better, and with it, the lives of countless Africans.

Kate and a team of more than twenty-five ARP representatives traveled to the Dakar Summit. By force of habit more than anything else, the people who worked in the IAU office went together. Guy, Sam, Nigel, and Kate made the first part of the journey in a convoy of seven armored SUVs that traveled from Tarfaya to Laayoune, where the team boarded a flight to Dakar. Max Burke, who had been in the lead vehicle of the convoy, saw them safely into the airport and returned to the ARP compound.

Later that evening, Kate and Guy found themselves standing together at the pre-summit reception. Sam and Nigel had wandered off in search of food and drink, leaving Guy and Kate to fend for themselves.

"I hate these things," Guy said. "I mean, I get that it's important to provide information to people and organizations who are going to shell out millions or billions of dollars, but why not just get straight to the point? Why do we always have to waste money on parties? It's not like the World Bank isn't going to make a loan if they don't get some canapés and shrimp cocktail.

"Don't you think it would do a lot more good if we gave all this food to the poor kids we passed on the way from the airport?"

Kate could see peril both in agreeing and disagreeing, so she decided to do neither. She spied Ebiere Olani, whom she recognized from COPS32, and excused herself to go say hello.

Ebiere, however, was locked in a heated debate with the Senegalese Minister of Public Works. From COPS32, Kate was familiar with Ebiere's argument that African countries needed to be more careful about taking on too much debt, but the Senegalese Minister was having none of it.

The Minister said, "It's easy for you, a Nigerian, with all your plentiful oil, to tell your poorer neighbors how to get along without taking on debt."

"I am not saying that all debt is bad. But I don't understand why Senegal needs to build a new international airport when your citizens are too poor to fly anywhere. And why build a new port to bring in goods they can't afford to buy? I'll tell you why. Far too many African leaders are lining their pockets with bribes from the construction companies who build the ports and the airports. We've seen this movie before, and we know how it ends. You know as well as I do that none of these projects will generate enough revenue to pay for the debt, and eventually those loans will go into default and the lenders will take control of the infrastructure as collateral. We will be in the same place we were with colonialism—with foreigners controlling everything that matters—except this time we will have sold it to them willingly for a few well-placed bribes."

The Minister was not the slightest bit perturbed by the accusation. He replied, "Perhaps you are right. Maybe we would be better off without roads, or ports, or airports. Maybe it would be better to remain poor and to have nothing to show for ourselves. Many African countries have unemployment rates close to 50 percent. Are their leaders wrong to try to do something about that?"

"I am not saying that you should do nothing. You don't have to be corrupt to believe that an aid package will make the lives of Africans better. But surely you must see the risk of taking on so much debt that you know cannot be paid back."

The Minister countered, "But I believe in the old saying, 'If you owe the bank a million, the bank owns you; if you owe the bank a billion, you own the bank.' My point is, yes, it is possible that in a perfect world, the things that we are building now could have been built a bit more cheaply. But the wheels turn slowly in that perfect world, and the people of Africa need progress now."

"Yes," Ebiere huffed. "The people of Africa are desperate for fifth-generation telephone systems so they can watch videos on their phones of Westerners living lavish lifestyles. When will you people see that your corruption is not helping the people of Africa, it is only helping the elite of Africa, China, and the West?"

As optimistic as Kate was about the good that could come from foreign investment in Africa, she was not about to jump into the middle of this dogfight. She returned to where she'd left Guy to find him and Sam Fischel deep in conversation with Makram Abd Alsalam.

Guy was explaining his vision for the role of plasticized sand in the Trans-African Highway program. "We've had a very good response from the United Nations Economic Commission for Africa and the African Development Bank. As soon as we get access to enough plastic waste, we intend to start what we're calling the 'Highway School,' where we'll teach students the complete life cycle of building roads with plasticized sand. There are massive stretches of highway, especially in the interior of the continent, that we believe are excellent candidates for PS roads."

"But don't you see a logistics problem? I get that one of the main ingredients is sand, and that is going to be readily available in most places in Africa, but where are you going to get all the plastic you need? You told me that you're only getting a couple of tons a month from your ocean plastic recovery project."

"That's true, we won't be able to get anywhere close to enough plastic with what we're recovering from the ocean, but most of the places we will be working have plastic waste of their own readily available. We are working on creating a land-based version of our plastic recovery system that can extract plastic from landfills. We'll do something similar to what we do in the ocean, but we will leave it in pellet form instead of converting it to bales. We'll haul those pellets to the job site. The pellets will be melted and mixed with sand on location and the road will be extruded right onto the roadbed."

"But I don't see how you're going to power that with solar panels."

"We'll have to use fossil fuels, but we will be reusing plastic waste and we will be building roads. Both of those are important."

"Or you could just wait for the Chinese to come in and let them take over. They'll build all the roads for you."

"So, it's true?" Kate asked. "The Chinese are going to make a major investment in ARP?"

"I don't know the exact amount, but I think it is going to be big," Makram offered.

"That's interesting. I had no idea. When do you think it will happen?" Guy asked.

"I can't say for sure," Makram said, "but I've been told it will occur within the next few weeks. My firm is one of the few companies in Morocco that is licensed to import firearms, and we're expecting a shipment of weapons and other security equipment for about four hundred Chinese soldiers any day now. If they are planning to have a security force that is as large as the entire population of ARP today, they must be planning a big investment. I'm told the decision has already been made and that the announcement will come tomorrow or the day after, once the Chinese formally commit."

Guy looked at Kate. "I wonder if Max Burke is aware that the Chinese are planning to take over security at the compound."

"Talk about burying the lede," Kate countered. "The Chinese are about to make a $2 billion investment in ARP, and you're focused on who's going to do security? This is huge. It will put ARP on the map in a big way."

Makram nodded in silent agreement, but not for the reasons Kate supposed.

CHAPTER 7

FOR SEVERAL DAYS AFTER THE DAKAR SUMMIT, Guy stayed busy preparing for the arrival of the remaining people assigned to the IAU workspace. When he received an email notifying him that two individuals who worked for the Chinese-American Green group would be sharing IAU's trailers, he was certain that the rumors about Chinese investment were true. He decided to attend the weekly orientation briefing to meet Brenda Bullock and Li Ming. Nearly everyone who came through orientation found it shocking, and he thought he could take some of the edge off by meeting his new arrivals and escorting them around.

But his motives weren't completely focused on easing the adjustment of the new arrivals. First and foremost, he wanted to meet the two CAG employees who would be assigned to his workspace. CAG's website suggested its goals aligned very well with IAU's, but he was concerned that big organizations and big money had a way of trying to push everyone else around. If Brenda and Li Ming were the first emissaries of a coming wave of CAG bureaucrats, he intended to do his best to show them the virtues of ARP as it was—a collection of like-minded idealists trying to solve hard problems to make the world a better place. He also wanted to attend the orientation again to brush up on his AK-47 skills. The trip back from the Laayoune airport after the Dakar Summit had been eventful, with a couple of hoodlums in a beat-up Toyota truck forcing their way into the convoy and brandishing weapons.

After the orientation session, Guy offered to escort Brenda and Li Ming to their residential trailer. Brenda seemed particularly overwhelmed. “Was that guy intense, or what? Is it really dangerous here or is he just full of himself?”

“It’s hard to say,” Guy replied. “If you think he’s intense in a training session, you should try sharing a trailer with him. He’s my roommate.”

When the trio turned the corner near the compound’s swimming pool, Li Ming, who normally treated words like coins—to be used only when they could purchase something—laughed out loud at the sight of Peanut at the center of a gaggle of young women. “What kind of dog is that?” she asked, dropping her suitcases and joining the group gathered around the pug-Chihuahua mix. “She’s so cute! May I pet her?”

One of the women said, “Sure, but if you start, she won’t let you stop. She’ll put her nose under your hand to make you keep petting her, so be prepared.”

Li Ming turned to Guy. “Do you mind? We will only take a minute.”

Peanut seemed to sense what was at stake, because she walked directly up to him and rolled over, offering her belly. She looked up at him with plaintive eyes, and he couldn’t resist.

“She likes you,” Li Ming said.

“Not any more than anyone else. She just knows me because she stays in my trailer, with Max. She’s kind of the camp mascot, and she spends her days in the various workspace trailers. When we first got here, there was a sign-up sheet to get Peanut during the day. The IT guy, Sam Fischel—you’ll meet him later today or tomorrow—updated that to an online request system. It's pretty funny, but she's very popular."

Once the ladies were situated, Guy headed to the gym, where Max and Sam were in the middle of a workout. As usual, they were digging in on the opposite sides of a social issue. Sam was doing a set on the bench press while Max spotted him.

"Look, man, you need to get that chip off your shoulder. Not everything that happens to you is necessarily because you're a gay black man. People don't really care.

"The reason people treat you the way they do sometimes is because you act like an asshole. In a better world, your friends would tell you straight up when you're acting like a dick, but because of political correctness no one is willing to say anything to you. They don't want to be branded as racist or homophobic, so they just ignore you.

"A real friend would call you out."

Sam finished his set and sat up on the bench. He looked over at Guy, who was standing a few feet away doing curls. "For real, man? Do you agree with him or do you think he's full of crap?"

"I'm just here to work out. Leave me out of this one, okay?"

Max started his set, easily lifting the 225 pounds six times in rapid succession without obvious strain. "Okay then, Sam, if you don't think that political correctness is what keeps people from calling you out, why is it that the left goes so hard after Christians for their anti-gay stances, but doesn't say anything when Muslim countries kill people for being gay?"

"So now we're going to play a game of whataboutism, are we?" Sam shot back. "Why is it that whenever someone points out something you do wrong, you point to something worse and say, 'What about that?' Just because something else is worse, doesn't mean that what you're doing is right."

"Who defines what's right and wrong?" Max asked. "I mean, until a few years ago, there was a consensus that marriage was between a man and a woman. Now, it's okay for men to marry men and women to marry women. Who changed the rules?"

Sam was back on the bench now, straining to complete six reps with the 225-pound weights. "Oh, so you don't think that gay marriage is right? Are you okay with black people walking around free, or should we all be slaves?"

"See what I mean about you being a dick? I'm just trying to have a conversation with you, and you got to play the race card. I didn't say anything about race. Not everything has to be about race."

"Said the white man."

"Look, I agree that race is an issue. I remember when I first entered the Marine Corps. The old timers would tell stories about race riots on military bases, when they had to go out with a buddy, so they didn't get jumped. Those were bad times, but the Marine Corps taught people to be colorblind. There were no black Marines or white Marines. Every Marine was green, and they were either light green or dark green. The point was that color wasn't important. What was important was whether the Marine could shoot, move, and communicate. It didn't matter if you were black or white, so long as you did your job.

"But who is it that has the authority to say, all of a sudden, that gay marriage is the same as being black—just another thing for the Marine Corps to teach people to deal with?"

Sam took the question seriously. Based on personal experience, he knew the black community could be just as bigoted against gays as everyone else. He didn't have an answer and let the question marinate for a while until Max filled the void.

"I'm not saying that gay marriage is right or wrong. Personally, I don't care what people do in the bedroom as long as they don't try to do it to me."

"Don't worry, Max, you're not my type," Sam interjected, trying to lighten up the discussion.

"Well, thank goodness for that," Max replied, only half in jest. "I guess I'm trying to say that I don't think that everything should be enforced by the government. There are some things that should be decided by society and some things that should be decided based on faith."

Guy had wrestled with similar questions but didn't have answers either. "Like what?" he asked.

"Well, let's start with an easy one," Max replied. "Catholics don't eat meat on Friday and Muslims don't eat pork at all. Those are clearly religious questions and those rules should apply only to the people who practice that religion. You wouldn't think it reasonable for a Catholic president to suddenly issue an Executive Order saying no one could eat meat on Fridays, right?"

Sam and Guy nodded in agreement. "But what is an example of something where society sets the rules?" Sam asked.

"Cursing. My mother would wash my mouth out with soap if she heard me cursing, but now it's everywhere, especially on social media. The rules used to be clear—you didn't curse in public. Now, people say things in public that would make a sailor blush."

Guy cast a knowing glance at Sam. "Well, I'm not sure that's a good change. But I'm glad that most people still realize it can be offensive to others and, if asked, they will clean up their language."

"That's my whole point," Max added. "There was a time when people didn't curse in public because they knew it was impolite. They put restraints on themselves because they felt they had a duty to act a certain way. For the most part, people knew what to do because they were raised a certain way and that was that.

"But now, cursing is fine, but don't even think about calling someone by the wrong pronoun or you could lose your job."

"What do you mean?" Guy asked.

Sam answered for Max, "What he means is that there are certain words you just can't say anymore, or the thought police will come get you. Everybody knows that a white person can't use the N-word and a straight person can't call someone a faggot. If they do, they can get fired for it, and they should get fired for it."

"That seems a bit extreme, don't you think?" Guy countered.

"Really?" Sam asked. "How can you ask that with a straight face when just a couple of weeks ago you threatened my job if I didn't quit cursing all the time?"

"Wait a minute—I *didn't* threaten your job. Just the opposite. I offered to double your salary if you did what I asked."

"And you don't see that as being the same as threatening my job? What if you wanted to go out on a date with me? Do you think it would be any different if you offered to double my salary or if you threatened to fire me? In both cases, you're using the power you have over me to change my behavior."

"Well, as the owner of the business, I think I have certain rights to establish the rules of conduct. I would never tolerate someone who works for me using his or her position of authority to prey upon a subordinate for sexual favors. And I don't think it is appropriate for people to use foul language."

Guy recalled his conversation with Janet just a few months before, and realized he was taking the opposite position on the question of whether businesses should be the enforcers of society's rules. He decided to come at the issue from a different angle. "Okay, so I get it that this is a complex issue, but I think it's important to realize that we have to differentiate between the rules that society, as a whole, has agreed to, and what a few people want the rules to be. When society agrees on something, and they want it to be enforced, they pass a law. For example, it's against the law to discriminate against you because you're black, and it would be against the law for me to use my position as the owner of the business to get sexual favors from you. But we're seeing demands now from people who want things enforced that aren't established as law."

"Like what?" Sam asked, wiping sweat from his forehead.

"Well, look at the Masterpiece Cakeshop case."

"Wait, I know that case," Sam interjected. "But there *was* a law. Colorado had a law against discrimination, and the guy who owned the bakery wouldn't bake a wedding cake for a couple because they were gay."

"Right, that's the one. And the Supreme Court overturned the decision of the Colorado Civil Rights Commission, because they violated the owner's right to free exercise of religion."

"So, what you're saying, then, is that the Supreme Court said it's fine to be a bigot so long as you do it for religious reasons?"

"That's not what I'm saying at all. What I'm saying is that sometimes we may need to step back a bit and decide whether we really want to bring a social issue into the legal system. I think it would have been perfectly acceptable for that gay couple to tell the owner of the bakery that they didn't agree with his views. And they could have taken their business elsewhere. If enough people agreed that the bakery owner was wrong, the guy would have gone out of business. The world may not be exactly the way I want it to be, and I might have a right to something, but it isn't necessary to call in the law every time someone does something I don't like.

"And, doesn't it seem odd to you that these cases of discrimination against gays never get filed against Muslim bakeries? Do you think a Muslim bakery would make a cake for a gay wedding? I doubt it. So why aren't there a slew of lawsuits against Muslim bakeries?"

"I don't know," Sam said, "but you've obviously got a theory, or you wouldn't bring it up."

"Well, I can't say for sure, but I do think that there is a backlash against Christianity in America today. And I think, oddly enough, that Islam is treated differently. I don't think it would be fair for me to weigh in on the motives of the people who see the world that way, so I'll just leave it at that. I think the left is going after Christianity and they're giving Islam a pass on the same issues they're blasting Christians for."

Max, who had been listening quietly and doing curls with forty pounds in each hand, weighed in. "Have you ever heard the expression, 'The enemy of my enemy is my friend'? I think we're seeing a bit of that. I was a teenager when 9/11 happened, and I couldn't understand why anyone would want to attack us. What had we, as Americans, done that would justify attacks on New York and Washington? I joined the Marines because I believed that those attacks were unjustified, and I wanted to defend our country."

Sam was lost. "So, what does that have to do with gay wedding cakes?"

"Nothing, directly, but the question isn't about gay wedding cakes; it's about why people who criticize the behavior of Christians give Muslims a pass for doing the same thing. For better or for worse, the United States has framed the war against terrorism in religious terms. There were a lot of attempts by senior leaders, both military and political, to prevent that from happening, but people don't go to war for complex reasons, they go to war for things that can be boiled down to very simple terms: good versus evil, us versus them. And in the case of post-9/11, it got boiled down to Islam versus the West. But don't think that this was happening only in the West. The terrorists were making it all about Islam as well. How do you fight the 'Islamic State' without being against Islam?

"So, when the people in the United States who opposed the war saw that it was put in terms of the West versus Islam—and they were against the elite in the United States who had made the decision to go to war—they saw Islam as the enemy of their enemy."

Sam grew visibly agitated and said, "That's complete bullshit, man. It's a cop-out."

Seeing this could quickly spiral out of control, Guy tried to steer the conversation back to safer ground. "Okay, Max, so keep going with this theory you have about different spheres of influence. So far, you've defined the rules of religion and the rules of society. What else is there?"

"The third sphere, if you want to call it that—which I guess would make my philosophy 'Spheritualism'—is the rule of law.

"So, let's go to the other end of the spectrum. Everyone agrees that murder is wrong. Every religion I know of says it's wrong to kill someone, and society is against killing people, but the reason we have laws is so that we can enforce rules against murder. You wouldn't want the First Baptist prison, and you wouldn't want a neighborhood retribution squad. I mean, those things happen sometimes, but the point is that when a society or a religion wants to do something punitive to someone else, there must be rules that everyone agrees to. There is a proportionality to what each one of the different spheres can enforce. Religion gets enforced in the religious sphere. If you're a Muslim, don't eat pork, but Muslims don't have the right to tell others not to eat pork. If you don't like cursing, you can ask the people around you not to curse, but you don't have the authority to make them not curse."

Sam calmed down a bit. "I see where you're coming from. I mean, it makes sense to me, but what does it matter? Pretty soon we'll all be speaking Chinese anyway, and who the fuck knows what they believe."

"What are you talking about?" Max asked. "I've been told that the Chinese are considering a big investment here and that, if they do, they're going to send about a thousand people, including four hundred or so that will augment the security force, but nobody has said anything about the Chinese taking over."

Sam wiped the sweat from his brow and said, "For a guy who sees himself as the great observer of the world, it seems funny to me that you haven't noticed what the Chinese have done to the rest of Africa. Name one place where the Chinese have gone in that they didn't end up taking over. Maybe not the government, but effectively they are in charge once they move in. How can you not see that?"

CHAPTER 8

AS FEBRUARY TURNED INTO MARCH, THE DAYS grew warmer and the evenings were pleasant enough that the ARP employees began to socialize at the compound's pool after work. On this Tuesday evening, when Guy and Kate came out from the dining hall, they were surprised to find the IAU team, plus Brenda and Li Ming, gathered in a small circle around Max Burke, who was telling stories of his days in the Marines with Peanut asleep in his lap.

One of the IAU employees was asking Max about his time in Iraq. "Is it really like it is in the movies?"

"Depends which movies you're talking about. I haven't seen them all."

"But what about everybody getting a nickname like 'Tex,' or 'Stretch'? Is that how it really is?"

Max stroked Peanut gently between the ears, "I don't know that everybody gets one, but some do."

"Did you have one?"

"Yes."

"What was it?"

"Socrates."

Sam Fischel chimed in. "Did they call you that because you asked deep probing questions, or because you were a smelly, obnoxious old goat?"

Over the laughter, Max replied, "Maybe a little of both."

"Well, out with it. Tell us the story. It's not like we've got anything better to do."

"Okay, but there's a little bit of military history that you need to know for this to make sense, so bear with me.

"As most of you know, I was in the infantry. Sometimes the infantry is supported by artillery, and as an infantryman you need to know how to do a 'call for fire.' That's how you tell the artillery folks where to shoot.

"When I was in training to be a forward observer—the guy who makes the call for fire—we were issued binoculars. Now, military binoculars are different than regular binoculars. They have a reticle pattern, a set of marks on the lens that allows you to measure distance. But the reticle pattern isn't on both lenses. It can be on either eye, but usually it's only on the left lens, and that didn't make sense to me, since most people are right-eye dominant. So, I asked the instructor, 'Why put the reticle pattern in the left eye if most people are right-eye dominant?'"

Sam was following up to this point but had never heard the expression "right eye dominant." "What does that mean, 'right eye dominant'?" he asked.

Max didn't seem perturbed by the question and asked the group to do a little drill. He said, "See that light across the pool?" and pointed to a lamppost on the opposite side of where the group was sitting. Everyone looked and nodded. "Now, with both eyes open, put your thumb over that light and cover it up. Be sure to keep both eyes open. Got it?"

Everyone held their thumb up to the light and moved it around a bit. After a few seconds, Max continued, "Now, close your right eye. What do you see?"

Brenda was the first to speak. "Wow, that's really weird. When I looked at it with both eyes, the light was covered up, but when I closed my right eye, it's like the light moved to the left and my thumb moved to the right."

"That's because you're right eye dominant."

Sam was still having a little trouble. "I don't get it. When I close my right eye, nothing happens. And what does this have to do with calling in artillery, anyway?"

"You sound just like the instructor. Apparently, he didn't know the answer either, so when I asked why the reticle pattern was in the left eye if most people are right eye dominant, he said to me. 'I don't know, Socrates, why *is* it the left eye?'

"Everyone in the class, except me, got a big kick out of that, and they started calling me 'Socrates.' It stuck, and that's how I got my handle."

"So, did you ever find out why they put the pattern in the left eye?" Sam pressed.

"Yes, I did. As it turns out, there's a very good reason for it, too. You need to use both eyes for depth perception, to tell distance. If you look with only one eye—and there is a tendency for people to use their dominant eye, just like you did when you covered up the light on the other side of the pool—you'll have a harder time telling how far away something is. Putting the reticle pattern in the left eye forces people who are right-eye dominant to use both eyes to measure distance. If you're looking out at the target and you don't see the reticle pattern, it's because you're only using one eye and you won't be getting an accurate range. You need to learn to force yourself to look through both eyes."

One of the IAU employees, a young man from Houston, still didn't get it. "So how does it help you to know how far away the bad guys are?"

For the next ten minutes, Max held a seminar on the "adjust fire, polar" call for fire. He explained how it was the easiest of all the methods of calling for fire because the person making the call only had to describe the direction and distance from his own location to the target. If the artillery unit knew where the call for fire was coming from, it could easily plot the target location.

Sam listened intently, with a mix of admiration and envy. He had grown to know Max over the past few weeks and had concluded that his initial impression—that Max was a racist homophobe—wasn't correct, but still, he didn't have the guy completely figured out. Max was complex, to say the least. On the one hand, he was a demanding taskmaster. It seemed that in every orientation class, Max would find some excuse to read the new employees the riot act—just like with Sam. He would also randomly quiz employees on the location of the rally point, and what they were supposed to do if they were outside the gates when the compound came under attack. But the same guy who was a beast about security rules was a creampuff when it came to Peanut. He treated her like a little princess, always doting on her as if she could do no wrong.

But Sam was smart, and he knew there was no benefit to getting on Max's bad side. For one thing, Max seemed to be dialed in on almost everything, and was a great source of intel. Sam decided to prod a little bit. "So, Max, what's the latest on the Chinese takeover here?"

"You keep saying they're going to take over, but nothing I've heard leads me to believe that'll happen. From what I hear, they are definitely going to make an investment—probably a very big one—but it's being held up while they negotiate with the Moroccans about creating an economic zone that includes the solar farms south of Marrakesh."

Here, Guy perked up. "You mean the Noor complex at Ouarzazate? Why would they want to include that?"

"I don't have any inside information or anything, but if you look at a map, it makes a lot of sense."

"How so?"

"Well, suppose for a minute that China wanted to really expand their influence in Western Africa. The Moroccan government isn't likely to fall into the Chinese sphere of influence. The

Moroccans are firmly in the Western camp. Did you know, for example, that Morocco was the first country to recognize the United States when it declared independence?"

"I did!" Kate exclaimed. "I did a tour in public affairs at the US Embassy in Rabat, and that fact was in nearly all of our press releases about Morocco. It's also interesting that the peace treaty with Morocco is the longest standing peace treaty between the US and any country, and the building that used to be the US Consulate in Tangier is the oldest US diplomatic outpost in the world."

"Okay, guys, thanks for the history lesson, but I still don't see how any of this would make China want to include the solar power farm in Ouarzazate in any kind of deal, and why they would want to take over ARP," Sam said.

"Like I said," Max responded, "I don't have any conclusive proof, but sometimes if it walks like a duck and it quacks like a duck, it might just be a duck."

"What the f—" Sam caught himself. "Uh . . . what the *heck* is that supposed to mean?"

"I'm not sure how much you follow the history of this region, but there's an ongoing dispute between the Moroccans and the Polisario over control of an area just south of here called Western Sahara. For a long time, nobody paid any attention because the whole area is pretty much desert. In the mid-1970s, the Moroccan government just took over the region, and they built a bunch of walls to protect against guerilla attacks. Where we are here in Tarfaya has always been part of Morocco proper, but when we go down to Laayoune, we're crossing into what used to be part of Western Sahara. That's why we go in convoys of armored SUVs. The threat isn't as bad as in some places, but these kinds of things have a habit of kicking up when you're least expecting it. Just ask the guys who were in Benghazi about fifteen years ago, or the guys in Cairo two years ago. Everything seems fine, then one day you wake up and there's a bunch of guys outside who want to kill you."

"No, no, I get that," Sam said impatiently. "This place is dangerous. You've convinced me. I know where the rally point is, I got my AK-47, I'm ready for the bad guys. But I still don't understand what this has to do with the Chinese."

Max pushed back a little bit. "You're the one who keeps saying the Chinese are going to take over. I'm just explaining what I think could be a plausible reason. May I continue?"

"Sure," Sam said, sheepishly.

"Okay, so if I'm the Chinese, and I know the Moroccan government is never going to join my camp, but I still want to have strong allies in the region, how do I get them? I have at least two ways of going about it. First, if I want to be really aggressive, I can form an alliance with the Polisario, and I can support their claim for control of Western Sahara. That's a kick in the face to the Moroccans, but they were never going to be on my side anyway. And the Polisario, which has been trying to get recognition for the better part of fifty years, is going to be very grateful for my help, so they become my best friend.

"On the other hand, if maybe I don't want to be so aggressive or if I want to keep my options open while I am putting myself in a position to be more aggressive, I can make a big investment here and I can *threaten* to form an alliance with the Polisario. I wouldn't even have to form an actual alliance. If I'm the Chinese, and I want to take over the Western Sahara, do I really want to establish a new government there that is friendly to me, or do I want to be able to get control without having to form a new government? If I actually set up a new government, they may or may not remain loyal to me. But if I just make the Moroccans think I am going to ally with the Polisario, I get the benefits without the risk. The Moroccans are more flexible in dealing with me because they don't want me to actually support Polisario control in the Western Sahara, and I keep the Polisario guys on a string with the promise that someday, if they're good, I'll help them take control of Western Sahara."

"But what proof do you have of all that?"

"Like I said, I don't have any proof, but when I put my 'Socrates' hat on, I have to ask the question, 'Why would the Chinese be sending four hundred soldiers to guard the ARP compound when we're currently doing it with less than a dozen security personnel?' Sure, they're going to be putting a lot more people in here, so there is a need for more security, but not four hundred soldiers. And that's just here—that doesn't include the four hundred or so they're going to send to Ouarzazate."

Kate saw the connection Max was making. "But if I'm the Chinese and I want to be able to prevent the Moroccan military from getting involved, sending in a couple of battalions of Chinese soldiers would do the trick. If I had a small security force and there was a firefight between them and the Moroccans, it could all be explained away as a misunderstanding. But if there are close to a thousand Chinese soldiers in southern Morocco and the Chinese decide to declare that Western Sahara should be an independent country, the Moroccans are going to think twice before using their military to do anything about it."

"Exactly," Max said, and took another sip of his beer, bringing that part of the discussion to a close. Most of the group that had gathered underneath the date palm tree took the opportunity provided by the lull in the conversation to call it an evening, but Sam and Guy stuck around. They both wanted to learn more about what Max knew—or at least what he thought.

After everyone else had cleared out, Sam was the first to speak. "That's depressing, man. Why would anyone want to fight over a shithole like this?"

"Well, I don't want to burst your bubble or anything," Max replied, "but that's the way it's been since the Second World War. If you look at the damage that World War I and World War II did to Europe, it's not too hard to figure out that the major powers don't want to take each other on directly anymore. They want to fight proxy wars. If you were the President of the United States and you had to choose between fighting a war in Iraq or Afghanistan and fighting one in Virginia, which would you choose?"

"But that's not a fair comparison," Sam shot back. "In Iraq and Afghanistan, we weren't fighting the Chinese or the Russians. We claimed that we were fighting Islamic terrorists in Afghanistan and then we claimed we were after weapons of mass destruction in Iraq, but that turned out to be wrong, so I am not even sure that anything I've been told is true. I don't know who to believe or what to think."

"If you think it's hard to make sense of here and now, sitting by the pool in this little research project, just try being on the ground where the rubber meets the road, as they say. How do you think my Marines and I felt when we were walking down the streets of Kabul or Mosul?

"When we looked at the people staring back at us from inside their mud huts or their cinder block houses, we had no idea whether they were just looking at us just because we were something to look at, or if they were waiting to blow our brains out."

"So, which was it? Were they just looking, or were they waiting to blow your brains out?"

"Sometimes it was both. But the point I'm trying to make here is bigger than just my experience. If you try to understand the world as other people describe it, I don't think you'll ever understand it. There is a tendency to personalize everything, good guys versus bad guys. And if I don't like the politics of the person in the White House, I might have a hard time doing what Marines are supposed to do—which is to close with and destroy the enemy by fire and maneuver. If I think that the president is selling me a load of crap, how am I supposed to do my job?"

Sam could identify with the question. "I don't know. I don't trust any politicians. They're all full of shit. So, what did you do?"

"Well, I learned the importance of history. It's easy to think that the time we're in is unique, and that there's never been anything like it before, but if you study history and philosophy, you can see the bigger picture."

"I mean, I get the bit about history, but why philosophy? How does studying Aristotle, or Plato, or your man Socrates help you see the bigger picture?"

"I can't speak for everyone, but for me, if I was going to have to kill people, and there was no way I could do my job without killing people, it was important to have some way of knowing that I wasn't just a tool in someone's power play."

"And?"

"After reading philosophy and history, it became very clear to me that our fight with Islamic radicals is justified, and it's one we can't afford to lose."

"You know I'm Muslim, right?"

"Gay, black, *and* Muslim. Now, there can't be too many of those."

"Not many that I've met but finish your story. Tell me how philosophy and history helped you deal with killing all the people you had to kill." Too late, Sam realized how flippant and insulting his words must have sounded, but Max answered before he could apologize.

"The way you said that, it wouldn't be too hard for me to think that you're making fun of me, but even if you are, it just goes to prove what I learned from my studies: I don't have to solve every problem in the world. There are some problems that are just going to keep on existing no matter what I do."

"That sounds like another cop-out to me," Sam said, not meaning it to sound as harsh as it did.

"Actually, it's just the opposite. It's the only way I could stay sane, and it's what helped me put the world in context. If you look to society to solve every problem, you won't find answers. If you look to the government to solve everything, same deal: There are some things that the government just doesn't have answers for.

"So, to boil it all down, I learned two simple rules that I try to live by. First of all, not everything in the world is going to be the way I want it. That doesn't mean that I just ignore the things I think are wrong. I don't. I try to understand what's right and I try to fight for what's right.

"But that leads to the second rule, which is that you shouldn't try to turn a screw with a wrench."

"You have some of the strangest damn expressions I ever heard," exclaimed Sam. "What does that even mean?"

"It means," Max replied calmly, "that for every issue there is a place where it gets decided. You can call it what you want to, but I call them spheres. There is a sphere for religious things, one for social things, and one for government. Sometimes they overlap, but you need to know which set of rules to apply when you're trying to decide the right thing to do. And you have to realize that, depending upon the sphere you're in, other people might have legitimate views that differ from yours."

Guy was about to ask a question when Max said, "Sorry, gents, but Peanut is looking at me like she needs to go for a walk. I've got to swing by the trailer and pick up a pooper scooper so she can do her business before we call it a night. See you tomorrow."

As Max stepped away, Guy turned to Sam. "I was hoping to talk to Max about security between here and the airport at Laayoune, but I guess I'll just have to find out when I go there."

"What do you mean?"

"I've got to go back to the States for a few days. I've got some things to sort through at headquarters."

"If you need me to take your place, I could use a trip back to DC. There's a pub at Twelfth and Pennsylvania that has the best nachos I ever tasted. The food here sucks, and they don't know squat about making nachos."

Guy chuckled, "Thanks for the offer, Sam. There are a couple of meetings that I'd happily let you take for me. But for the rest, that's not an option. I should be back by early next week. Try not to piss Max off too bad while I'm gone, okay?"

CHAPTER 9

LUCINDA HORNBUCKLE WAS GETTING NERVOUS. Over the past several weeks, she had made no progress in her attempts to take control of IAU. Her plan to get David Gordon on the board had stalled because he had thrown away the script and increased his settlement demands from half a million to a million dollars. Brenda Bullock had completed her training in China and was in place at ARP, but nothing she reported was proving useful. Making matters worse, Brenda seemed fixated on some guy named Max, who—depending upon when she was reporting—was either a hero or a Nazi. It seemed to change from week to week and Lucinda just didn't have time to sort it all out.

It was after six in the evening and Lucinda was due to have dinner with Guy in less than an hour. She was getting desperate for some kind of leverage to bring into that meeting. She was about to call David Gordon, hoping to browbeat or bribe him into accepting the offer on the table, when she saw Heather Alston emerge from the elevator.

The way Lucinda's office was positioned, combined with its glass walls, gave her a clear view of the entire path from the elevator to Heather's office. Lucinda also had the habit of keeping the lights low in her office to avoid feeling like she was in a fishbowl, so people in the passageway generally didn't notice when she was there, especially after normal working hours.

Based on the way she was dressed—in tight black yoga pants and a skimpy pink tank top—it seemed likely that Heather had just come from the gym in the basement. Heather behaved as though she thought she was alone, or at least unobserved, and sauntered toward her office casually, stopping to stretch. She leaned against the doorframe and stretched one leg at a time, grabbing her ankle and pulling it up behind her. After working both legs, she turned so she was facing away from the elevator, and away from Lucinda's office. She reached down to grab her ankles, bending at the waist. Then she leaned forward slightly and placed her palms on the floor, giving Lucinda a full view of her exquisite derriere.

Lucinda felt flushed. She was drawn to Heather like a kid to an ice cream truck; the bell rang, and she had to come running to see what flavors were on offer. But Lucinda was smart enough to know that it wouldn't be a good idea for Heather to know that.

Heather stepped into her office and Lucinda waited a few seconds so she could at least create the impression that she hadn't seen Heather stretching. She walked down the hallway and stopped at Heather's door. "What's got you working so late tonight?"

Heather, of course, had known full well that Lucinda was in her fishbowl and watching, and had put on the display for just that reason. She, too, however, didn't want to let the full truth be known. She feigned mild surprise at Lucinda's question, and responded with a fib, "I didn't know anyone else was still here. I just came up to catch up on some emails. What are you doing here this late?"

"I'm just hanging around to go to dinner with Guy Pearle at the Capitol Café at seven. I think we've got him by the balls this time," she added with false bravado and nothing to back it up. She stepped into Heather's office and moved over toward the couch but didn't sit. She stood with both hands casually in her pockets, waiting for Heather to respond.

Heather's response was non-verbal. She stood up from behind her desk and walked over to the couch where Lucinda was standing. She leaned toward the couch, reaching into her gym bag, ostensibly in search of a comb, trapping Lucinda between herself and the couch. While Heather rummaged, she brushed against Lucinda, who could feel Heather's firm breasts against her. It took all of Lucinda's self-control to keep her hands in her pockets. Heather knew full well the effect that she was having on Lucinda and lingered twice as long as necessary. She had found the comb she was searching for almost immediately after she placed her hand in the gym bag but wanted to give Lucinda a good dose of her own medicine.

After ten seconds or so, Heather stood up so as not to give away her intentions and walked back around to her chair on the opposite side of the desk. Lucinda just stood there, unable to move, barely able to speak. All her alarm bells were ringing. She knew that propositioning a subordinate would expose her to potentially damaging lawsuits and could ruin her career. But the jingle of the ice cream truck was strong, and Lucinda ran into the street without checking both ways for traffic.

"I knew you were fit, but this is the first time I've ever seen you in anything but office clothes. If you work out dressed like that, you must get hit on by half the men in the gym."

"And a few of the women. The women are much more subtle about it, but that just makes it more interesting."

"Really? I didn't know you were . . ."

"Oh, yeah," Heather fibbed again. "I think there's something very beautiful about a young woman's body."

"Definitely."

"I really took to heart what you said about the power of sex. That's why I've been working out almost every day. God gave me this instrument, but it's up to me to keep it in tune. I want to hang on to what I've got as long as I can. It's so unfair. Men have it easy, but women have to work much harder to stay in shape. If they're not careful, they can lose everything by the time they're forty. I mean, you must know what it's like to have to fight that battle against gravity."

Lucinda was so intent on keeping her place in line among the jostling kids at the ice cream truck window that she didn't notice the pointed jab. The way that Heather had said it, in a "we're all in this female-power thing together" kind of way, made it possible for Lucinda to interpret it as something other than a direct shot.

Heather, on the other hand, had calibrated her comments carefully. She knew that misogynistic women tended to react to "negging," the use of slights or minor insults to undermine a woman's confidence and make her want to win the shamer's approval. She'd had more than her fair share of losers try that with her, and she'd seen a number of her friends succumb to it, too. She was pretty sure that Lucinda was at a point in her life where she was particularly vulnerable to negging, and she was right.

Lucinda responded in the only way she knew how: She tried to impress Heather with her power. "So, at dinner tonight, I am going to drop the hammer on Guy Pearle."

"Oh, yeah? How so?"

"Well, first of all, I'm going to force him to take David Gordon back on the board. David is asking for twice what was previously agreed upon, but I'm going to make Guy pay up and take him back."

"Really? A million bucks? That's a lot of money. How are you going to get Guy to pay that?"

"I've got leverage. I've got some emails that I'm sure he doesn't want to see the light of day."

"You mean the ones we talked about before, with the silly jokes and stuff?"

"No, I've got some that are much worse than that," Lucinda said. It was a bald-faced lie, but she was desperate to prove to Heather that she was winning her battle against Guy. Somewhere deep inside her psyche, Lucinda knew that Heather would not be attracted to her physically, but perhaps she could be attracted to her power.

For her part, Heather sensed that she was about to confirm a long-held suspicion—that Lucinda was responsible for sending the virus that had compromised IAU's servers. But she knew that if she told anyone about her suspicions, it would be her word against Lucinda's. She needed proof, and she had a plan to get it. She sent herself an email, and when her cell phone dinged with the notification, she picked it up. She hoped that Lucinda would think it was a text message rather than an email, which she could just have easily answered on her desktop. Lucinda was too deep in her own thoughts to notice what was going on, so Heather picked up her cell phone and pretended to answer the text message when, in fact, she was turning on the voice memo recorder.

"So, let me get this straight," Heather said. "The emails I saw during my interview with Brandon Leather aren't the ones you're going to use to pressure Guy Pearle to take David Gordon back onto the board of IAU so he can be your asset.

"That's very impressive—kinda sexy, actually," she cooed, standing up and leaning over her desk. "How did you get them?"

Lucinda was so focused on getting the ice cream that she walked directly in front of the oncoming car. "Let's just say that I managed to plant a little bug in their system. I've got access to everything they're doing, and I'm going to use it to bury them."

CHAPTER 10

BY THE TIME SHE REACHED THE CAPITOL CAFÉ AT Sixth and Pennsylvania in downtown Washington, DC, Lucinda had calmed down a bit. The restaurant was practically across the street from her office, but she had done a bit of extra walking, up Pennsylvania toward the Capitol, to clear her head. Now, as she passed her office again and crossed the street to the restaurant, she was working hard to regain her composure. She didn't want to give Guy the impression that she was anything other than 100 percent in control of her emotions.

By nature, Lucinda was a control freak, always in charge, always "on," but she knew that whatever had just happened with Heather Alston was a potential disaster. It all boiled down to whether or not she could trust Heather. Lucinda surmised that if nothing came of the conversation within the next day or so, she was probably in the clear.

Even if nothing came of the encounter, however, Lucinda knew that she had to regain control of her relationship with Heather, and she always needed to be on her guard. At least part of what Heather had said was true: Heather *had* clearly taken Lucinda's advice to heart and was now willing to use her sexuality to get what she wanted. What Lucinda couldn't tell, and what she was desperate to know, was what Heather could possibly want.

As she stepped through the revolving glass and wood door into the Capitol Café, Lucinda told herself that she'd deal with the Heather problem later. Right now, she needed to deal with Guy Pearle.

She waited in the short line for the maître d's desk and announced, "Hornbuckle, party of two."

The waiflike woman behind the desk searched the reservations list. "Yes, I have you down for 7 p.m. I can seat you now if both members of your party are here. If not, please feel free to have a seat at the bar and we'll try to work you in when your guest arrives."

Lucinda spied Guy at the bar, engrossed in conversation with a young woman, late twenties or early thirties, who was leaning forward conspiratorially to tell Guy something or other. She had her hand on his shoulder and was whispering in his ear.

Lucinda recognized the type. This woman was flirting with Guy, so he'd pay for her drinks. He was an easy mark—a good-looking guy with a nice tan, a sharp suit, and a fancy watch.

She could empathize with the woman. *What girl hasn't flirted with an older man to get a few free drinks? It's a fair trade. She gets her drinks, and he gets his ego stroked, if nothing else.*

But she was surprised to see Guy falling for it. *That didn't take long. His wife has only been dead a couple of months and he's already trying to get back in the saddle? Have some class!*

Lucinda waved impatiently, and eventually succeeded in getting Guy's attention without losing her place in line. Guy took the young woman's hand from his shoulder, threw a handful of bills on the bar, and walked over to join Lucinda. He greeted her with a handshake, but they exchanged no words until they were seated at the table.

Lucinda broke the silence. "Guy, I was so sorry to learn about Janet's death. It must still be devastating to you, only a few months later."

Guy was completely unaware that she was being passive-aggressive and mistook her comments for genuine sympathy rather than the bitchy dig that she intended. He thought that perhaps she was ready to turn over a new leaf and act like a civilized human being.

"Thank you. I appreciate your kindness. It's been difficult, but I've been very busy with work and that has helped a lot to take my mind off of . . ." His voice trailed off.

Lucinda thought, *I can see that. Poor woman's barely cold and you're already cuddling up to some woman half your age. What is wrong with you?* Instead, she said, "Well, I'm glad you're able to get some relief from it all."

"Thanks, but we're not here to talk about me. I want to see if we can find a way forward. My experiences in Africa have really opened my eyes to some things, and I want to be more supportive of David. I realize that he's been through a hard time, and I want to see if we can find a way to help him. If he'll drop his demand for a million, and accept the half a million we originally offered, we'd be willing to cover his costs for a six-week inpatient drug rehab program. If he completes that successfully, we'll be willing to put him back on the board, with a few minor conditions."

"Like what?"

"He would have to submit travel requests in advance, and they would have to be approved by IAU management before he could travel. And he won't get an IAU credit card—for at least six months, maybe a year."

Lucinda was pleased. She was confident she could get David to agree to those terms. "Give me a couple of weeks to get it done," she said. "I assume that I can work with Nigel Winston and that you'll let him know all of this?"

"Yes, I'll make sure he's ready when you and David are."

"So, tell me about your adventures in Africa. How are things going over there?"

"They're going pretty well, I guess. It certainly is different. I remember last time you and I spoke, we got crosswise because you wanted me to use IAU as a platform for social change. I was pretty resistant, and I still have my reservations, but at least I'm starting to get a better understanding of why you feel the way you do."

"Really, how so?"

"Being in Africa, seeing the way things work there, has given me a whole new appreciation for how good we have it in the United States. More importantly, it has helped me to see how things work here—or at least, how they're supposed to work."

"I don't follow."

"Well—and when I describe things, forgive me if I mix up what I've learned from interactions with Africans, and Arabs, and the Chinese, but all of those have had an impact on my world-view. And some of this is influenced by a guy I'm working with called Max, who used to be in the Marines and is now our security chief at the compound."

"Okay, I get it—it's complicated, but you mentioned that your worldview has changed, and you see my point of view now. Or at least, that's what I thought you were trying to say."

"That's close, but not quite. Let me try to put it this way. Everything I've experienced over the past few months—from Janet's passing to the moment I walked in here tonight—has taught me a couple of very important lessons."

"Okay, like what?"

"First and foremost, I need to make sure I don't spend so much time focusing on what I *want* that I don't leave any time to appreciate what I *already have*." He spoke slowly, then paused to let his words sink in. "That's why I agreed to meet with you. I want to do the right thing by David. IAU has already succeeded beyond my wildest dreams, and it would be selfish of me not to share some of that with David. He was one of our earliest investors, and he stuck with us through some lean times. I won't go so far as to say that he deserves it, but I want to do it."

"What else? I mean, I appreciate what you're going to do for David, and I will make sure it happens, but you make it sound like there's been something more profound than just agreeing to bring back a board member. Let's hear it."

They paused to order their food, then Guy continued. "I still don't have a good way to explain it all, but I'll do the best I can. The way Max describes it, there are three spheres of influence. One is social, the second is religious, and the third is legal or governmental. Each of these spheres has its own set of rules for how decisions are made. Sometimes the spheres overlap, but if they come into conflict, there is a logical way to sort out where the decision gets made."

"Sounds like rock paper scissors to me."

"Don't be facetious. I'm about to get to the part where I almost agree with you."

"Do tell!"

"Societies are constantly changing. Their value systems are constantly changing. And I believe there should be a robust debate. What was accepted yesterday may not be acceptable today, and what we agree upon today may not be appropriate tomorrow. And I agree with you that *everyone* should be a part of that debate."

Guy was about to make the point that while everyone should be part of the debate, only the government should have the authority to make rules with punitive consequences, and those rules should be in the form of laws. The American system—unlike everything else he had seen—had enough checks and balances built in to keep one faction or the other from imposing their will unjustly on everyone else. It was possible that unjust laws could get through both houses of Congress and signed into law, and it was also possible that excellent laws might get bottled up in partisan bickering. But the side of the argument that didn't get its way could always come back later, at the next election, or the one after that, to get another bite at the apple.

Guy wasn't sure he could explain this to Lucinda, but he didn't have to. Before he could marshal his arguments and start laying them out, she cut him off. "I knew you'd eventually come around. There's the Guy I used to love."

Guy was so relieved that he just blurted out, without much thought, "Oh, you used to write me wonderful love letters."

Lucinda softened a bit. "Those were the days, weren't they? Where did those days go? How did we lose that friendship and end up like this?"

"Well, I think there was a time when I was in love with you—genuinely in love with you. Later on, I think I was in love with the idea of you, or with the idea of being in love with you, but one of us or both of us had changed. Eventually, we grew apart so that what we had wasn't strong enough to hold us together anymore."

"Yeah, but when and why?"

"I don't know. Sometimes I go back, and I read your old love letters. I've looked for specific moments when we were starting to grow apart, but there wasn't anything I could really pinpoint."

"You kept my letters?" Lucinda was shocked and wondered what Janet had thought, or whether she had even known.

"I kept them, but not as love letters necessarily. If you remember, we were revolutionaries back then. We were lovers who wanted to conquer the world. We had everything figured out, and we spent as much time explaining how we were going to fix the world as we did professing our love."

"But you still have my letters?"

"Yep, sure do!"

Lucinda was growing agitated now, thinking of one letter in particular. From the vague, romantic way Guy was speaking, there was a possibility he didn't recall this one. But if she mentioned it, she would lead him straight to the evidence of a false sexual assault allegation she'd made against her political science professor. For reasons she could never quite explain—hubris, complete infatuation with Guy, and a misguided sense that he would never do anything to harm her, as well as a dozen other things she couldn't put her finger on—she had sent Guy a detailed account of the time she decided to falsely accuse her professor, just to see if she could pull it off.

The man had never done anything to her. It was a large class, a requirement for her major that had dozens of students in each section. There was a good chance the man couldn't have picked her out of a lineup, much less fallen in love with and made a pass at her. But she made her allegation and it stuck.

At the time, Guy had been shocked, but he never said or did anything when the man was summarily punished on nothing more than Lucinda's word. Back in the day, she was so beautiful that it wasn't hard to imagine a professor falling in love with her. Because there wasn't any proof, the dean of the political science department helped the hapless professor get a teaching position at another university, so the damage to his career wasn't lasting, but the impact on Lucinda was transformational. She learned that she was powerful—if only she was willing to use that power.

But Lucinda couldn't be sure that she was interpreting Guy's comments correctly. She knew that if *she* had such incriminating information, those words would be a thinly veiled threat, "Do what I want, or I will use this against you."

Lucinda decided to do what she had learned to do when she was out of options: She threw a fit. She stood up and stepped aside from her chair. "All right, Guy," she said. "You win this one, you son of a bitch. I'll get David Gordon to agree to your terms, but don't expect me to do anything else for you!" She grabbed her water glass and threw it in his face before storming out of the restaurant.

Guy was beyond puzzled. He had no idea why Lucinda had suddenly become enraged. It never dawned on him that she might have been triggered by the mention of the letters. As it was, he had no memory of the incriminating letter.

He chalked it up to Lucinda being Lucinda. They had ordered dinner, but their food had not yet arrived, so—for the second time that night—Guy tossed a handful of bills onto the table and walked away.

CHAPTER 11

GUY FELT AS THOUGH EVERYONE IN THE RESTAUrant was staring at him. He used his napkin to dab as much of the water as he could from his shirt and jacket. He made has way back to the bar and took a seat next to the young woman he'd been chatting with before Lucinda's arrival.

"That went well," she said.

"Oh, yes, that was fun," Guy replied, putting on his best self-deprecating humor. He was humiliated but tried to see the humor in the situation.

"Buy me another drink and I promise I won't throw it in your face."

"Sounds like a plan. I'm Guy, by the way."

"You can call me Ronda."

"All right, Ronda, what are you drinking?"

"Appletini," she said to the bartender.

As they waited for Ronda's drink, Guy took stock of the situation. He was exhausted. His internal clock had long ago adjusted to Moroccan time, and his body felt that it was past midnight. He was running on fumes. The last thing he'd had to eat was airplane food, and that had been several hours ago. Most importantly, however, he didn't want to be alone right now. After the thrashing he'd just received from Lucinda, he wanted to talk to someone, to just have a normal conversation about everyday things.

And Ronda looked like she might fit the bill. She was much younger than he was, probably in her late twenties. She was attractive, but not overly so. And it was clear that she was dolled up for an evening that hadn't gone as planned.

"So, when we spoke before my night went to hell, I thought you said you were waiting for someone. What happened?"

Ronda took a sip of her Appletini. "Oh, just some prick on a dating app stood me up. I should've known better. That app sucks and most of the guys on it are losers. His pics were hot, and he said that he was a Senate staffer working in the Majority Leader's office on climate change issues. If he had showed up and turned out to be who he said he was, he was in for a sure thing. But his loss." She waved her left hand from her face down to her waist. "He could've had this, but instead he's probably jerking it to some Barbie porn or anime."

For the next half hour, Guy listened while Ronda explained how dating worked in her generation. It sounded like a foreign language. The thing that surprised him most was the casualness of it all, particularly when it came to sharing intimate details. Ronda showed him several of her dating app profiles, and nearly all of her pictures showed her in various stages of undress. She casually thumbed through conversations on the apps where she had exchanged pics with prospective dates, including some that Guy found highly inappropriate. He thought back to his courtship with Lucinda and later with Janet. Both relationships had involved a substantial amount of passion and steamy sex, but that was something that remained private, between lovers—not shared with strangers at a bar.

As the conversation continued, Guy couldn't help noticing that Ronda was getting more flirtatious. She was rubbing against him on various pretexts. At one point, she opened the photo app and scrolled down to several topless shots. She leaned close to him and whispered into his ear, "What do you think of those? I got a boob job last summer with a bonus I got at work. Nice, huh?"

Guy was very much out of his element, but he could still appreciate a fine-looking woman. "Very."

"Okay, then." Ronda said. "You got a place somewhere close? I know you said you're in town on business, so I assume you're staying in a hotel. Is it close by?"

"It's just a few blocks away. My company has a membership at an Executive Club downtown. We use it for meetings or to put up visitors from out of town."

"Let's go have a drink, shall we?"

For the third time that night, Guy laid out a handful of bills to cover his tab. As they walked the six blocks to the Executive Club, Guy found the cool night air bracing. He had a vague sense of what was about to happen—she had left little doubt in that regard—but he lacked the sense of anticipation that he had grown to expect and appreciate. Even after twenty years of marriage, there had always been some amount of buildup to his amorous interludes with Janet. As he got older, he had grown to enjoy the romance as much as or more than the sex, but now he found himself on the verge of being intimate with someone he had known for less than three hours. *How does that even happen?*

When they reached his room at the Executive Club, Ronda wasted no time. As she started removing her clothes, she asked him to pour her a drink, which she threw back like it was a sip of water on a hot day.

Then she was on him like an octopus devouring a fish: Pulsing, probing, spinning, flailing, grinding—all while he lay there with a general sense of what was going on, but not quite comprehending what was really happening. Mostly, he was wishing it would just end.

Soon enough, it was over. Ronda got up almost immediately and started to get dressed. Guy remained on the bed, watching her with no clue what to say.

When she finished dressing, she turned to Guy and said, "Okay, that was fun. You're nice."

Guy mumbled something and then, stricken by a vague sense of obligation, he asked her if she wanted to have dinner sometime.

"Thanks, honey, but you're a little old for me. If I had seen your profile, I would have swiped left, but I got stood up tonight, so you got lucky. I saw how your date blew up and felt sorry for you. She seemed like a real bitch and you seemed like a nice guy, so I decided you were the one for tonight. You've probably heard the saying that a two at ten is a ten at two? I wanted to get laid tonight, and I did. Now I'm going to go back and see if I can have any luck finding someone hotter and younger."

As the door closed behind her, Guy sat up on the bed. He was shocked by her brazenness, but more than that he was devastated that his first time after Janet had been so transactional. He felt like he had dishonored her memory. He was sure Janet would not have wanted him to remain celibate for the rest of his life, but he knew she would have been mortified by what he had just done.

CHAPTER 12

GUY RETURNED TO AFRICA WITH A NEW SENSE OF purpose. Soon he would need to return to the US permanently to manage IAU, but first, he wanted to ensure that the team he would be leaving behind in Morocco was positioned for success. One of his biggest concerns was creating a means of capturing the rapidly growing knowledge base that was developing within the IAU team. For that, he took a two-pronged approach. First, he had Sam create a knowledge management portal to capture lessons learned. For all the concerns he had about millennial work habits, Guy was pleased to discover that they were naturals when it came to capturing information in the knowledge base. For them, it was just another social media platform where they could share their experiences.

The second part of Guy's plan was to get the team to stay together longer. The idea of two- and three-month stints at ARP made sense if people were simply rotating through workaday jobs. But IAU's projects required problem-solving and having those problem solvers onsite for more than a couple of months would greatly increase the odds of success. To address employee concerns about the austere living conditions at ARP, Guy sweetened the pot: If they would agree to stay at ARP for a period of six months, IAU would fund a week of vacation every two months.

The first period of R&R would be the team trip in Morocco, and it would be a working vacation. There would be a weekend visit to Agadir, followed by a trip to Casablanca to arrange logistics for additional shipments of recycled plastic from Egypt, and then on to Ouarzazate for a look at the Noor solar power plant.

Employees who stayed an additional two months beyond that would get a free one-week trip anywhere in the Mediterranean, with a per diem rate to cover meals and hotel. To keep costs down, Guy funded only economy class tickets. At the end of four months, employees would be allowed a one-week trip back to the United States, or any destination of their choosing so long as the airfare was less than or equal to an economy-class ticket to the States.

Guy discussed the plan with Sam before presenting it to the group. He wanted to make sure he had structured the incentives in a way that would be attractive to the group, which was comprised mostly of young idealists right out of college. It had been Sam's idea to offer an option of going somewhere other than back to the United States at the end of four months, and he was able to put everything into an online application that tracked when employees arrived, when they were due for their R&R breaks, and what their planning budgets would be.

Within two weeks, Guy was ready to make the pitch. The employees were already eagerly using the knowledge management system, and Sam had a very crude version of the R&R tracking system up and running. Since the first R&R would be a group trip, Sam had at least two more months to complete the application before it got any serious use. All he really needed for the briefing was a working shell that demonstrated the key principles.

When everything was ready, Guy gathered the team in the IAU workspace, just opposite from where Kate Mulgrew, Brenda Bullock, and Li Ming had their offices. Sam had created a presentation with the key details of the R&R plan and was projecting it on one wall of the space. The desks had been removed to a different room, and the chairs were arranged in rows facing the projection.

As the group filed in, one of the younger employees said, "Oh, great! Movie night. Who's got popcorn?"

Guy took that as his signal to start. He explained why he wanted the employees to stay at ARP and what he was prepared to offer as an incentive. He laid out the upcoming trip that would start with a weekend in Agadir.

The plan was well-received and all except one young woman agreed to stay on for an additional six months. One of the employees noted that if they all stayed for six months, IAU would still face a brain-drain when everyone rotated out at the same. He suggested that Guy offer additional incentives to get some from the original group to stay longer to prevent a complete crew turnover. Guy accepted in principle, and the employees agreed that they would work it out among themselves to ensure that there was an orderly rotation plan. Guy was pleased that the group had coalesced so quickly into a team, and he was thankful that Sam had been able to create the system on such short notice. That alone had proved to the team that the company appreciated their dedication.

After the meeting, Sam headed to the gym where he ran into Max, who was already halfway through his workout.

"Hey, man," Sam joked, "Do you do anything besides work out and harass new trainees?"

Max grinned. "The great Sun Tzu said, 'The more you sweat in peace, the less you bleed in war.'"

"There you go again with all that military history crap. You are so stuck in the past that you can't see what's going on now."

"I think I see what's going on," Max replied. "But I find that history helps me deal with it better."

"What do you mean?"

"Well, here's a simple test: Do you like what's happening in the world?"

"Hell, no! I don't know anybody who likes what's happening in the world. It's like everybody has gone crazy."

"Right. But if you study history, you'll see that—for the most part—what we're experiencing isn't unique to our time. We think that we're in the worst moment in history and that things have never been worse, but the truth is that everything comes full circle. Wherever we are now, as a society, there's a good chance we've been here before. We just need to look to history to learn that."

"I remember you said something like that a couple of weeks ago out by the pool. But your whole argument was that you look to history to help you accept what's going on. I don't want to accept it. I want to change it."

"Then you should be a politician."

"What? Me, a politician? No way!"

"Why not? You're young, you're smart and articulate, and you're passionate about what you believe in. You'd make a great politician."

"But I can't."

"You can't, or you don't want to?" Max pressed.

Sam paused and considered how much he should tell Max. It wasn't something he liked to talk about, and he wasn't sure Max would understand it, but he thought it might help him to deal with it if he explained it to someone else. "The short version of why I can't be a politician is because I'm anti-abortion. I'm liberal, black, and gay, and I agree with the policies of the Democrat Party on almost every other issue, but I wouldn't last ten minutes as a Democrat because of my views on abortion."

"But what's to stop you from changing your views on abortion? Politicians change their views all the time. They go to Washington to represent the views of their constituents, not to push their own views on the world. If your constituents are pro-choice, why can't you just go with the flow on that one issue?"

"I haven't told very many people this story," Sam answered, "but hear me out and I think you'll understand. I was raised by a single mom. My dad left us when I was just a few days old. She never talked about him, just said that he walked out on us.

"Then one day I was jogging in Rock Creek Park listening to one of my favorite podcasts, a true crime series about criminals who left forensic evidence at the scene without realizing it. They always get caught on that show.

"The episode I was listening to that day was about a murder that had happened right around the time I was born, in the town where I grew up, and when they gave the name of the murderer, it was my dad's name.

"When I got home after my run, I called my mom and asked her why she never told me. I was pretty pissed.

"She said, 'I was afraid to tell you because I didn't want you to grow up with that hanging around your neck. Your grandmother and grandfather, and all your uncles and aunts, said I should terminate my pregnancy. They were afraid that your father's 'murdering gene' might get passed down to you. They said that it just wasn't safe to take a chance that you'd turn out like him. And they pointed out how difficult it would be for me to raise a son without a father. But I knew in my heart that you would be different than your father, that you deserved a chance to be better. Your father had already killed one man—I couldn't let him be the one who killed you, too.'"

Sam paused for a few seconds to catch his breath. "She said, 'I never told you because I didn't want you to feel what you're feeling right now. I wanted you to grow up like you did, to be a strong, wonderful, loving, caring young man.'"

"My Momma could've gotten rid of me. Everyone was telling her to, but she decided that I was worth the risk. After all that, I just can't support abortion. I don't mean that women shouldn't be allowed to have an abortion, I'm just against it personally, and that puts me way outside where most Democrats are on the issue today."

Max was silent for a moment as he searched for a response that matched the occasion. He couldn't find words that expressed what he felt. Sensing that Max was struggling, Sam changed the subject. "Hey, are you going with us on this road trip?"

"Yeah, Guy mentioned it to me, but I thought it was still in the early days of planning. I didn't know it was a done deal."

"We locked it down this morning. I think there will be close to a dozen people going, including you, so we'll need two or three of the armored SUVs. Can you spare them?"

"I think we can make it work. I'll coordinate with Guy to confirm, but I really want to see the operations at Noor and talk to their security chief there. They were supposed to get the Chinese security forces first. I think they may already have them, and I want to see what the chief of security there thinks about it all."

CHAPTER 13

AFTER COORDINATING ROAD-TRIP LOGISTICS WITH Max, Guy needed a break. He'd had a long day. He was making great progress with the IAU team at ARP, but now he needed to think about how he would re-engage with the US side of the company when he returned to DC for good later in the summer. He had a nagging suspicion that there was more to Lucinda's demand about bringing David Gordon back than she was letting on. Finding it difficult to think about such things in the crowded work trailers, Guy headed for one of the solar greenhouses just outside the walls of the compound.

When he first entered the greenhouse, he was glad to see he was alone with his thoughts, but once he got deeper inside, he spotted Kate Mulgrew sitting in a chair against one of the outer walls, and partially hidden by a row of tomatoes.

"I'm sorry, I didn't mean to intrude," he said, turning to leave.

"No, please stay. There's something I wanted to ask you."

"What is it?"

"I've heard through the grapevine that you're planning a trip to a few cities north of here this weekend. Do you have room for one more?"

"I think so. I've literally just worked out the logistics with Max and we did a headcount so we would know how many vehicles we would need. We've got a couple of extra spaces, and you'd be welcome to come with us if you'd like."

"Thank you very much. I could use a break, and if the rumors are true that the Chinese are going to merge the Noor Power Station with the rest of ARP, it would be helpful to know more about it."

"Sure, we can make that happen."

There was only one chair, and Guy felt awkward standing there with nothing further to say. He had just decided to leave this greenhouse and check to see if the neighboring one was empty, when Kate broke the silence.

"What are the boundaries?" she asked.

"What boundaries?"

"They always say you should write what you know, but how will the readers know where the boundaries are between something I'm making up and something I'm writing about because I know it?"

"Still a little lost here."

"Oh, sorry. This isn't a work question. Actually, I am writing my first novel and I'm struggling with the boundary between fiction and reality."

"If it's a novel, why do you care if people wonder whether it's real or make believe? The purpose is to entertain people, so just write something that will entertain them."

"But when you read something and one of the main characters does or says something truly awful, what does that make you think about the author? Doesn't it make you think that he or she must be a bad person?"

"Not really. I mean, no one goes around arresting murder-mystery writers. And what about science fiction or fantasy? No one ever thinks those things actually happened."

"I know, I know, but that's not what I'm talking about."

"Then what are you talking about?"

"I want to write a novel that has meaning—one that takes on contemporary issues and forces the reader to question his or her values."

"Why on earth would you want a reader to question their values? Then you're saying their values aren't what they should be. Why would anyone read a book that points out their own moral inferiority? That doesn't seem like a very good way to sell books."

Kate paused. Guy's comments mirrored her own struggles, but she had to find a way ahead, regardless. "It's just that we're so divided as a country. People associate with people who agree with them and refuse to listen to any other point of view. And it's not enough to just *ignore* those other viewpoints. Social media has made it so easy to trash-talk anyone and everyone. Everything is immediately subjected to a tribal filter—liberal or conservative—and is accepted or rejected on that basis alone."

Guy decided to play devil's advocate. "That actually makes it easier, then. Just pick a side that you feel comfortable with and write your novel for them. Half the country will agree with you and the other half will ignore you, and even if they trash-talk you, you can ignore them."

"But that's the whole point. I want to write something that makes people on both sides question their own point of view, or at least be willing to consider the other side. If I just play to one side or the other, all I'm doing is adding another log to the fire. I might sell a few books, but sales alone aren't what's important.

"When I read the classics—the ones that have stood the test of time—I can't help but notice that they reflect the time in which they were written. Fictional stories about someone standing up to racism in the Deep South, or a politician who goes to Washington and is honest for a change—those become classics because they capture the struggles of the era in a meaningful way. I think someone needs to write a story like that about our time, about how we are on the verge of taking differences of opinion and turning them into something much worse, something that will tear our society apart. I want to write that story so people will know it doesn't have to be that way."

The solar-powered fans whirred in the background, and the greenhouse's irrigation system began spraying a fine mist over the produce, forcing Guy to move away from the row of tomatoes he'd been leaning against. The disruption gave him a moment to ponder whether or not he really wanted to say what he was thinking. It would definitely come across as a direct challenge, and Guy didn't want to seem adversarial, but he did feel that he owed her honesty. "It seems to me you have two choices. You can write something so pure, so right, so perfect that both sides will see the 'truth' in it. You trust your readers to see that while you're not saying there's anything wrong with their point of view, there is another, more enlightened viewpoint they may want to consider. In that case, you don't have to worry about boundaries, because your readers will see the virtue in what you're writing."

"What's the other choice?"

"There are no boundaries."

"Meaning what?"

"Meaning, you figure out where you're willing to go and that's the boundary."

"That's helpful. Almost as helpful as the advice I got from Simon Johnston."

"Simon Johnston, the famous author?"

"Yes, the famous author."

"Really? You met him and he gave you advice on your novel? How did that happen?"

"When I was working on the Hill, before I went to the State Department, I was the press secretary for a Midwestern senator. I accompanied my boss to an admiral's funeral at the Naval Academy in Annapolis. After the service, we headed to the graveside, and as we were walking there, I heard someone say, 'Look out!' It was Simon Johnston, pointing to a pile of horse manure people were about to step in. At the time, I was working on the outline of this novel I'm still trying to write, so the way I tell the story now is: 'I was working on my first novel when I met Simon Johnston and he gave me some really good advice.'"

Guy chuckled. "That's funny. You should put it in your book. I'd love to hear more but I've got to go check on a shipment of plastic coming into the port. We're doing large-scale tests on the sonic welder tomorrow, and I need to get the bales of plastic hauled from the port to our warehouse. Maybe I'll see you later. I think there's a DJ playing at the pool tonight. Might be fun to hang out there."

"Sure, see you there."

For the rest of the afternoon, Guy concentrated on getting the two large bales of plastic from the port of Tarfaya to the warehouse. All the previous loads of plastic had been used to create wall, floor, and ceiling panels with plasticized sand. They had received just enough plastic to date to build a one-thousand-square-foot residence. This new load of plastic should be enough to allow them to do a full-scale demonstration of how quickly a house could be built using pre-formed parts and sonic welding.

After dinner and some paperwork, Guy made his way to the date palm tree near the pool and found himself searching the crowd for Kate.

He felt a hand on his shoulder and turned to see her. The DJ was playing a slow song, and she said, "Let's dance. It's easier to talk that way."

"You know, I thought some more about what you were saying this afternoon, about how you wanted to write something that makes people question their point of view. Have you ever thought about just writing for yourself?"

"I have, but it seems to me that writing for myself is a fallback position in case I can't get published."

"That's not exactly what I mean. Let me try again. If you had to choose between writing a bunch of novels that were commercially successful—meaning they made you a ton of money—and writing a single novel that was controversial because it made people think but wasn't a commercial success, which would you choose?"

"Oh, my God, I don't even want to think about writing more than one. I just don't think I have enough to say to justify more than one novel."

"Well, let's come at it from a different angle. If you had a choice between writing a novel where you got a million dollar advance, but the book never really took off—by that I mean, nobody read it—and giving away a million copies of your book for free, but knowing that they were going to be read, which would you choose?"

"Why does it matter?"

"I'm trying to understand why you're writing. There are many reasons to write, and each one might lead you down a different path. Are you writing to become rich and famous? Are you writing because you like to write? Or are you writing because you want to share an important message?

"I mean, think about it. If you're writing just to get published, you've got to understand that there's a certain amount of luck involved, and sometimes getting published isn't always a sign of success—at least not in a meaningful way."

"How so?"

"Well, how many times have you seen a movie so bad it made you wonder how it ever got made? Didn't you ask yourself, 'If they made this movie, who are they turning down?'"

"Quite a lot, actually, but what's your point?"

"My point is that you can't necessarily use commercial success as a benchmark when it comes to writing. It is perhaps the easiest benchmark to measure, but if you're writing, for example, to share an important message, you could do that perfectly and still not achieve commercial success. A lot of crap gets published, and a lot of crap gets turned into movies. At the same time, you can probably assume there's a lot of good stuff out there that isn't getting published or turned into movies. It's a bit of a crapshoot, so to speak."

"I hadn't really thought about it that way."

"Well, it's just a thought. I toyed with the idea of writing once, and I did a little research on the topic. What I learned is that the number one category in terms of sales volume is romance. If you want to write for commercial success, you should write romance novels for women. That's what sells."

Kate wondered if Guy was serious or had just chosen a very ham-fisted way to bring up the topic of romance in the context of their relationship. She played it straight. "What do I know about romance? I've never had a relationship that lasted more than six months. Every time I get close to someone, it turns into a complete disaster. For whatever reason, I seem to be attracted to broken men. I'm just not sure I'm cut out for romance, and if I can't do it, I probably can't write about it."

"Maybe, maybe not. I've had my share of romance and the lessons I've learned are mostly negative."

"Like what?"

"I realize this is a complete cliché, but love can make you do crazy things. Nice people can still fall in love with very bad people."

"Amen to that. I've been down that road a time or two. You said *lessons*, so what else have you learned?"

"Another cliché, I know, but it's true: Love hurts. Losing Janet was the most painful thing I've ever experienced. There were days when I didn't think I could get out of bed in the morning. I certainly didn't want to. But the world kept turning, and everyone else went on, and I had to keep going, too.

"What I learned from that is that I don't ever want to fall in love again. I don't have the strength for it. I'm not sure I could ever form a bond with another woman like the one I had with Janet."

Kate listened without speaking; it was as though he was talking to himself, and she was just his sounding board.

"But even when you think you're starting to get over it," he continued, "you do something stupid that hurts you even more."

"Like what?" Kate asked, gently.

"When I was back in the States recently, I hooked up with some woman I met at a bar. It was beyond pathetic. She actually told me it was pity sex. Can you believe that?"

Kate rolled her eyes. "It just goes to prove cliché number three about love. Men are horndogs. Don't confuse love with lust—they're two completely different things. Even when men know they don't want to get emotionally involved, they're still always on the prowl for sex. This may come as a shock to you, but you're just like most men in that regard."

"What makes you say that?"

"Do you remember that Saturday afternoon about two weeks ago, before you went back to the States? I was reading by the pool, in my orange bikini, and you came up and started talking to me. You were checking me out."

"I was not!"

"Yes, you were. Your eyes were roaming everywhere, and I could tell you were enjoying the view."

"How?"

"The same way I can tell that you're enjoying dancing with me now," she said, pressing her hips against him just enough for him to catch on.

Guy blushed and tried to turn away, but Kate held on tight. "I'm not trying to embarrass you," she said. "I just want to let you know that I've noticed, and I don't mind. I'm not looking for a relationship, but I'm not looking for a one-night stand, either. Let's just be friends and acknowledge there's something there worth exploring.

"Today is here. We're in this moment, and all we need to do is enjoy it. Don't make it complicated."

CHAPTER 14

ON FRIDAY MORNING, THE THREE ARMORED SUVS pulled out of Tarfaya at 8 a.m. sharp. The trip was going to take more than seven hours, so leaving just after breakfast gave them the best chance of reaching Agadir before dark.

They took RR109A for a short distance before turning onto RN1, the main road along the west coast of southern Morocco. It was not the most direct route, but it was in the best condition, and Max wanted to stay on well-traveled roads in case of trouble. For the first two and a half hours, they traveled east-northeast, very close to the coast, and after a brief rest stop in Tan-Tan, the crew got back on RN1, which headed well inland for the rest of the way.

Salim Hadithi, one of the newest members of the IAU team, drove the lead vehicle with Max Burke riding shotgun. Salim was Moroccan and knew the area well. He spoke Arabic, English, and some Berber. Max carried his AK-47 and several spare magazines, along with a short-range commercial radio that allowed him to keep in touch with the other vehicles in the convoy.

Nigel Franklin drove the second vehicle, with Guy in the passenger seat. Nigel was not with IAU, but the organization he worked for needed him to take some paperwork to the British Consulate in Casablanca. Kate Mulgrew was in the backseat, handling the radio.

Sam Fischel was driving the last of the three SUVs. Brenda Bullock, in the passenger's seat, refused to hold her AK-47. She left it wedged between her seat and the console and had relegated all the spare magazines to the rear seat with Li Ming.

By the time they reached Guelmim, they were in the southern regions of the Anti-Atlas Mountains. The R1 was well away from the coast at that point, and they would not get close to the ocean again for several hours. After another break at Tiznit, the convoy finally arrived at the hotel in Agadir a little after five o'clock. They were tired and hungry, and after a brief team meeting with instructions to re-group on Monday, everyone went their own way for the evening.

Guy and Kate put their belongings in their rooms and met up downstairs for a walk. As they were heading out, they spotted Sam, Brenda, and Li Ming. "We're going for a walk on the beach. Would you like to join us?" Kate asked.

Sam was first to respond. "No, I'm not much for going to the beach, especially around here. I've done some reading, and the population of the area around Agadir isn't too keen on gay people, so I'm not going to push it. I'll just hang at the pool or, if there's a section of the beach that the hotel runs, I might go there."

Guy briefly considered pushing Sam a little harder. He didn't understand why Sam was so sure everyone would automatically assume he was gay and subject him to some sort of discrimination, but he dropped it. He half hoped Brenda and Li Ming would decline, too, so he could be alone with Kate for a time.

But Brenda spoke for herself and Li Ming. "We'd like to go, if it isn't an imposition."

Guy realized exactly what Brenda was implying but didn't know how to respond without confirming her suspicions. Kate also recognized the hidden question within Brenda's statement, and didn't want to seem overly eager to deny the implication. She said, "No imposition at all. Please join us."

The four of them exited the marked-off section of beach in front of the hotel and walked north for a couple of hundred yards before anyone said anything.

Guy, who wanted to ensure that Brenda and Li Ming had a positive impression of IAU's projects, saw an opportunity to advance his cause. "I'm really glad you guys were able to join us on this trip. There's a lot of change coming to ARP over the next several months, and it's a good thing that you're here at the beginning, to see what it's like now.

"I'm sure you've heard a lot about what we're doing—kind of hard to avoid it, given the cramped conditions—but I imagine you don't have a full picture of what we're up to. Do you have any questions about IAU's projects?"

Brenda, who was under orders to get as much information as she could about Guy and IAU, also saw an opportunity. "Well, first of all, I want to thank you for inviting us on this adventure. You're right, the trailer is incredibly small, and the walls are really thin, so I heard almost all of your R&R announcement meeting.

"I think I also have a pretty good understanding of your projects. I mean not the technology so much, but the impact, what they're going to contribute to society, and I think it's pretty cool.

"But there are a couple of things I don't understand, if you don't mind."

"Sure, I'll do my best."

Brenda laid her cards on the table. "So, I get why your company is doing these projects. They're important for the environment, and they have the potential to solve big problems. It does seem a bit unusual that a small company is so heavily involved in green technology. Most of the time it seems like it's the really big companies that do these kinds of things, but that's just my impression.

"But I do know that it is unusual for the CEO of a company to be so far away from home, or headquarters, or whatever it's called. I guess the short version of my question is, 'Why are you here instead of back in DC?'"

"It's a long story, but essentially, I came here to deal with some personal issues. I lost my wife just before Thanksgiving. At the same time, we were planning to take IAU public. As you noted, it is unusual for small companies to get into this type of technology, and we were planning to use the funds we raised from going public to expand our footprint in the green technology space. But we had to put the IPO on hold."

"Why?"

"That's a little more complicated," Guy replied, starting to question the wisdom of his promise of transparency. "A lot of things contributed to that decision, but I think the most direct answer is that I wasn't ready. I needed some time to regain my focus. Being here at ARP has given me the break I needed, and when I leave here in a few weeks I intend to restart the IPO process."

Pay dirt! Brenda thought. There was no way Lucinda was aware of this, and Brenda could hardly wait to get back to the hotel so she could call her. She grabbed Li Ming by the hand and said, "Oh, we forgot to put on sunscreen, so we should really be getting back to the hotel."

It was well after six in the evening, and the sun was already sinking low over the Atlantic Ocean, so Guy and Kate both knew that whatever was going on with Brenda, it had nothing to do with sunscreen. Guy was unaware of the relationship between Brenda and Lucinda. Had he known, he would have been more circumspect and would never have mentioned restarting the IPO.

Kate was pretty sure Brenda's haste didn't involve her, and she welcomed the opportunity for a few minutes alone with Guy. When Brenda and Li Ming were out of earshot, Kate said, "I've learned more about you and your company in the past five minutes than I have the whole time I've been in Africa. I guess I'm not asking the right questions."

"I'm sorry," Guy replied, sincerely. "I'm not trying to hide anything, but, truth be told, I think I just got a little bit out over my skis."

"What do you mean?"

"I may have gotten ahead of myself about restarting the IPO. The last action of the board was to postpone it. We can't restart it without a formal vote, and I haven't even discussed it with them. I've been mulling over the idea since I got back, but this is the first time I've actually told anyone about it.

"I'm not sure why I told them. In part, I suppose it's because I want to make sure that I've got allies when the Chinese come in. I don't know what it'll be like to work for the Chinese, if they do take over, but I don't want to find out. I'm trying to lay the groundwork to keep IAU independent, regardless of what the Chinese do. I thought if I could make the case that we're on the verge of going public, maybe it would help us stay independent."

"I see." Kate realized she had no special right to be the first to know such things, but that didn't stop her from wanting Guy to confide in her. She chastised herself for not being more clear-eyed about their relationship and resolved not to let it get any deeper.

They walked back to the hotel in silence, allowing more distance between them than they had on the way out. Both Guy and Kate realized that the plans he had just described were in direct conflict with the idea of allowing their relationship to continue to evolve, but neither wanted to talk about it. Guy was riven with guilt for developing any sort of emotional attachment to another woman so soon after Janet's death. As for Kate, she just added another name to her long list of broken men. She was grateful to have learned the truth before she got in too deep.

By mid-morning on Saturday, most of the group had congregated around the hotel pool. Max was reading, Sam was playing a game on his cell phone, and Brenda and Li Ming were soaking up the sun.

Brenda was doing her best to get Max's attention without being too obvious about it. He was significantly older than her, but she was drawn to him, nonetheless. When Guy joined the group just before noon, she took the opportunity to initiate a conversation that she hoped could signal, indirectly, her interest in Max.

She believed, correctly, that Max assumed that because she was a young woman, she must want to have children someday.

She also assumed that, because Max was older, he wasn't interested in children at his age. To keep things simple, and to improve her chances with Max, she decided she would take the issue of children off the table right away. "Well, thank goodness it's so peaceful here," she said to no one in particular. "I'm so glad there aren't any children around, splashing and making noise," she added.

Max didn't look up from his book, but Guy replied, "I take it you're not a big fan of kids, hey?"

"Not really, especially not at pools. They always seem to have a meltdown, and their parents just let them scream, and whine, and throw a fit. They make so much noise that you can hardly think. I think if they're going to be at the pool, the parents should control their kids so everyone else can enjoy relaxing in the sun."

"Or reading a book," Max said, pointedly.

Brenda was offended, and she lashed out. "What? Are you saying that I'm acting like a child?"

"No," Max replied calmly, not even looking up. "I'm just saying that I'm trying to read, and it's difficult to do with you going on about how children make too much noise. Ironic, don't you think?"

Brenda focused her rage on his military background. "I think you're a goddamned baby-killer, that's what I think. How about that?" Brenda spat back at him.

Max finally fixed his gaze directly on her. "I've always wondered what happens to those kids who're allowed to throw fits at the pool. I've wondered what they grow up to become. Now I know."

That pushed Brenda over the edge. For the next two minutes, she vented about men, about the Marine Corps, about guns, about anything she thought held meaning for Max. She was alternately yelling and sobbing, making everyone in the group entirely uncomfortable. He had rejected her, and she was not going to let him off easy.

Max, on the other hand, never lost his cool, but decided he needed to shut her up before someone from the hotel came out to check on the situation. "You know, Brenda," he said. "I spent most of my life in situations where the people who didn't like me were trying to kill me. They shot at me and planted bombs on the side of the road to try to blow me up. From those experiences, I learned how easy it is to put up with words. You seem to want everyone to believe that you're a strong woman, a feminist who doesn't need men, but here's a little something for you to chew on.

"Somewhere, there's a bright young man—and I can assure you that it is a man—who is working overtime to make a realistic sex doll. And when he's done, you'd better look out, because from that moment on, men will never put up with the likes of you just so they can get laid."

Brenda completely lost it. She flew into a white-hot rage and lunged at Max, but Li Ming stepped in front of her, saying, "It's okay. He's not worth it. At least now you know what he's really like. Just be glad you found out when you did."

Guy and Sam were unsure of what to do. They were surprised by the rapid escalation. Sam tried to broach the subject with Max, "Man, that was a little harsh, don't you think?"

Max returned to his book and said, "I'm trying to read."

The rest of the weekend was uneventful. Max spent another day reading by the pool, and everyone else kept to themselves. Guy took the opportunity to call Nigel Winston to discuss the idea of restarting the IPO.

After a brief greeting and a lengthy apology for disturbing him on a Sunday, Guy described his plan.

"I think it makes sense," Nigel said. "We finally got David Gordon sorted out. I've got an airtight non-disclosure agreement in place. If he breathes a word about being let go, about his rehab, or about his travel restrictions, he's gone, and he's got to pay us back twice what we paid him. I don't think he'll be a problem."

"What about Lucinda? What do you think she's up to?"

"The only thing I can say for sure is that she got David to invite her to speak at the next meeting of the board. It's not formal, but she has something she wants to pitch them."

Guy spat out a series of rapid-fire questions, not waiting for Nigel to answer. "And they've agreed? Do you know what she plans to talk about? Why didn't anyone ask me?"

"Like I said, it's an informal meeting. Carl Underhill, who you designated as acting CEO in your absence, approved it. He called me last Friday to see what I thought, and I said I thought it would be okay. I mean, Lucinda is a real bitch, and she's difficult to deal with, but I don't see what harm she can do just by talking to the board. Now that I know you'd like to restart the IPO process; this meeting might prove useful. I'll attend the meeting, and I'll brief the board on restarting the IPO before she speaks.

Then, when she talks, I'll keep an eye on her, and I'll let you know what she says."

"Okay," Guy said. "That makes sense. She can't do too much harm in an informal meeting, and it would be good to take the board's temperature on restarting the IPO process. I'm going to be here for a few more weeks, at the very least."

"Be safe, my friend." Nigel signed off.

CHAPTER 15

THE AIR WAS TENSE THE NEXT MORNING WHEN the group gathered for the second leg of the trip. The original plan was for Guy to take one of the vehicles up to Casablanca so he could meet with Makram Abd Alsalam about finding additional sources of recycled plastic. But Brenda refused to travel in Max's group and demanded to go to Casablanca with Guy. So, Nigel Franklin and Guy took the driver and passenger seats, and Brenda and Li Ming took the back. Guy kept the AK-47, but since they were now well north of any reported terrorist attacks on passenger vehicles, he placed it in the very back with the luggage. And knowing they would quickly be out of radio range as well, Guy added the radio to the cargo pile, too.

The group going to Casablanca took the A3 expressway, a four-lane divided highway that climbed through the High Atlas Mountains to Marrakesh and then on to Casablanca. The A3 was a modern roadway, as good as any in the West, and the group made excellent time.

The two-vehicle convoy going directly from Agadir to Ouarzazate had a much slower go of it. They traveled along the RN10, which stayed largely on the southern side of the Atlas Mountains. They headed almost due east and turned back south, onto RN9, just north of Ouarzazate. They checked into their hotel in Ouarzazate, not far from the power plant, and settled in to wait for Guy's group.

Meanwhile, in Casablanca, it took less than fifteen minutes for Nigel Franklin to drop off his DFID paperwork at the British Consul, and the group made it to the offices of Sahara Freight Express by early afternoon. Makram was expecting Guy and ushered him into his office. Brenda and Li Ming, who didn't have any formal business to tend to, headed to the loading dock, accompanied by Nigel.

As they were watching the freight handlers move the boxes and crates, Brenda noticed that one of the forklift drivers was visibly nervous. She mistakenly assumed he was unhappy because of her and Li Ming's presence, and she was about to suggest that they leave when she heard the forklift driver ask a question of a man who appeared to be the foreman. She couldn't quite make out the question, but she heard the foreman's answer quite clearly. He waved his hands in the direction of a distant vehicle and said, "*Kunbula lil ARP.*"

Brenda wasn't sure she had captured the first two words correctly, but she was positive the man had said "ARP." She wished for a moment that Salim Hadithi was here with them. She wasn't sure if the man was speaking Arabic or Berber, but there was something about the way he'd said "ARP" that unnerved her. She considered sharing her concerns with Guy but decided against it. He was too chummy with Max.

If it had been an option, Brenda would have gladly flown back directly to the compound, but doing so would have deprived Li Ming of the chance to see the Chinese-built solar power plants at Ouarzazate, and despite her seething rage at Max, Brenda didn't want to do anything that would negatively affect Li Ming. So, she'd decided to do her best to ignore Max.

Guy's business with Makram took less than an hour, and they were back on the road again by early afternoon. The first part of the journey, down to Marrakesh, was on the A3 again and so they were able to cover the distance in less than three hours. They hoped to be at Ouarzazate before nightfall, but unfortunately, the road from Marrakesh to Ouarzazate was in poor condition, and so it was another four hours, and well after dark, until they arrived.

After breakfast the following morning, the two groups reunited and reformed their three-vehicle convoy for the six-mile trip to the Noor complex. Brenda insisted on being in the last vehicle to be as far as possible from Max. By this point, everyone on the group had heard about the incident at the pool in Agadir. They quickly re-organized themselves to accommodate her wishes.

They were greeted at the Noor complex by a Chinese man wearing a hardhat and goggles. From the bed of his pickup truck, he pulled helmets and goggles for everyone in the group to wear during the tour.

While they geared up, Salim Hadithi listed a few fun facts about the plant and the town of Ouarzazate. "The word 'Noor' means 'light' in Arabic, which makes it a fitting name. Ouarzazate has three full-scale movie studios, and a lot of movies are filmed here. Whenever you see a desert scene, there's a good chance it was filmed around here."

The Chinese plant supervisor was all business, not even bothering to give his name. He exhibited an air of superiority and seemed annoyed at having to play tour guide. For that reason, the word "tour" was a bit of a misnomer. Rather than shepherd the group around the complex, as they had anticipated, he stood right next to his pickup truck and pointed to the various major components of the complex.

He began what was obviously a well-rehearsed speech. "The Noor complex is the largest solar power plant in the world," he said with obvious pride. "There are four different phases here, with three different types of solar power. Altogether, these four plants generate nearly six hundred megawatts of electricity, which is enough to power more than two million homes.

"The first phase is a wet cooled molten salt plant that generates 160 megawatts of power. Phases two and three of the complex were built by my company. They are dry cooled plants, which is a big benefit because we use much less water than in phase one. The other advantage of our two plants, which makes them much more useful, is that they have a seven-hour storage capacity. The original phase only had a three-hour capacity."

As the man spoke about phase one, he pointed to the northernmost of three sets of mirrors. Each one was positioned so that the sun's rays were focused on the uppermost portion of a tower in the center of the mirrors. Even in mid-morning, the reflection was intense enough to create a shimmering mass of air surrounding what looked like a ball at the center of the tower, where the light was concentrated.

The middle set of mirrors, which was nearest to the group, did not create the same heating effect on its tower. The reflectors were turned almost perpendicular to the ground, while dozens of workers cleaned the surface of the mirrors. Like the plant foreman, they all wore khaki trousers and blue work shirts with a helmet and goggles. Interspersed among them, and in larger numbers at the outskirts of the rows of mirrors, Guy could see dozens of armed guards in desert-tan camouflage and combat helmets. Most of them wore sunglasses rather than goggles. Guy couldn't tell if they were protecting the facility from attack or if they were guarding the workers. He glanced at Max and saw that he was focused on the soldiers, as well.

Nigel Franklin was not sure if questions were allowed, but he decided to ask one anyway. "Why does it matter how much storage capacity they have?"

The Chinese plant manager gave him a stern look but paused his set speech. "Because the sun only shines part of the day. The salt is heated during the day, and we use it to turn water into steam to make electricity.

"If we did not have a storage capacity built into the plant, we would lose our ability to generate steam soon after the sun went down. The more storage time we have, the longer we can generate steam, and the longer we can generate steam, the longer we can provide power to the grid.

"If we can extend the storage cycle long enough, we can provide main power to the grid from the solar plants. If we can do that, we will be much greener than we are today because we will greatly reduce our greenhouse emissions. Just as importantly, we will be able to reduce Morocco's dependence on foreign-supplied fossil fuels."

The foreman continued, "The fourth and final solar facility here is a photovoltaic plant. It is much smaller than the other three types, at only seventy-two megawatts.

"Each of the three concentrated solar power plants you see here cost between two and three billion American dollars to build. During the next phase, which has already begun, we will build a fourth concentrated solar power plant that has double the storage capacity of the best of these three. This new Chinese technology will allow the plant to operate around the clock, with storage capacity of at least fourteen hours."

He pointed to an area well to the south, where bulldozers were leveling the ground and half a dozen water trucks were spraying the ground to keep the dust down.

"Thank you for that explanation," Nigel said, genuinely grateful for the information.

The foreman continued, politely, "We are also proud to note that the building of these plants created more than thirteen thousand jobs for local laborers."

Li Ming, thinking that Nigel had broken the ice on questions, decided to ask one of her own. "What happened to the locals once the plants were completed? From what I can see, there are Chinese workers cleaning the mirrors on the plant closest to us, and it looks like there are Chinese men on the construction site to the south. What are all the local workers doing now?"

The plant manager glared at her and hissed something in Mandarin. She bowed her head and stepped back. "That is the end of the tour," he said in a tone that made it clear he was done with questions, too.

After they turned in their headgear and goggles, the plant manager drove away, leaving them standing in a semi-circle next to their SUVs. Guy said what was on everyone's mind. "I know you're probably disappointed to have come all this way to get about as much information as you would find online. I'm sorry. I hoped this would be a lot more informative."

Max shared what he'd picked up during his dinner meeting with the security chief the previous evening. "What we saw today is how it is here now. My buddy told me last night that since the Chinese took over, they've really clamped down on the information flow. When it was just the Chinese construction company here, things were more or less normal, but the Chinese–American Green group has been a lot less cooperative. They forced out quite a few of the local workers and replaced them with imported Chinese labor. And they've really beefed up security, as you can see. It's not clear to me whether they're protecting the facility or guarding the workforce. My buddy has heard rumors that they're using prisoners for some of the work, but he doesn't have any solid proof. Prisoners or no, if this is what we've got to look forward to at ARP, I can't say I'm all that keen."

Everyone in the group looked at Li Ming and Brenda, hoping for something to challenge the impression that they had just drawn from the surly Chinese plant manager. Li Ming, who knew that the truth was just as bad as, if not worse than, the rumors Max had heard, remained silent. She was worried that the plant manager might send a negative report about her to China and that she would be fired or else called back to Beijing. She wasn't about to say anything more that could lead to negative reports getting back to her supervisors.

With Li Ming completely silent, Brenda felt all eyes on her. She needed to change the direction of the conversation, so she took a chance. Earlier, she had asked Salim Hadithi what the expression "kunbula lil ARP" meant. Salim had told her that she must have misheard because "kunbula" meant "bomb." Ignoring Salim's words of caution, she cast a wary glance at Li Ming, and said, "Well, at least these guys aren't planning to blow us up. When we were in Casablanca, I heard the men in the warehouse talking about bombs for ARP. If Max was any good at being in charge of security, he'd know that, and he'd be dealing with it."

Ordinarily, Max would have asked Brenda what she meant, but he'd had more than enough of her. He climbed into the lead vehicle and waited for word from the last vehicle that everyone was loaded up and ready to head back to the hotel for an early lunch and an afternoon of sightseeing.

CHAPTER 16

AS SOON AS LUCINDA HAD MANAGED TO GET David Gordon back on the board of IAU, she had asked him to set up an informal meeting of the board so she could pitch a merger between IAU and the Chinese–America Green group. The group, which was far more Chinese than American, had recently incorporated in the United States and was positioning itself to go public on the New York Stock Exchange. A merger with IAU would allow the company to immediately meet the operating and revenue requirements of the NYSE and would allow them to go public much sooner than they otherwise could.

Lucinda hadn't known that Guy was considering restarting the IPO process when she'd put the wheels in motion to promote this merger, but when Brenda told her, she was quite pleased. Her reasons for pushing the merger were twofold.

The first was financial. *Social Tech* was not doing well. Her business model, which was just one step removed from extortion, was not providing enough operating capital. She had overextended herself and needed a quick infusion of cash. The merger between IAU and CAG was her brainchild, and she had pitched it to the Chinese as a way to speed up the IPO process. Of course, she had explained, the odds of success with the merger would be much greater if she were given a prominent position in the merged entity, with the proper monetary incentives. She had persuaded them to grant her a million options at a strike price of five dollars per share. If the company went public at twenty dollars a share, and the share price stayed there through the mandatory six-month waiting period before she could exercise her options, she could pocket a quick fifteen million bucks. That kind of money could put *Social Tech* back on firm financial ground and set her up for a comfortable future.

Her second reason was more personal. She hoped, or perhaps more accurately, she *intended*, to use her new position within the merged entity to oust Guy Pearle. Once the merger happened, the Chinese would quickly begin to assert themselves, and it would be a simple matter to get Guy removed from his position as CEO. It might take a bit longer and a few more steps—such as an interim CEO from China—before she could take complete control, but removing Guy was the real prize. Everything else after that was just a bonus.

Since it was only an informal meeting, Lucinda knew she could not be straightforward in presenting the idea of a merger. The bylaws of IAU required the board to be in regular session before it could address such issues, but her plan was to paint a picture that would make them want to explore that option on their own. If she planted the seed properly, it would take root on its own.

When she and David entered the boardroom, he was greeted like a returning hero. Although he was quirky and irascible, the members of the board genuinely liked and admired him. They knew that behind his irritating mannerisms was a brilliant mind, one that had made them millionaires.

After much handshaking and backslapping, David ushered Lucinda to the head of the conference table and stood to her left. The table was positioned so that the windows were to his back, and he hoped the shadows on his face would mask the tears in his eyes. He was grateful to be back, and he was thankful to everyone who had played a role in his return, especially Lucinda.

"Thank you all for the very warm welcome back," he began. "I'm a little overwhelmed by your kind words, and I can't tell you how much it means to me. But the main reason we are here today is to hear from this remarkable woman, my friend Ms. Lucinda

Hornbuckle. Many of you know her outstanding publication, *Social Tech*. She is a pioneer in the field of online tech media, and everyone who is anyone in the field reads her publication—so, if you're not advertising there already, you should be."

After a brief round of quiet laughter, David continued. "In all seriousness, Lucinda is one of a kind. She is smart, fierce, and loyal, and I'm so happy to be able to count her as a friend. She is here today to tell us about her latest adventure with an organization called Chinese–American Green. It's pretty exciting, but I don't want to steal her thunder, so, Lucinda, please . . ."

Lucinda mumbled thanks to David and shook his hand before he took his seat. Then she leaned forward, placing her hands on the conference room table. The gesture was intended to draw in her audience and to signal her seriousness. "For those of you who don't know about CAG, I'll give you an overview. The company, and I say 'company' because we just incorporated in Delaware this month, began as a nongovernmental organization focused on green technology. As you may also guess from the name, there are Chinese and American components to it. They began in China five or six years ago, as a late addition to the Chinese national strategy that has been called One Belt One Road, or the Belt and Road Initiative. The idea, as most of you probably know, was to revitalize the ancient Silk Road—the main trade route that linked China with the rest of the world—but to do so in a modern way. For the Chinese, modern means environmentally friendly.

"I can see some of you have doubts about hearing the words 'Chinese' and 'environmentally friendly' in the same sentence. I know the Chinese have a reputation for promoting growth at the expense of everything else—including the environment—but this is precisely why they formed the CAG. The leaders of the Belt and Road Initiative realized how much they still have to learn in the area of environmental stewardship, and they understood that the United States is a world leader in green technology. Since its inception roughly five years ago, the CAG has experienced tremendous success, financing massive green projects all around the world, including at the Africa Renaissance Project.

"I have been working with CAG for the past few months. Among other things, I've helped them to navigate the regulatory and business environment here in the US. As I've already mentioned, CAG has recently incorporated in Delaware. The goal—in about three years, when we meet all the requirements—is to take the company public on the NYSE."

Lucida looked around the room to see if anyone had made the mental leap she was hoping for., but based on their facial expressions, nothing was registering. Nigel Winston, who was sitting immediately to her right, glowered at her. She couldn't tell if he had understood what she was inferring and was opposed to the idea, or if he just didn't like her and wasn't hiding it very well. She thought the latter was substantially more probable, so she pressed ahead. She wanted to establish why it would be good for IAU to have a Chinese partner.

"Of course, you all understand the benefits of going public. I know that you were considering going public yourselves." She let it hang just for a second to see if anyone would offer up what she had already learned from her spy—that IAU was about to restart the IPO process.

No takers. She would have to be a little more direct.

"I believe that when CAG goes public it will set a new standard for how public companies are governed. They plan to implement a model of social responsibility that is unmatched anywhere in the world.

"If you're not persuaded that we have anything to learn from the Chinese, let me remind you of a few facts. You only have to go back as far as 1980 to see how much China has grown, and how rapidly. Their gross domestic product in 1980 was roughly $300 billion. Today, it is over $35 trillion. They surpassed the United States in GDP in 2015 and have been the fastest growing economy in the world for several years running. The Chinese are world leaders in almost every category you can name, from automobiles to cell phones to energy—you name it, and the Chinese are at the forefront.

"I know that many of you have a hard time accepting these facts. You grew up in an era of 'American exceptionalism' and it just can't be true that the Chinese are beating us. But they are, and I'll tell you why.

"Some like to say that the Chinese are doing so well because they are cheating. They just create money out of thin air, and they manipulate their currency to keep it isolated from the checks and balances that would normally punish them for their inflationary spending. Others say that what the Chinese are doing isn't really communism—it's command capitalism. What does that matter? It doesn't! What matters is that the Chinese have become the largest economy in the world, and we'd better learn to deal with it."

Nigel Winston had reached the point where he couldn't sit idly by any longer. "So, what's your point? The Chinese are successful. Good for them."

"What's important," Lucinda replied, "is not the fact that the Chinese are successful. What's important is *why* they are successful."

"And I suppose you're going to enlighten us?" Nigel poked back.

"I'll tell you what I think. Whether you find it enlightening or not is up to you. But before I get into that, I'd like to ask you a couple of questions. Do you think it's important that women have the right to vote?"

Everyone, including Nigel, nodded.

"And what about the civil rights movement? Do you think that was a good thing?"

More nodding.

"So why did it take so long?" It was a rhetorical question and she continued before anyone had a chance to answer. "I'll tell you why it took so long to give women the right to vote and to protect the civil rights of African Americans. It took far too long to fix these problems—these things that we now look back on and wonder how they could have ever been the norm—because the power over such things rests in the hands of the government. And, in the United States at least, the government is *designed* to move slowly. With three branches of government, each of which is equal to the other and can throw a wrench in the works of progress, everything happens slowly, too slowly."

Nigel was beginning to see where she was going. He remembered the discussions he'd had with Guy regarding how Lucinda thought that companies should be at the forefront of policymaking on social issues. "So, I suppose you're going to tell us that the Chinese have it all figured out, and we should adopt the Chinese model of having the government run companies?"

Lucinda looked directly at David. It was the signal he had been waiting for.

"That's an interesting thought," David mused, trying to move the conversation from Nigel's rejection to an explicit statement that the two companies should merge, without stating it directly. "Even if we wanted to adopt the Chinese model—and I'm not saying that we should, I'm just saying that the Chinese have been very successful with it—we don't have the kind of experience necessary to bring it here. I look around the room and everyone here, including me, is used to the traditional American model of corporate governance. We wouldn't have a clue how to adopt the Chinese model, unless . . ." He trailed off, waiting for someone to pick up the thread.

"Unless what?" Otto Milner asked. He was one of the senior members of the board and had a strong reputation as an innovator.

Susan Cole, who had been on the board for three years, made the mental leap. She was a lawyer with vast experience in workplace sexual harassment and had been brought on board for the express purpose of drafting and implementing a set of policies suitable for a public company. She had been appalled that IAU had almost nothing in the way of policy regarding sexual harassment, racial and gender discrimination, or anything else for that matter. Ironically, she had been the one to insist that David be fired for using the company credit card to hire prostitutes, and now she believed that what she was about to propose would ensure that the "good old boy" network could no longer protect such behavior in future.

"Unless we merge IAU and CAG," Susan said, boldly putting forth the idea as if it were her own.

"Now, wait a minute," Nigel shot back. "Why would we even consider something like that? It doesn't make one bit of sense."

Lucinda considered whether to jump in, or to just leave it to Susan and David to outline the next steps. She was concerned that Susan's distaste for David would cause her to reject anything that David might offer, so she stepped back in. "I realize it's not my place to make recommendations to the board, but since the question has been asked, I think I can shed some light on how IAU would benefit from a merger, if you don't mind."

"Please do," Susan said.

"There are three clear reasons that an IAU merger with CAG makes sense. First, as we've just discussed, the Chinese have been very successful in growing their economy. Their style of corporate governance is a major contributor to that growth. A merger would allow IAU to tap into that corporate governance model.

"Second, merging IAU with CAG and then following the Chinese model of corporate governance would be a first for an American company. IAU is already at the forefront on green technology development. A merger would also make IAU a leader in social responsibility.

"Finally—and I know this is less important to you than the other reasons, but it is worth considering—a merger between IAU and CAG would create a corporation that is many times larger than IAU is now. If you look at comparable IPOs, this would put you, as members of the board, in a whole new category." She was too polite to say it, but she knew they understood her point precisely. They would do well if IAU's IPO proved successful. If the two companies merged and then went public, however, they would do exceptionally well. "Social media IPO" well, perhaps.

Susan Cole put the final piece of the puzzle in place. "I realize that, because this is an informal meeting of the board, we can't take any action. However, we've been made aware of a potential merger possibility and, as members of the IAU board, we have a fiduciary responsibility to consider whether or not it is the best course of action for the company. I will form a small working group of no more than three people to explore this opportunity and we will report to the board at the next meeting. Who would like to join me in this working group?"

Otto Milner raised his hand. "Okay, that's two," Susan said. "Anyone else?"

Lucinda, who had sat down as soon as the discussion had become self-sustaining, kicked David Gordon under the table. He raised his hand.

Susan looked down the line, ignoring David. "Anyone else?"

Lucinda nudged David again. "Me!" he said. "I'll be in the working group."

"Okay, then. We've got our committee," Susan said, then added in a tone that did not match her words, "great."

CHAPTER 17

WHEN HE RECEIVED HAKIM AL-WAHID'S PANICKED phone call reporting that the Chinese had stationed four hundred soldiers at Ouarzazate to protect the solar power plants, Makram Abd Alsalam feigned surprise. He had been on the Chinese payroll for months as a consultant, informant, and freight forwarder, and he was well aware of their extra security at the power plants. In fact, he had been the one to suggest it, and had forwarded on the soldiers' weapons and equipment. But he couldn't let Hakim know this.

Makram was motivated primarily by a desire to see the territory that had once belonged to the Sahrawis returned to them. If they could also break off a little bit of southern Morocco—the part to the south of the Atlas Mountains, perhaps—to make up for all the years of hardship the Sahrawis had endured, that would be fine, too. Makram was not an Islamic fanatic, and he didn't see the Chinese or the people at ARP as the enemy. If everything turned out as he hoped, the facilities that the Chinese and others were building would become the cornerstone of a new economic future for the Sahrawi Arab Democratic Republic.

That put him at odds with Hakim al-Wahid, one of the most vocal leaders of the half-dozen or so organizations that were loosely allied together in what outsiders derisively referred to as Terrorists and African Nationalists, or TAN. Although they had been meeting regularly for close to a year, they had not yet been able to agree upon a set of goals and objectives, or even a proper group name.

To maintain as much control as he could, Makram called for a meeting of the "brothers"—the term they used for the leaders of the allied groups. He offered to host it in Casablanca.

"No," Hakim replied adamantly. "We must call the meeting of the Islamic State in Africa here in Tindouf."

Makram was genuinely surprised that Hakim had taken it upon himself to create a new name for their loose alliance, which unfortunately put Islam front and center. There would be little room for debate about the charter of an organization with "Islamic State" in its name. And he was equally alarmed that Hakim would insist on holding the meeting in Tindouf, the Algerian town near the borders with Morocco, Western Sahara, and Mauritania. Meetings in Tindouf—and there had been several over the past year—were more heavily attended by refugees from the Sahrawi camps. The refugees were more often than not conservative Muslims and, as a rule, were more willing to support aggressive measures. Meetings in Casablanca, on the other hand, were more often attended by the moderate group leaders.

Makram knew the venue of the meeting would have a huge impact on the outcome, so he decided to focus on that instead of confronting Hakim about the new name.

"Yes, brother," Makram said. "We will call an emergency meeting of the Islamic State in Africa to deal with these troubling new developments. But, may I suggest that we hold the meeting here in Casablanca? It will be easier and faster for the brothers to come here than it will be for them to reach Tindouf. Tindouf is an especially difficult trip for our brothers from Nigeria."

Hakim held firm. "No, we must hold the meeting here, and it will be two days from now. I have spoken to most of the leaders already, and they are on their way. You are welcome to come, but if you cannot make it, we will take the necessary actions without you."

Makram had been outmaneuvered. Now he had no choice but to travel to Tindouf, and he had to hope that he could prevail upon the other members of the group to avoid doing anything drastic. He was in a precarious position; everything he had hoped and planned for rested upon the outcome of this meeting.

When he arrived at the camp in Smara—one of the five administrative regions into which the Sahrawi refugees were divided—Makram was dismayed to see that, just as he had feared, only the most hardline brothers were in attendance. And Hakim clearly wanted it that way. After their call two days before, Makram had called a few of the more moderate members of the group to determine if they would be able to make it to Tindouf on such short notice, and most had never even been informed about the meeting. When he called the hardliners, however, every one of them confirmed that they had already been contacted by Hakim and that they planned to attend the meeting.

Hakim called the meeting to order. "The purpose of this emergency meeting is to decide a course of action in response to recent measures taken by our enemies."

With framing like that, Makram realized where Hakim was headed, but he didn't see an obvious response. Better to let Hakim set the stage and find a counterargument after all the cards were on the table.

"I have been informed," Hakim continued, "that the Chinese have added a security force of four hundred armed soldiers at the Ouarzazate solar power plants, and that they intend to do the same at the Africa Renaissance Project at Tarfaya within the month."

Actually, it's more like two weeks, Makram thought, but kept it to himself.

A group leader Makram had never seen before but who was clearly a resident of the refugee camps picked up where Hakim had left off. "The time for action is now. We cannot wait for the Chinese to set up additional security at Tarfaya. We are not strong enough to fight the Chinese.

"We have been stockpiling weapons and fuel for our vehicles. It is only one night's driving distance between here and Tarfaya. We need only one or two days to gather the brothers from throughout the region. We are ready to take action, and we must take action."

"What are you proposing?" Makram asked, hoping Hakim had not laid the groundwork for an all-out assault on Tarfaya.

Much to Makram's dismay, Hakim resumed control of the discussion. "There can only be one action. We must destroy the infidel camp at Tarfaya and everything they have built there. And we must do it *now*, before the Chinese security forces arrive."

Makram searched for an approach that might tamp down their bloodlust. He decided that it would be better to sacrifice the people to salvage the infrastructure. "But, brother Hakim, if we destroy everything, what will we have won? The wind farm alone is worth billions. At the very least we should take it as a bargaining chip. If we destroy it, there will be nothing to prevent them from adopting a scorched earth approach to retaking the area, and we know they will not simply withdraw after we take over Tarfaya."

Makram could see from the looks he was getting that his ideas were gaining traction. They knew—to a man—that the Moroccans would not allow Tarfaya to fall without a counterattack.

The original plan—the one they had been discussing for nearly a year—was to target a larger, more defensible section of southern Morocco. Now, they were talking about attacking nothing but the ARP compound at Tarfaya. If they laid waste to it, they would be in control of only a tiny fraction of land that, taken alone, was virtually worthless.

All eyes turned to Hakim, who was prepared. "Again, we have a brother who is recommending that we go slowly, attack gently." Hakim raised his voice and shook his fist. "But there is no such thing as a gentle attack! We must act decisively, and in a way that will force the world to take notice!"

He looked around at the eager eyes, playing to their years of pent-up frustration. "All of the world watched as the Moroccans deprived the Sahrawis of their birthright, a state of their own. We have been pushed into camps here in southern Algeria and we have been fed crumbs. And the world has done nothing. No one cares about us, and no one will help us. We must take care of ourselves, and the only way to do that is to demonstrate to the Moroccans—and to the rest of the world—that we are a formidable fighting force.

"If we are gentle, they will know that we are weak. If we are fierce and strong, they will know that it will cost them a great deal of blood to reclaim what we will take. The outsiders are weak, and they are tired of fighting against Islam. They will not come to the aid of the Moroccans.

"So, we will be dealing only with the Moroccans, and we know that the king will not risk a fight against the Sahrawis. It was his father who orchestrated the Green March on Western

Sahara. He cares nothing about it, and—if we can prove that we are strong—he will fold."

Hakim was making a strong case. Makram had only one more card—one that would be dangerous to play. "I agree that no one will come to the aid of the Moroccans if we take Tarfaya. They will abandon them as surely as they have abandoned the Sahrawis. But there may be an option to get what we want without a fight."

"And what might that be?" Hakim asked, barely hiding his disgust.

"I have sources close to the Chinese government who have told me they are sympathetic to the idea of a Sahrawi Arab Democratic Republic. As you know, the Moroccans have been very supportive of the Americans in all of the international organizations. If we could form a government in exile for the SADR and get the Chinese to recognize it, the Moroccans would be left powerless. There is a strong historical argument for including some portions of Morocco—everything south of the Atlas Mountains—in the new SADR. If we laid a claim to the SADR on those boundaries, we could include the Chinese soldiers at Ouarzazate. The Moroccans would never attack the Chinese."

The scruffy Sahrawi refugee from earlier chimed back in. "And what would the Chinese ask in return?"

"I believe they would request two things. First, they would demand that we do no harm to the infrastructure they have developed in the region. They have invested billions of dollars in these projects, and their first concern must be to protect them. They would negotiate with the Moroccans for agreements to sell the power generated by the plants. The taxes on those revenues would be the primary source of income for the SADR, so the government would not be dependent upon foreign aid. The second thing I believe they would ask for is that we align with them in international organizations such as the United Nations."

Makram began to believe that he had won the argument and that the attack on Tarfaya might be put off, but Hakim stood and pointed an accusing finger at Makram. "Jasoos!" he exclaimed, labeling Makram as a spy. "Do you believe that we are unaware of your secret dealings with the Chinese? When our brothers go to your warehouse to pick up our shipments of weapons and explosives, do you think we do not see the crates of arms and ammunition bearing Chinese shipping labels? You do not have a source within the Chinese government. You *are* a source for *them*."

Within minutes, the meeting broke up and the brothers filed out. Makram made his way back to the airport, hoping against hope that the wave of destruction that was about to be unleashed would not spiral out of control. His only reason for optimism, strangely, was the notion that TAN might be too incompetent to carry out a successful attack on Tarfaya.

CHAPTER 18

WHEN GUY HUNG UP WITH NIGEL WINSTON, HE was seething. He was angry at Lucinda for yet another attempt to insert herself into his life and his company. He was livid at David Gordon for repaying kindness with betrayal. But most of all, he was furious at himself for running away to Africa rather than staying to fight. As long as he was in Africa, Lucinda would be able to outmaneuver him. But he needed at least another two weeks before he could turn over operations at ARP to Sam Fischel and head back to resume control of IAU.

But it wasn't as though there was nothing he could do in the interim. Apparently, David Gordon had clearly implied to the board members that he had won his Phishhook case against IAU—the case that had started this whole mess. David hadn't come right out and said, "I won, and they had to pay me and put me back on the board," but his comments were unmistakably designed to leave that impression. What else would a member of the board conclude when they heard David claim, "I'm back on the board, and I just bought a new boat—you do the math"?

Nigel was doing his homework to see if there was a cause of action against David for violating the non-disclosure agreement. And, following the establishment of the committee exploring the possible merger, Guy had reached out separately to Susan Cole and Otto Milner.

His conversation with Milner had gone quite well. Otto had told him, in no uncertain terms, that he was opposed to the idea of merging with the Chinese and had volunteered to be on the committee so that he could keep an eye on Susan and David.

Guy's conversation with Susan was not so reassuring. Their relationship had always been strained. He respected her legal acumen and her considerable accomplishments, but he had never been able to shake the feeling that she resented him.

His assessment was spot on. Susan didn't care for him. She thought he was far too unsophisticated to lead a modern tech company. He lacked knowledge of gender and racial norms for the modern workplace, and he seemed remarkably uninterested in educating himself. It seemed as though he was content to just delegate everything in that area to her and let her run with it. Such an approach granted her great latitude, which she did appreciate, because it allowed her to develop policies that she thought were among the most progressive on the East Coast. But Guy never really embraced the mindset she was advocating, and Susan resented that fact.

Based on his conversation with Susan, Guy was certain the committee would put forward a positive recommendation to merge with CAG. Otto was against it, Susan would be in favor, and David would be the tiebreaker. Since David was Lucinda's puppet, the committee was likely to make a two-to-one recommendation for the merger.

Guy was certain, or at least he hoped, that he could dissuade the board from voting for the merger, but he needed to meet with them face to face. He'd have to move up his timeline for returning to the States.

The day after making all those calls, Guy asked Sam to meet him in the sonic welding and sand plasticizing machine warehouse.

"Well, Sam," Guy said, "if you'd asked me a few weeks ago if we'd ever have this conversation, I would have laughed in your face. But things have changed a lot since we first met. I know you and I have very different personalities, and we see the world in very different ways, but you have two qualities that I find very important. First, you're a very hard worker, and second, I trust you."

"Sounds like you're about to ask me to marry you," Sam joked.

"Not quite," Guy replied without missing a beat. "But I do need you. I want you to run the IAU operation here at ARP. I'm not asking you to stay here forever, but I need you to stay here at least another six to eight months. It might be slightly longer, depending on when we're able to complete the IPO, but I need you to stay in place at least through that and for a couple of months after."

Sam was touched. "First of all, thank you for trusting me. It means a lot to me. A few weeks ago, you thought I was a snot-nosed punk with bad manners and an attitude."

"Oh, don't get me wrong," Guy quipped. "I still think you've got an attitude. I've just learned to look past it."

Sam flashed a big smile. "Ha! Touché! But that sounds like a lot more responsibility than my job now . . ." He trailed off.

Guy took the hint. "Yes, it is a lot more responsibility and it does come with a raise. But I'm also going to do something even better—I'm going to give you some skin in the game."

"What does that mean?"

"Options."

"What kind of options?"

"Stock options."

"How does that work?"

For the next several minutes Guy explained the concept of granting stock options. He defined terms like "strike price," "reverse split," and "waiting period" so that Sam had a good understanding of the potential benefits of getting stock options. He would be granted options at a price substantially below the anticipated face value, but he would not be able to exercise those options for at least six months after the IPO. If he then decided to exercise the options, he could sell them and pocket the difference between the strike price and the sales price. If the stock did really well, he could make a lot of money. If it lagged, he could hold onto his options until it recovered. There was a lot of potential upside and very little downside risk.

Sam agreed to stay on through the IPO, and most of the other members of the crew had already extended their contracts at ARP, which meant that Guy had accomplished one of his primary tasks. But there was one more thing he needed to take care of before he could depart.

Guy knew that Kate Mulgrew preferred to spend her free time in her favorite solar greenhouse, and after the trip to Agadir and their awkward conversation on the beach, she had been spending more and more afternoons there to avoid running into Guy.

When he entered the greenhouse, she was busy at work in her usual spot, with her laptop and her cell phone.

"Hello, Kate," he said as he drew nearer.

She looked up at him briefly but did not respond. She returned to her laptop and waited for him to continue.

"I wanted to apologize for what happened in Agadir. I'm really sorry that I didn't share my plans with you before I announced them. You've been a good friend, and you deserved better from me. I'm sorry."

"Don't worry about it, Guy," she replied. "You don't owe me an apology, or an explanation. You don't owe me anything. We're just two people who had a moment, but that moment is gone, so now we'll just move on."

"Look, I'm not trying to defend myself here, or maybe I am, but I just want you to consider what I've been through. I hope you'll understand that I didn't act the way I did out of malice or disrespect. I just didn't realize what was happening until it was too late."

He inched closer to her and softened his voice, trying to get rid of the defensive edge that even he could hear. "Do you remember the conversation we had where you asked me about the rules?"

"I believe it was boundaries," she replied.

"Either way, I'm just asking you to understand that I'm struggling with something similar in terms of the rules for emotional relationships. I lost my wife only a few months ago. I still miss her very much. When I met you, I wasn't expecting to develop feelings for you. And the fact that I have makes me feel guilty. I know that the way I've treated you isn't right, but I don't know what I should have done instead. I just don't know what the rules are, and I wanted you to know that I'm sorry."

"Like I said, Guy, we're good."

Guy grew more desperate. "If it means anything, I want you to know that I seriously considered staying. I'm being forced to go back to the United States to save my company. I don't think I should be punished for something that is beyond my control, and I wish I didn't have to make a choice. I wish you'd say something to let me know that you want to find a way . . ."

"What part of 'we're good' don't you understand?" she cut in with a chill in her voice Guy had never heard there before.

"But, Kate, I don't want it to end like this."

Kate stood up, shut her laptop, and slid her cell phone into her pocket. She barely looked at Guy, and as she walked by, she left him hanging with, "You know what they say, Guy: You can't always get what you want."

CHAPTER 19

AFTER THE DISASTROUS ATTEMPT TO SETTLE things with Kate, Guy needed some time to think. He asked Sam to accompany him to the demonstration site where they had built a single-family home out of plasticized sand in less than two days. They grabbed a short-range commercial radio and their AK-47s and headed to the motor pool to check out a vehicle.

The demonstration site was only fifteen minutes from the ARP compound, but it might as well have been another planet. As Guy and Sam drove out of the compound and then outside the city limits of Tarfaya, Guy couldn't help noticing that they were surrounded by crushing poverty. The homes were shoddy and unkempt. On the outskirts of Tarfaya, the residential streets quickly turned from macadam to dirt, and the passing of their vehicle stirred up yet another layer of dust.

As they approached the sand house, they were amazed to see that it had already taken on enough dust to blend into its surroundings. In its original form, plasticized sand was a dark color, somewhere between green and brown, but now, after only a few days, the house already looked like it had been standing there for the last hundred years.

As they walked up to the front door, Guy was shocked to discover that someone had already moved in. He had no objection to the house being occupied—they had planned from the beginning to donate the house to a local family—but it shocked him that someone had apparently just taken it upon themselves to move in.

Rather than disturb the family, Guy and Sam got back into their vehicle and drove a few miles toward the edge of the wind farm. Guy parked facing east, looking out into row upon row of giant wind turbines. Their massive blades turned slowly and seemed to perfectly capture the pace and spirit of the western edge of the Sahara.

"Before I go back, Sam," Guy began, "there's something personal I'd like to discuss with you."

"Personal for you, or personal for me?" Sam asked.

"It's about you. I don't mean to pry, and if you want to tell me that it's none of my business, I'll drop it, but I wanted to talk to you about your gay thing."

"My 'gay thing'?" Sam bristled. "What the hell is that supposed to mean, and why do you think you're qualified to talk to me about anything related to being gay?"

"I'm not saying I'm qualified to talk to you about being gay. I'm trying to talk to you as a friend."

"Well, I'm pretty sure you have no idea what it's like to be a gay black Muslim. Last time I looked, you're a rich white dude—but go ahead, bro, let's hear it. Tell me the wisdom of the world. I'm listening."

"I'll admit I have no idea what it's like to be you, but what I'm about to say is based on many years of watching other people interact. If it's useful to you, I hope you'll take it on board. If not, feel free to ignore it."

"Okay, man, I'm listening. Shoot!"

"I guess what I'm trying to say is that you have a lot more going for you than you realize. You're a brilliant person. I've met a lot of IT people in my line of work, and you're one of the best I've ever seen. And you're an incredibly hard worker. You might think I never noticed, but I know for a fact that when you were developing the R&R and knowledge management systems, you took your laptop back to your trailer almost every night and worked until one or two in the morning. That's the kind of dedication that separates you from everyone else."

"What does that have to do with me being gay and black?"

"It has *nothing* to do with you being gay or black. You're a good person, because you're a good person. People don't see you as a gay black man. They see you for what you can do. You're the one who is always bringing in the gay black stuff, and—to be honest—nobody wants to hear it."

Sam was silent for a moment. He thought about telling Guy some of things he'd shared with Max about his upbringing, about his father's criminal past, but before he could decide what to say, a loud crack shattered the air.

"What the fuck was that?" Guy asked, not even realizing he had cursed.

The answer came not from Sam, but from one of the distant turbines. They could see a cloud of black smoke rising from the base of the turbine, and it began to lean—almost in slow motion—to one side. After a couple of seconds, the wind turbine collapsed to the ground, and a dust trail raced across the desert in their direction.

Sam was first to react. "We need to get the hell out of here, Guy. I don't know what's happening, but it ain't good."

"Call Max," Guy shouted. He put the vehicle in gear and raced back toward the compound.

"Max, this is Sam. I'm with Guy and we're outside the compound, out toward the wind turbines near the sand house. Something just happened. We're not sure, but it looks like an attack. There's a vehicle coming toward us and we're not sure if it's friendly or not, but we're not taking any chances. We're coming back to the compound now."

Max's voice came over the radio a few seconds later. He was calm, without a hint of stress. "Yes, that's right. We're under attack. I don't know how many people we've got coming after us, but they're attacking in multiple places. I'm outside the wire, too. I just talked to my deputy at the compound and they're getting hit pretty hard. It's not safe to go back there. I'm on my way to the rally point. If you can make it to the rally point, you should try. Don't try to go back to the compound. My guys there are weapons-free until further notice."

"Roger that," Sam said, channeling some of Max's calm.

"And, Sam, make sure you're clear before you go to the rally point. If you have someone following you, it's important that you don't lead them directly to it. You've got to lose them or fight them off, but don't lead them to the others at the rally point. Okay?"

Guy nodded at Sam to acknowledge Max's instructions. They had enough of a lead on the vehicle behind them, but Guy didn't want to take any chances. He turned away from the rally point and headed for the port, first, where they drove through enough traffic to lose any vehicles that might be following them.

As they approached City Hall, Sam said to Guy, "We need to split up. You can go right up to City Hall. I'll take the vehicle and ditch it, then join you."

"But I don't think we were followed," Guy said.

"Are you willing to bet everyone's life on that? Are you that sure?"

"No, I'm not sure, but even if we do split up, why should I be the one to go straight to the rally point? I don't want you to be outside any longer than I am."

"Guy, for a smart man, sometimes you can be one oblivious motherfucker. Look at the locals, and then look at me. If you haven't noticed, *I'm black too*. If the two of us are out on the street, and these guys are trying to shoot all the foreigners, which of us do you think has a better chance of not getting shot?"

Guy couldn't argue against that logic, so he pulled the vehicle to a stop outside City Hall and jumped out, leaving the engine running. "I'll see you inside."

When Guy made it to the second floor of City Hall, he spied Max and a few others who were already there. Most of them were unarmed, and Max was issuing weapons and ammunition from the small armory. Guy was relieved to see Kate, too, but he knew he needed to keep his mind on the business at hand.

"What can I do?" he asked Max.

"I need a lookout." Max handed Guy a set of binoculars and pointed him toward the row of windows on the east side of the building. "Look for our people and for the bad guys. Shout if you see either one."

Guy took a place in front of the middle window, but Max barked, "Not there. Go to one side or the other. You'll be too easy to spot in the middle."

Guy moved to the left side of the bank of windows and began his sweep with the binoculars. Almost immediately, he saw Brenda Bullock and Li Ming making their way toward the rally point from the north. They were bent over and moving slowly. He said, "Max!"

He didn't listen for Max's response but kept up his sweep. To the south, he could see Sam trying to appear casual, walking calmly toward City Hall. Guy was scanning back to check on Brenda and Li Ming when he saw the small Toyota pickup with a machine gun mounted on the back. It was directly to the east, moving slowly. The man behind the machine gun was swinging it from side to side, firing at random. It would be on top of Brenda, Li Ming, and Sam before they could make it safely inside. "Max!" Guy yelled as loudly as he could.

Max grabbed the binoculars and saw exactly what Guy had seen. But he also made a decision. "We've got to take out that vehicle before they see our people. If they get another hundred yards closer, they'll see Brenda and Li Ming, and they'll probably see Sam, too, and then all our people are as good as dead."

"Can't you just go out and bring them in?"

"I won't be able to get to all of them. Our only chance is to take out that vehicle."

Max ran out of the building onto the street. He waved at Brenda and Li Ming, signaling them to pick up the pace, and then he turned to give Sam the same urgent signal. He headed along the street toward the technical vehicle, hiding his AK-47 behind him and keeping his head down so that his face was covered by the brim of his baseball cap. He was hoping the terrorists would not see him as a threat before he was ready to act.

When Max was about seventy-five yards from City Hall and slightly more than that from the technical, he could see that they had detected Brenda and Li Ming. The man with the machine gun swung it toward the two women and ripped off a burst of fire. He missed but they darted in terror behind the closest building.

Max's current position was exposed, and if he opened fire now, he'd be an easy target. But if he didn't take immediate action, the terrorists would radio in about the foreigners gathering at City Hall. If he allowed that to happen, the place would be crawling with terrorists in a matter of minutes.

So, without hesitation, Max swung his AK-47 from behind his shoulder and engaged the technical vehicle, focusing first on the driver to keep him from touching his radio. That gave the gunner enough time to draw a bead on Max and open fire.

As soon as Max saw the driver's head explode in a flash of red, he shifted fire to the gunner. He was a better shot and took out the gunner with his second round, but not before taking a round in the chest. It hit just above his SAPI plate, the Small Arms Protective Insert, which would have been strong enough to protect him if it had hit there. Instead, the round penetrated the Kevlar webbing and entered his chest. He went down hard.

Guy ran down the stairs and, just as he exited the building, spotted Sam. "Come with me! Max has been hit."

A few seconds later, he and Sam carried a mortally wounded Max Burke into City Hall. They took Max to the rear of the room and slumped him upright against the wall. Looking down, Max could see the pink froth bubbling through the hole in his ballistic vest. "That's not good," he said, trying to play it cool to keep everyone from panicking.

"Guy, I need you to listen to me. I don't know who these guys are, or how many of them there are, but they've got a lot more firepower than we do. They will eventually overrun our position at the compound, and they'll find us here and kill us all. We don't have enough force to fight them off. You've got to find a way to get help."

Kate Mulgrew volunteered what she knew. "I spoke to one of my friends at the embassy in Rabat recently. She said they'd heard chatter about the security situation but didn't have anything firm. She said they were moving a Marine Exploratory Unit into the area."

"Expeditionary Unit," Max corrected her. "It's called a Marine Expeditionary Unit, and they've got enough firepower to deal with these assholes. Figure out how to get in touch with them, and hopefully they can get here in time to save your bacon. I'd help, but I'm pretty much done for."

Max pulled Guy close and whispered, "Guy, I'm not going to make it. I don't know how much you know about sucking chest wounds, but this is what they look like. This is the end of the road for me."

Guy tried to offer encouragement, but he knew that Max was fading fast.

"I just want you to promise me one thing," Max said. He relaxed his grip on Guy's arm and stuck out his hand as if to shake on a deal. "Promise me that you won't let those bastards get Peanut."

Guy nodded. Max squeezed his hand. "I want to hear you say it. Promise me that you'll take Peanut out of here with you."

"I promise," Guy said.

"All right, then," Max exhaled, and leaned back against the wall.

The next four hours passed in a blur. Kate was able to contact her friend at the embassy in Rabat, who patched her through to the Defense Attaché Office there. The DAO was able to put her in contact with the command group of the MEU.

They established contact with the Marines just as a second wave of attacks began at ARP—according to radio communications with the security team at the compound. Kate relayed details to the MEU command group, but both positions were in danger of being overrun.

"We can have LCACs on the ground in half an hour," the Marine commander said over speakerphone. LCAC stood for Landing Craft Air Cushion. It allowed the Marines to move quickly from ship to shore and could carry several armed vehicles. If the ARP could get some LCACs into the fight, their odds of surviving would improve significantly.

"I don't think that's going to be quick enough," Sam said, pointing to a line of vehicles raising dust in the distance. There were at least a dozen of them, all headed toward City Hall.

Sam barked into the cell phone, "Adjust fire, polar!"

The Marine commander was surprised and responded instinctively, lapsing into radio protocol. "Say again, over."

"I said, 'adjust fire, polar.' I was told you'd know what that means, and you could help us."

"That's the artillery call for fire. We won't have artillery on the ground for at least an hour, but if you can give me what I need with a polar call for fire, I can get a couple of gunships to you in about three minutes."

Over the next ten minutes, Sam and the Marine commander worked together, and got two AH-1Z Viper attack helicopters to rain down death and destruction upon the terrorists. The arrival of the Marine gunships was a turning point, and the terrorists broke off and retreated.

The Marines established blocking positions to the east and set up an exfiltration point on the soccer field next to City Hall. In all the commotion, everyone had lost focus on Max, who was still slumped against the wall, and Sam and Guy headed over together to tell him that help was on the way.

But within a few seconds, it was clear that Max was gone. Guy was too shocked to accept that Max was dead, so he focused instead on the promise he had made.

"Sam," he said, "I need your help. We need to find Peanut. I've got to go get her, but I don't know where she is."

Sam took out his cell phone and checked the Peanut app he had created to track who was taking care of her for the day. "She should be in the accounting office. I'll go with you."

They ran to where Sam had left the motor pool vehicle and raced back to the compound. They talked their way past the Marine stationed at the entrance and made their way to the accounting office, where they found Peanut asleep on her traveling bed, underneath one of the desks. She stretched and wagged her tail as Guy approached. She rolled on her side, begging for a belly rub, but Guy said, "Not now, Peanut. We've got to go."

They made their way back to the landing zone just as the last of the civilians from the rally point were being loaded aboard a V-22 Osprey tilt-rotor aircraft. They were to be ferried to the ships at sea and onward to safety from there. Guy walked up the ramp with Peanut in his arms, but the loadmaster stopped him and said, "I'm sorry, sir, but we can't allow you to bring the dog aboard. You'll have to leave it here."

Guy looked past the young Marine to the body bag lying on the floor of the aircraft. He said, "The man in that body bag was a Marine. He saved all of our lives. Before he died, he made me promise to save his dog, and I've done that, unless you intend to stop me now."

The young Marine waved him aboard and said, "Okay, sir. Semper Fi."

PART III – DISCOVERY

CHAPTER 1

THE ATTACK ON TARFAYA MADE HEADLINES around the world, but the impact was short-lived. The terrorists had quickly retreated and dispersed, so it was over almost as soon as it had begun. Their encounter with the AH-1Z Viper gunships had persuaded them that they weren't ready to take on the West—at least not until they were better armed and better trained. The damage to ARP was significant, but not irreparable.

After the incident, the CAG followed through on their plan to beef up security. Only a few days after the Marines evacuated all international workers at ARP, the CAG brought in a security force of nearly six hundred soldiers. But ARP became, for all intents and purposes, a ghost town. The people who had worked there were scientists and idealists. They had no desire to fight it out with Islamists and nationalists, so they abandoned their green projects, leaving everything.

After a couple of days at an American naval base in Rota, Spain, the civilians were repatriated. While different countries had different mechanisms for getting their people home, the Americans were transported on a Navy aircraft back to the United States. Most of them hailed from the East Coast, so when they arrived at Andrews Air Force Base it was relatively easy for them to restart the lives they had left only a few months ago.

Guy Pearle offered all of the IAU employees full-time positions back in the United States. Everyone accepted his offer, except Salim Hadithi, who was Moroccan and wanted to stay close to home, and Sam Fischel, who got a job managing the IT infrastructure at the *Washington Note*. Sam's decision stung a bit, but Guy understood that the job at the *Washington Note* was a big career move for Sam and he had no hard feelings.

Guy also offered positions to a few others, including Brenda Bullock, Li Ming, and Kate Mulgrew. Of course, he hadn't expected Brenda and Li Ming to accept, since they had positions waiting for them at the American arm of the CAG, so he was neither surprised nor disappointed when they politely declined.

Kate's decision to accept a position at the Millennium Challenge Corporation was more painful. The MCC was a US foreign aid agency that had been established in the early 2000s to explore a new approach to development aid. Her choice made complete sense—it was a natural place to apply her public affairs talents in an environment that promoted a pro-business approach to foreign aid.

What was painful for Guy was that she never even bothered to acknowledge his job offer, much less explain why she was turning it down. She simply acted like Guy didn't exist.

Guy didn't realize he was being tested, and because of this, he failed—miserably. Kate had seriously considered his offer, but she didn't want to be treated as just another member of the IAU crew. She felt that if Guy really wanted her on his team, he would have approached her independently and made the offer on a more personal level—one that acknowledged the potential difficulties of working together when they had feelings for each other.

His failure to broach this subject made her feel that he was no longer interested in exploring something more than friendship—that whatever might have happened in Tarfaya, there was no future for them. In that case, working at IAU would only remind her of what might have been, and she had no desire to put herself through such daily emotional torture.

For his part, Guy never really thought it all the way through. He had been sincere in wanting Kate to work for IAU. He respected her talent, and he knew that when IAU went public, they would need someone with her skills to manage investor relations and press affairs. But he wasn't going to chase her. Their last interaction in the greenhouse had left him with the impression that he was interested in pursuing a relationship, but she wasn't. As the CEO of a publicly traded company, he simply couldn't afford to have an unrequited affection for one of his employees.

Guy was also going to be extremely busy preparing for the IPO, and the drive to and from Annapolis would take a heavy toll. He also had to think of Peanut, whom he had inherited after Max's death, so he decided to rent an apartment in Crystal City just across from the IAU offices. That way, he was able to pop over at lunch and, if he planned to work well into the evening, later in the afternoon, to take her for a walk and feed her.

By late May, Guy had settled back into a routine. He thought frequently about Max, and the sacrifice he had made, but the whole world of ARP and Tarfaya become more distant and surreal with each passing day. Sitting in his cushy office just off Crystal Drive, it was both easy and tempting to suppress the memories of what had happened there.

On days when he knew he would be working long hours, Guy brought Peanut to the office with him. Pets weren't allowed to walk through the Crystal City underground, so Guy bought a small carrier that looked like an oversized briefcase and carried her to work in that. She often fell asleep on the way to the office. He purchased several dog beds, including one that fit easily beneath his work desk, and she spent many days lounging at his feet.

But Peanut was the only one getting plenty of rest. As Guy had expected, Susan Cole's special committee recommended that the board pursue a merger between IAU and CAG. The good news for Guy was that a merger wasn't something that just happened overnight, and it wasn't something the board was ready to vote on until it had more information—a lot more information. In this case, Guy maintained an appearance of neutrality and let Nigel do the heavy lifting. And even Nigel didn't have to show all his cards when he pushed back. He simply pointed out that there were numerous filings that the Securities and Exchange Commission would require in the event of a merger prior to the IPO. He recommended, and the board unanimously agreed, that no decision be made on the merger until CAG had gathered the information necessary to complete the amended SEC forms.

On CAG's behalf, Lucinda Hornbuckle expressed confidence that they could gather the required information within ninety days. The board agreed to consider the merger at the next board meeting, with one caveat—the information from CAG would have to be delivered ten days prior to the board meeting so that everyone would have time to review it before voting on the merger. Lucinda agreed and the clock was ticking.

Nigel and Guy met privately to discuss their options. "What, if anything, can we do to stop this?" Guy asked.

"So far, I'm not seeing a lot. To be honest, I'm not seeing anything. I was hoping there was something we could do related to David Gordon. There's absolutely no doubt in my mind that she maneuvered us into putting him back on the board for the express purpose of opening the door to this merger. If that isn't a conflict of interest, I don't know what is, but it doesn't seem to violate anything in David's employment agreement. I've also done a lot of research on the case law regarding non-disclosure agreements, and what David said at the last board meeting doesn't violate his NDA. The bottom line is that so long as he maintains that a merger would be good for IAU, there isn't anything we can do."

Guy stared out the window overlooking the Washington National Airport. "So much for our airtight NDA."

Nigel pushed back a bit. "Let's be honest about what we're really up against. What we're trying to prevent—at least the way I see it—is losing control of the company to Lucinda Hornbuckle and the CAG through the merger. That problem didn't start with David Gordon, and there's nothing we could have put in his NDA that would help us keep control of the company."

Guy walked back to his desk. As he sat down, he said, "I know. I'm sorry. I didn't mean to take it out on you. Please keep pressing ahead. Maybe something will turn up in the CAG books that will sour the board on the idea of a merger."

When Nigel left, Guy leaned back in his chair and gazed at the skyline. As he had done many times in the past, he watched the planes appear as specks in the distance and morph into aircraft readying to land, hoping that something about that process of evolution would help him find a solution.

He was deep in thought when his cell phone rang. He didn't recognize the number, so he sent it straight to voicemail. A moment later, the phone rang again so he answered. It was Sam Fischel.

"Oh, hi, Sam. I didn't recognize the phone number and thought it was spam."

"Yeah, I'm calling from a pay phone. There's something I need to tell you and I didn't want to call from my office or personal cell."

"No problem. What's up?"

"Okay, so you know I do IT at the *Washington Note*, right?"

"Yes."

"Well, yesterday I was doing a remote session with one of the reporters, a woman named Arlene Tann."

"I know her. She's written a couple of articles about IAU, including the most recent series about what happened in Tarfaya."

"Right. So, while I was helping her regain control of her computer from some malware she'd picked up, I saw an email pop up on her screen with a subject line that said, 'Maryland US Senate Seat, 2028.' I could see that the sender was a Lucinda Hornbuckle. Do you know her?"

"I know her," Guy replied, shortly. "But I don't see why you're calling me about this."

"Well, you know how you can configure your email program so that part of the email is visible in a side panel of the screen?"

"Yes." Guy wondered if Sam was ever going to get to the point.

"I saw your name in that email."

Now it was getting interesting. "In what context?" Guy asked.

"I couldn't read the whole thing, but basically Lucinda was saying that the article Arlene did on you after Tarfaya was helpful, but she—meaning Arlene—would have to do more or you would be 'too strong to stop' for the US Senate seat for Maryland in 2028."

"I'm not planning to run for Senate next year. Why would Lucinda tell her that?"

"I don't know, I couldn't see the rest of the email, but there were a couple of attachments that were emails between you and someone named Nigel Winston. Does that ring a bell?"

"Yes, he's my lawyer. Why would Lucinda have our emails, and why would she be sending them to Arlene Tann at the *Washington Note*?"

"I don't know, and I've got to be careful poking around. I saw what I saw, but I don't have a good reason to go looking for anything else. I thought you'd want to know."

"Yes, Sam. I do appreciate this information very much."

"Okay, I've got to go. I took the Metro up to Columbia Heights so I could call you from a pay phone. I need to get back to the office before they notice I'm gone."

"All right. We'll catch up another time. Thanks again for the info, it's very helpful."

As soon as he hung up with Sam, Guy dialed Nigel. "I think we may have something."

Nigel said, "I'm on the Metro, so I might lose you, but what have you got?"

"Do you remember the stories that the *Washington Note* ran right after the terrorists attacked the ARP compound in Tarfaya?"

"Yes. They were way out of line with all the other coverage. Most of the press was pretty friendly and focused on the good work that people were trying to do at ARP, but it seemed to me like the *Washington Note* was trying to make you out to be some kind of moron for being there and involving your company in such a dangerous place."

"I think I know why."

"Lucinda?"

"How did you know?" Guy asked.

"Just a good guess. But if she *was* behind the negative coverage, and we can *prove* it, we might have what we need to stop the merger."

Before Nigel could explain what he had in mind, the Metro car passed underground as it entered DC, and the call dropped.

CHAPTER 2

AFTER GUY AND NIGEL HAD WORKED OUT AN INvestigation strategy, Guy hosted a new product meeting at IAU. He loved these types of meetings, and this was the first since his return from Africa.

"All right," he began, "I know you've probably heard a lot of rumors about what's in store for us. So, I'll start with a couple that are true. First, it is true that we are in the process of restarting the IPO. If all goes as planned, we should be a public company within six months to a year."

One of the new software engineers interrupted him. "What about the merger with the Chinese company? Is that going to happen?"

"That's the second rumor," Guy answered. "As of today, the merger is not a done deal. The board has asked for additional information. The decision to merge will be made by the board after they receive and evaluate the information they have requested."

The young man blurted out, "But you're the CEO. Can't you stop it from happening?"

Guy did his best to maintain an appearance of neutrality. "Let's see what the facts are before we judge. The board is in the process of gathering information to support its decision about the merger. When all the information is available, I am confident that the board will do what is best for the company. I take it from your question that you're not a fan of the idea. If you have a reason that the merger should not go forward, feel free to share it here or prepare a memo for the board. I will make sure that all relevant information is presented so the board can decide what is best for the company."

The young man clearly had something more he wanted to say, but after an awkward silence, Guy continued. "Okay, so let's focus on why we're here today. This is pitch day. For those of you who haven't been through this process before, it's an internal meeting to decide which projects to fund for development. Today's pitch session is focused on software products, so I'll turn it over to Brandon Leather, our lead software engineer and senior program manager."

Brandon stood and took his place next to the large projector screen at the end of the conference room. The first project he described was the Public Search Index.

"Search," he began, "is one of the top areas of contention in the Internet world today. There are concerns that the people who manage the search engine have too much control over what users see. The core concept behind the Public Search Index, or PSI as we plan to call it, is that everything will be transparent to the public. We will accomplish this in two ways. First, the search algorithm will be available for the public to see, and, second, it will be 'tunable.' By that I mean the user will be able to adjust the search to find the results that are most likely to interest them."

One of the software developers had a question. "How do you make it tunable?"

"This will be a curated search engine. If you go back to the early days of the Internet, the idea of a search engine was to create a list of websites and allow users to find them more easily. That is what we will be doing here. If you look at search now, the big companies try to present the whole world to you, but much of what is out there is completely useless. The PSI will be created by users who find information and include it in the search engine. There won't be any porn, no violent videos, no social media pages with people trying to impress everyone with their vacation snaps."

The questioner was not impressed. "Isn't that just called Wikipedia?"

When the snickers subsided, Brandon went on. "The difference between what we are doing and what has already been done is that the curators will admit their bias. There will be people who identify as liberals and others who identify as conservative. They will be compared against others who self-identify in the same way, and they will achieve a score that shows how often they agree. You, as the user, can completely tune your search by deciding whose results you want to see. No one has done that effectively before."

"So," the software engineer countered, "you're going to create two different truths, one for liberals and one for conservatives? I am not sure that's going to make things better."

Guy had a question of his own. "How and where is this information going to be hosted? When you first start out, the total amount of information is likely to be relatively small, but as the search index grows and the number of users grows, you're likely to need a fair amount of storage space. How are you going to monetize this?"

Brandon had an answer, but he knew it wasn't likely to be persuasive. "Our current concept is to put this behind a paywall. The costs will be minimal, but we believe that people will pay for a tunable search engine."

One of the key aspects of pitch day was to encourage presenters to promote their ideas, with the promise that they would be given serious consideration. Guy could tell that the PSI concept was not being warmly received, and he didn't want the mood to turn sour. He looked for a soft segue. "That's very interesting. What else have you got for us today?"

"So, next up we've got the Memory Hole project, named in honor of George Orwell's famous novel *1984*. As you may recall, if you've read the book, the government constantly tried to rewrite history to make it conform to the official version of the truth. When something happened that caused a historical fact to be out of line with the official narrative, there were people whose job was to rewrite history to make that fact disappear. They put it down the Memory Hole.

"We've created an application that allows people to write their views on ten current topics. For example, a person could write an essay on the state of race relations in the country today. That essay gets locked in a vault, so to speak, and to unlock it, the owner has to write a new essay on the same topic."

Brandon explained the application, but nearly everyone had difficulty understanding how it would work. Guy found himself circling back to a familiar theme. "So, what is the value proposition we're offering, and how do we monetize it?"

Brandon was on more solid ground this time. "We see two potential revenue streams. First, we believe that people will pay for this themselves if we keep the cost low. I'm talking something on the order of a dollar a year. Second, we believe there will be a commercial market for anonymized data and predictions. There are a lot of organizations interested in finding people, or groups of people, who are better than chance at predicting trends. Over time, as users get higher ratings for accuracy, they will be asked to make specific predictions. They can get paid for that, and we can take a small piece of the action."

As was often the case in pitch meetings, the products being offered still had room for further development, so no one was surprised when Guy directed Brandon to put the PSI project on hold for the time being and to focus on the Memory Hole project. He requested that Brandon prepare a cost analysis and revenue model that would allow the internal investment group to decide whether to fund continued development of the project.

After the meeting, Brandon returned to his office and called Heather Alston. He planned to give her an update over the phone, but she asked if she could come to his office, as she had something she wanted to share that she felt safer discussing in person. Brandon was delighted, and after signing her in, escorted Heather to the new office he'd earned as part of a recent promotion. She closed the door behind them. Brandon was surprised, but said as casually as he could, "Okay, I've been able to trace the keylogging file back to the original IP address from which it was inserted. It wasn't easy, because there were several layers of anonymizers between here and there, but it's located at a public library in downtown DC. That's what took me so long."

"What can you do with the information you have now?" Heather asked, hoping that what Brandon had found would be actionable.

"Well, not a lot," he replied. "It has been useful to know that the threat is there so we can keep an eye on it, but until we know who is responsible, we can't really do much with it. I've briefed Guy and he has agreed to allow us to leave the keylogging program in place while we try to prove who's behind it. We know it's Lucinda, but until we can prove it, we have to be careful and hope that she slips up."

Heather pressed, "What would you do if I could prove to you that she is the one who put it there?"

"First, I'd want to know why she did it. Then I'd want to know how you can prove it. It wasn't that long ago that you were sent here to manipulate me into providing you with useful information, so why should I trust you now? What's changed?"

Heather knew she had to be honest. Completely honest. "The reason I changed my mind is because when I was doing what Lucinda wanted, I was becoming someone I didn't want to be. She saw me as a blond bimbo who could manipulate men. That's what I became, and I couldn't live with myself."

"So, this change of heart is about you becoming a better person? It has nothing to do with how you feel about me?"

"I do care about you," Heather answered, truthfully. "But not in a romantic way. I know that's what you want, and it's difficult for me to come here knowing that I'll have to tell you that I don't have romantic feelings for you.

"In some ways, I think it would have been easier for me to come here and lie to you, to tell you that I changed my mind because I fell in love with you. I have enough experience with men to know that you probably would have accepted that without question—wouldn't you?"

Brandon shifted uneasily in his chair. He knew that what she was saying was true. "Maybe," he said, "but that still doesn't solve our problem. I still can't prove that Lucinda is behind the keylogging file—at least, not in a way that would stand up in a court of law."

"I think I have a way to do that." Heather reached for her phone. She played the recording she had made of Lucinda in February, in which Lucinda removed any doubt about her role in planting the keylogging file on the IAU computers.

Brandon listened intently to the full recording. When it ended, he said, "I'm not a lawyer, but before we can use that, we'll have to figure out if it's even legal in DC to record someone without their consent. I just don't know. For the time being, let's just keep this between the two of us. I'll try to ask some questions in a way that doesn't throw you under the bus—just in case it is illegal. I'll get in touch with you when I find out, okay?"

Heather agreed and started for the door. She paused and turned back toward Brandon. "This may not be exactly what you want to hear, but I do want you to know that you were at least part of the reason I changed my mind."

"How so?"

"You're a really nice person. There are some people I wouldn't mind playing, if you know what I mean. They don't have any real interest in me; they just see me as a sex object. In my mind, they're fair game. They deserve to be treated the same way they would treat me—as a plaything.

"But you're different. You've been nice to me, even when I wasn't a good person. You've shown me respect that isn't solely based on what I look like. You've made me want to be the kind of person who earns your respect. I know I've got a long way to go, but I hope you'll keep giving me the chance to be the kind of person you seem to believe me to be."

Before Brandon could answer, Heather turned and walked out the door.

CHAPTER 3

WHEN LUCINDA HORNBUCKLE CALLED ARLENE Tann at the *Washington Note*, she was unaware that anyone else knew of her efforts to wage a negative press campaign against Guy Pearle. The notion that an IT employee at the newspaper had seen one of her emails to Arlene, and that he had happened to know Guy Pearle, was just too unlikely to even consider. In her mind, members of the press and their sources had an inviolable right to privacy, not only from the government, but from everyone. Confident that the press's veil of secrecy would protect her, and desperate for the IAU–CAG merger to occur, Lucinda was even more reckless than normal.

Lucinda knew that the story she was pushing—that Guy had an interest in the US Senate seat—was made up out of whole cloth, but she was confident that by the time the truth came out, the damage to Guy's reputation would already be done. She knew he was working behind the scenes to sway the board against the merger, and if the story were managed correctly, she could create the narrative that Guy opposed the merger because he was xenophobic and didn't want to have Chinese partners at the same time he was running for the Senate.

Arlene had been the one who first mentioned the Chinese–American Green group, and Lucinda hoped that would mean Arlene would be motivated to see the merger go through. She also knew that, if she played her cards right, she could get Arlene to mention Guy's potential candidacy as a "sources say" tidbit without going to Guy for confirmation. To do that, she needed to provide at least a hint of evidence. At present, she didn't have it—because it didn't exist—but she was hoping she could describe the situation in a way that Arlene would find both frightening and believable.

For her part, Arlene Tann was not sure what to believe. Lucinda had been the source of most of the negative information for the stories about the terrorist attack on the Africa Renaissance Project, and those had held up remarkably well. Lucinda seemed to have a source inside the organization, and that source had provided details about what occurred in Tarfaya. None of the facts in those stories had been disputed by Guy Pearle or anyone else.

What Lucinda was pushing now, however, was more significant. Arlene recalled the conversation they'd had several months before in which Lucinda had asked for dirt on Guy after the COPS32 conference. She remembered that Lucinda had described Guy then as a potential threat because he wasn't sufficiently woke, but Arlene was dialed in to the political scene and she'd heard nothing about a Senate run.

Arlene wanted to broach the subject gingerly, but only after setting a positive tone to the conversation. "When I mentioned CAG to you a few months ago, I had no idea you'd end up working with them to create a merger with an American company. That's just wild!"

Well, this just got a lot easier, Lucinda thought. *She's doing the hard part for me—she's building rapport that puts us on the same side.*

"Yes, isn't it something?" Lucinda gushed. "Who would have thought that a random snippet of conversation would lead to this? I don't know that I ever thanked you for bringing CAG to my attention. Everything's just been moving so fast. I should really take you out to dinner again and thank you properly!"

Arlene was conflicted. She was never quite sure if Lucinda was coming on to her or if she was just gregarious. All of that would have to wait, however, because she needed to remain objective if she was going to do a story with Lucinda as a source. "Perhaps at a later date. For now, let's focus on the story you've got in mind."

Lucinda decided to be bold. "First of all, let me remind you that everything I've told you in the past has turned out to be true. Do you agree?"

"Yes," Arlene admitted.

"So, I'm hoping that you'll give me a little latitude on this. I'm not in a position to reveal my sources here, and I know I'm asking you to go out on a limb. But, you know, from the first time we met, I felt a connection. I'm trusting you to trust me."

Alarm bells went off in Arlene's mind. She'd been a reporter long enough to know that establishing emotional ties was one of the oldest tricks in the book—one usually used by reporters to get sources to reveal more than they would otherwise. Now, the tables were turned, and Arlene went into defensive mode. "I do trust you, Lucinda. You've given me no reason not to trust you. I appreciate everything you've told me, and I find it fascinating that you were able to move so quickly to establish a relationship with CAG. I don't think I've ever met anyone more action-oriented.

"But what we're talking about here is a front-page story that will suggest that Guy Pearle is a candidate for the Senate when I've not been able to find anything to corroborate that. To be honest, it wouldn't be the first time the *Washington Note* published a thinly sourced story, but I'm also asking you to trust me. Tell me what your endgame is. I may or may not be willing to run with the story, but I don't see how I can move forward without understanding your motivation."

Lucinda was boxed in and she knew it. "All right," she confessed. "I believe I can make the case for why it would be bad for Guy Pearle to become a senator, but I'd like to do it in person, and I'd like to make the case to Malcolm Rutherford himself. Can you set that up?"

Arlene was both shocked and relieved that Lucinda was willing to go so far over her head, directly to the newspaper's owner. The action was consistent with Lucinda's history—never take a half-measure when a full leap is an option. But it also allowed Arlene to step back a bit from the story. If Lucinda could make the case to Malcolm, he would decide whether or not the story should run.

Surprisingly, Malcolm agreed to the meeting right away, and within an hour, the three were sitting in his corner office.

When Lucinda laid out the facts for Malcolm, she was candid. She admitted that her concern was not that Guy was actually planning to run for office, but that he would be extremely dangerous if he did. She painted a picture for Malcolm of what it would be like if someone like Guy, who had a strong tech background, got a seat on the committees that were responsible for antitrust matters. If anyone could make the case that the blurring of the lines between social media and traditional media smacked of monopoly, it would be someone like Guy Pearle.

She also made the case that if IAU merged with CAG, Guy would no longer be in a position to sound the antitrust alarm. The combined entity would be much larger than if IAU went public on its own. She hinted, but didn't come right out and say, that she was working behind the scenes to make sure that an IAU–CAG merger would result in Guy's ouster. She knew that Malcolm was smart enough to realize that there was only room for one tech billionaire on the East Coast, and she hoped he would see her proposal as the surest way to guarantee that Guy didn't become a competitor.

For his part, Malcolm was just as blunt. "You've made your case, but there's one thing missing. What's in it for you?"

Lucinda knew better than to bluff. "The short answer is cash. I've been so busy promoting positive social change—mostly in the form of the IAU–CAG merger—that I haven't been able to devote much time to revenue generation. Consequently, I'm seeing a cash crunch in the not-too-distant future."

Malcolm was already aware that she was facing a cash shortage. He also knew why. What she had failed to mention was that she wasn't getting as much revenue as she normally did from the companies she aggressively tried to extort into funding *Social Tech*. The reason for the cash crunch was because Malcolm had privately assured nearly all of her targets that they need not give in to her tactics.

"Well," Malcolm said, casually. "Maybe there is an opportunity for us to work together. I agree that an IAU–CAG merger is a good idea, but only if Guy Pearle doesn't remain CEO of the new organization. I also agree that it would be bad for IAU to do an IPO if Guy Pearle remains as CEO. But, as I'm sure you can imagine, I'm not in a position to interfere in such things directly. As you note, if he were to become a wealthy tech entrepreneur and decide to try his hand in politics, he might succeed. And if he did, he'd be in a strong position to retaliate against me for anything I did overtly during his rise.

"That's not a position that I want to be in. But you're well positioned to remain as a thorn in his side, and you can do that in a way that I simply can't. So, what we need here is a mechanism that allows you to focus as much energy as you need to on dealing with Guy. If cash is the issue, there are a couple of ways we can deal with that."

Lucinda perked up. "What do you have in mind?"

"Depends how much you need."

"Three million," she blurted, expecting him to counter. She was ready to accept one million.

Malcolm turned his chair to the window, pensively. Three million was pocket change to him. He had been prepared to offer ten. Still, he wanted to see what the terms would be, so he hesitated.

"Three million?" he asked, trying to give the impression that the figure was high.

Lucinda began negotiating against herself. "I know that's a lot, but here's how I came to that figure. To push through this merger, I'm going to need to focus on it almost completely. That, and getting rid of Guy Pearle. What that means is that I'll have less time for business development."

Business development, eh? Malcolm thought. *Most people would call what you do extortion.* But he let her continue uninterrupted.

"I have several sources of revenue and can cover most of my operations, but if the IAU–CAG merger and subsequent IPO takes a year or more, I'll need about three million to keep everything running smoothly until I can cash in my options. When that happens, I'll be able to pay you back, and I'll have more than enough cash to keep *Social Tech* solvent until I can start business development again."

"But," Malcolm countered, "if Guy is successful in preventing the IAU–CAG merger, you won't have a source of revenue to repay the three million, if we make it a loan."

Lucinda knew he was willing to part with the money. Now it was just a question of finding the right terms. "What do you have in mind? Are you thinking of making an investment in *Social Tech*?"

"The thought has occurred to me. If I understand correctly, you're the sole owner now. Do I have that right?"

"Yes, I am the only shareholder."

"It is notoriously difficult to value media properties. I don't know if you could find two experts who would agree on the book value of a single newspaper or online outlet. They defy conventional models, so if we're going to put a price on *Social Tech*, the main thing is to find a number that you and I can agree on."

"I agree that putting a value on *Social Tech* would be extremely difficult. You've obviously got a number in mind, so let's hear it."

"Well, like I said, this stuff is always subject to interpretation, so I hope you won't be offended, but I was thinking that the three million might get me a 20 percent stake in *Social Tech*. Does that seem reasonable?"

Now it was Lucinda's turn to play it cool. For three million, she'd been ready to go as high as 49 percent, just enough to maintain majority control. Twenty percent was far better than she had supposed possible.

"You're a tough negotiator," she deadpanned, wanting him to think she was surrendering. "But I believe that what we're trying to accomplish here is far more important than just numbers, so I'm good with 20 percent."

Within three days, the paperwork was in place that made Malcolm Rutherford a partial owner of *Social Tech*. Arlene Tann wrote and published a three-part series on the potential Senate candidacy of Guy Pearle, and Lucinda turned all of her energy to the merger.

CHAPTER 4

AFTER TWO DAYS OF RESEARCH ON VARIOUS ASpects of the relevant statutes, Nigel asked Guy to come to his office downtown to discuss the possibility of filing suit against Lucinda Hornbuckle. When Guy arrived, Nigel led him straight to a conference room, where a couple of paralegals were seated at the long table with laptops open. Their screens showed multiple web browser windows, with applicable statutes and case law at the ready.

Nigel started off with a simple truth. "Guy, I'm not seeing a slam dunk here. There are a couple of angles we could pursue, but I'd be lying if I told you that I thought we were sure to win."

Guy wasn't surprised. Lucinda Hornbuckle had never been stupid, so there was no reason to expect that her actions had exposed her to serious legal liability—or at least not anything easily provable. "Well, let's step back a minute and define the objectives of any legal action we might take."

"Silly me," Nigel shot back. "I thought the goal of filing a lawsuit was to win. What do *you* expect?"

"I'm not saying we don't want to win. I'm just saying we should define what 'winning' means."

"Fair enough," Nigel conceded. "Let me tell you the three things I think are potentially on the table, and we can decide what winning would be in each case. Is that reasonable?"

"Sure."

"Let me start at the end and work backwards. The first thing we should consider is damages. All three of the causes of action we're going to brief you on give rise to some sort of damages, but the damages I want to talk about first are for emotional pain and suffering. To sue for those, you'd have to win one of the other cases, but if you do, you can really ratchet up the pain for her by suing for emotional pain and suffering."

Guy could tell where Nigel was headed and wanted to cut him off before he went too far down that road. "I'm not interested in suing for that kind of damage."

"I wouldn't dismiss it out of hand," Nigel replied. "If you win one of the three suits we're talking about, you could be in for a big payout. I would remind you that we're on retainer, so I'm not pushing this idea to line my own pockets. You have led me to believe that you want to get her attention, to force her to back off. A multimillion-dollar award for emotional pain and suffering would get her attention in a big way."

"Nigel," Guy said, earnestly. "You're a dear friend and a damn good lawyer. I would never dismiss your advice without serious consideration. But you know me well enough to understand that I am not someone who sues for emotional pain and suffering. That's one of the biggest problems we've got in our legal system. You've heard me say that at least a dozen times. So, I'm not going to suddenly get on board just because *I* could be the one to get a boatload of money."

Nigel wasn't surprised. "I had a hunch that you might feel that way, but as your lawyer I felt obligated to bring the option to your attention. Now that you've indicated you're not interested; we'll focus instead on the three primary causes of action. I'll start with what I feel is probably the weakest."

"All right," Guy said, "but before we get too deep into all of this, I want to make sure you understand that I am speaking to you in your capacity as my personal lawyer. I expect that your invoices will be sent to me personally, not to IAU. As you are aware, filing a lawsuit of the nature we're discussing would require a vote of the board. I have no intention of bringing this matter before the board, so any action I take will be in my personal capacity. Is that clear?"

"Should I get rid of the paralegals?" Nigel asked, nodding to the two young ladies with laptops.

"No, they're fine."

"Okay, then, here we go. First up, we've got a potential lawsuit against the *Washington Note* for making an in-kind contribution to your opponent for the US Senate seat in Maryland in 2028."

"But I'm not running," Guy protested.

"According to three articles by a woman named Arlene Tann from the *Washington Note*, you are. And any person who reads those articles can only conclude that she is expressly advocating against you. Newspapers ordinarily have unlimited freedom of expression, based on First Amendment grounds."

"Then why are we even talking about this?" Guy asked, not bothering to hide the exasperation in his voice.

"These aren't ordinary times," Nigel answered, calmly. "And our objective would not necessarily be to get the Federal Election Commission to impose a fine on the newspaper for making an in-kind contribution."

"I don't follow," Guy said, blankly. "What would be our objective, then?"

"Discovery."

"Discovery of what?" Guy shot back. He clearly wasn't seeing whatever it was Nigel wanted him to pick up on, and he wished Nigel would quit beating around the bush.

"A little latitude, Your Honor, I assure you there is a reason for this line of questioning." For the next several minutes, Nigel laid out his theory of the case, beginning with the idea that the email Sam Fischel had described to them would be the predicate for a lawsuit against the *Washington Note* for two of the three causes of action.

"Let me get this straight," Guy said when Nigel finished his explanation. "We get Sam to swear an affidavit saying he saw an email between Lucinda and Arlene Tann that mentioned my name. The goal is to get the judge to let us file a discovery request against the newspaper demanding every email that mentions me or my run for the Senate, and the cause of action we would cite would be either an FEC complaint for an in-kind contribution or a defamation lawsuit. Is that right?"

"In my defense, I told you when you walked in the door that I didn't see any slam dunks lying around. I'm not responsible for what Lucinda did or didn't do, and I'm not responsible for the law. I'm just trying to tell you what your options are."

Guy was about to apologize, when Nigel continued, "Now, I told you that I saved the strongest case for last. Are you ready for some good news?"

"Not great news?"

"No, definitely not great news, but I think it's pretty good. We've got several additional pieces of information that we can bring to bear on the third case: tortious interference in a business relationship."

"That sounds interesting. Lay it out for me, please."

So, Nigel explained how Brandon Leather, with Heather Alston's help, had discovered the keylogging virus that Lucinda had planted on the IAU servers. He described the means through which Brandon had been able to trace the hack back to an IP address at a public library, and the fact that Lucinda had confessed to Heather, on tape, that she was responsible for the hack. The big finish was another email that Sam had seen on Arlene's computer when he was trying to remove malware. In that email, David Gordon had responded to Lucinda Hornbuckle without realizing that Arlene Tann was also copied. He bragged to Lucinda about how helpful he had been to her when he filed a lawsuit against Guy for wrongful termination and cheating him out of profits related to Phishhook. Most importantly, he admitted that the lawsuit was frivolous, and that Lucinda had put him up to it and paid his legal costs.

"So, where's the tortious interference? I can see that what he did was obnoxious, but I knew that from the start. I have to admit that if I'd known this when she was pushing to get him back on the board, I wouldn't have given in, but I don't see how this is something we can sue her for."

"Well, let's walk through the five elements of a tortious interference lawsuit. I'll state the law, and then describe the facts as they would apply in this case. I just ask that you hold your questions until the end, please.

"The first element is the existence of a contract. In this case, the contract in issue is the one between IAU and Advanced Capital Placement for running book on the IPO. The second element is the wrongdoer's knowledge of the contract. Both David and Lucinda were fully aware that IAU was in the process of preparing for an IPO and that ACP was running book. Third, the wrongdoer's intentional procurement of the contract's breach. We believe we can show that Lucinda's objective in getting

David Gordon to file the lawsuit was to prevent the IPO from happening. Toward that end, she put false information into the public domain to get ACP to back out of running book on the IPO. The fourth element is a lack of justification. On that score, David admits in his email that the lawsuit was frivolous and was for the sole purpose of stopping the IPO. And the fifth element is that damage resulted from the wrongdoer's actions. When ACP backed out of the agreement to run book, that was clearly damage, and I believe we can make the case that it was primarily because of Lucinda's actions."

Guy thought back to the time when he'd decided to pull the plug on the IPO. It was Janet's death that prompted him to postpone the IPO. "I'm not sure that all of the damage was done by Lucinda's actions."

"Well, I'm sure that will be her defense, but keep in mind we've got more than one goal here. The first goal is to make a strong enough case that we can get into the discovery phase. If and when we do that, we know we're going to find even more proof that Lucinda was trying to sabotage you."

"But what's our exposure here? I mean, if we do this, Sam will have to file an affidavit. He'll probably lose his job. And then there's Heather. She's been on both sides of this. Her original intent was to spy on us. If I were Lucinda's lawyer, how hard is it to make the case that Heather is just a disgruntled employee with a score to settle with Lucinda?"

"Well, now, we're back to where we started. I said right from the beginning that this wasn't going to be a slam dunk. With your permission, here's what I'd like to recommend. I'll put together the package and get it ready to file. You can look it over, and once you see the facts on paper, you can decide whether or not you want to file."

"All right," Guy said, getting up and making his way to the door. "Send it over and I'll take a look. There's no rush."

Nigel followed Guy into the hallway near the elevator, leaving the two paralegals behind in the conference room. "I know you say there's no rush, but keep in mind that this may be your only shot to do something to stop the merger."

"I know, but I need to think about it. There are other people who stand to suffer if we file and lose."

Nigel reached out to shake Guy's hand, not as his lawyer, but as his friend. Nigel said, "Guy, I know you'll find the right answer. The fact that you're struggling with it now rather than just jumping in regardless of the potential consequences for anyone else is what makes me sure that you will. And when you do, just let me know. I'll be ready."

CHAPTER 5

IT TOOK GUY A COUPLE OF DAYS TO DECIDE whether he should file the lawsuit against Lucinda Hornbuckle, David Gordon, and Arlene Tann of the *Washington Note*. He had hoped, perhaps naively, that the negative stories about him would stop and the damage would be limited to what had already been done. But while Guy was thinking things over, Lucinda was taking no chances, and she had planted yet another story claiming that Guy had carried on a wild affair with someone in Africa. He was certain that the story—which shielded the name of the woman as if she were a victim of sexual assault—was referring to his relationship with Kate Mulgrew. He thought it ironic that the only accurate thing in the entire story—the woman's identity—was the one fact that was conveniently left out. If the story had mentioned her by name, both Guy and Kate could have come forward to dispute it. However, by laying a veil of anonymity over the woman, the article was able to make dozens of baseless allegations.

For Guy, that was the last straw. He called Nigel and gave his permission to file the lawsuit in the state circuit court of Montgomery County, Maryland. Nigel had explained that, based on the facts of the case, there were several venues where they could file the lawsuit, but the Montgomery County Circuit Court was the most likely to give them a fair shake. Anything in the District of Columbia, where the *Washington Note* was located, was likely to favor the hometown newspaper. And, although David Gordon lived in Northern Virginia, trying the case there would be a crapshoot. Based on Nigel's research, the judges in Maryland's state courts were their best hope for fairness.

Although it was not required, Guy attended the first hearing. The first motion in the case was an attempt by the *Washington Note*'s lawyers to get the case dismissed by summary judgment. The primary complaint in the case was against Lucinda Hornbuckle, but the *Note* had played a significant role in publishing the stories that Lucinda was pushing, so Guy had agreed to include them in the lawsuit. Nigel had warned that doing so carried risks, though;

the paper, and particularly its owner, Malcolm Rutherford, could afford top-notch lawyers. This warning proved to be accurate. When the attorneys made their appearances, the three defendants were represented by none other than William Mayhew, Esq., one of the premier First Amendment lawyers in the country. He was one of the three principals of the high-dollar K Street law firm, Baker, Mayhew, and Hempstead.

"Your Honor," Mr. Mayhew said in his strong but melodious Boston accent, "we move for summary judgment on all counts. Because we believe that this entire lawsuit is a thinly veiled attempt to stifle a free press, we also move that the plaintiff be required to pay all legal costs for the defendants."

The judge who had been assigned to the case for the initial hearings was primarily there to decide which track the suit would be placed on in the differentiated case management system. According to Nigel, there were at least a couple of options, but some were better than others. He believed the best track they could hope for would be Track 5, which pertained to business and technology cases that were expected to be decided within seven months.

Nigel and Guy both knew that, for the purposes of exposing Lucinda to the IAU board, a trial under anything other than Track 5 was unlikely to be resolved before the decision on the merger. The IAU board had given Lucinda and CAG just under three months to gather the information to support the case for the merger. There were only a couple of weeks left and, based on what Guy had seen, nothing was turning up that was likely to dissuade the board from the merger. Shaking something loose in discovery was his last, best hope of proving that Lucinda was up to no good.

Before they could get that information, though, they had to pass two major hurdles. First, they had to hope that Judge Samuel Kincaid denied William Mayhew's motion for summary judgment.

Judge Kincaid was in his mid-seventies and held senior status, which meant that in most cases he simply handled the initial proceedings. In this case, the hearing was to address two issues. The first was the motion to dismiss. If Judge Kincaid granted that motion, the second issue—the scope of allowable discovery—would be moot.

The judge shuffled the papers before him and looked over his reading glasses at counsel for the defense. "Mr. Mayhew," the judge intoned, gravely, "I am aware of your prominence in the field of First Amendment law, and I read your brief with some interest, hoping to find something that would draw parallels between this case and your previous work. Failing that, I hoped to find some new, interesting angle that would make this case remarkable for some other reason. However, I was deeply disappointed when I found neither."

"Your Honor, if I may . . ." Mr. Mayhew tried to break in.

"You may not, Counselor. I have not finished.

"As I was saying, the First Amendment generally provides great freedom to the press. They are immune from charges of slander and libel except in the most egregious circumstances where it is proven that they failed to exercise due regard for the truth. The press may be wrong. That it is allowed. But they are not allowed to knowingly disregard the truth to cast aspersions on the good name of others.

"At issue today are two questions. The first question is whether the *Washington Note* was willfully negligent and acting in bad faith when the paper published articles, written by Ms. Arlene Tann, which claim that the plaintiff, Mr. Pearle, was actually the one who had used the company credit card to make illicit purchases, and that the firing of Mr. Gordon was an attempt to cover that up. The articles went on to say that the rehiring of Mr. Gordon was proof of wrongdoing on the part of Mr. Pearle. The plaintiff alleges that the articles constitute defamation in the form of libel for the articles and slander for verbal comments about them.

"The second question is whether the actions of the defendants, taken together, constitute tortious interference in a business relationship. Mr. Pearle notes that the articles, taken as a whole, have damaged his relationship with the company that was going to manage the IPO.

"You have asked for a summary judgment, stating that the statements in the article, which were later acknowledged as errors, were not known to be in error at the time of publication. However, I have a signed affidavit from an employee of the newspaper claiming to have seen an email in which your reporter was told—well before the article was published—that the information about Mr. Pearle was false.

"You also argue that the relationship between the plaintiff and Advanced Capital Placement, the firm that was originally slated to manage the IPO, was not damaged.

"On the state of the record, I do not see any case for making summary judgment against the plaintiff. The issues that you raise are exactly what we will address in the trial, so your order for summary judgment in your favor is denied.

"I further order that the case will be placed on Track 5 of the differentiated case management system, and that each side submit their requests for discovery by no later than next Tuesday."

The judge began pulling his papers together and paused, turning his attention to Nigel Winston. "Mr. Winston, I want to make sure you understand that, while I have not granted summary judgment against your client, you have raised some arguments that verge on being frivolous, and I will not tolerate this in my court.

"You argue that the *Washington Note* is making an in-kind contribution to the opponent of Mr. Pearle in the race for the US Senate seat from Maryland. Is that an accurate summary of your argument on that point?"

"Yes, Your Honor, that is the argument we are making."

"I thought so. And I believe you should know better. First and foremost, this is not the proper venue for a trial on that matter. Any such hearing would be a federal matter. Secondly, and—if you don't know this, I would like to know where you got your law degree—the press has substantial latitude to opine on matters of public policy and politics. By the argument you're making, every editorial that is friendly to one candidate or hostile to another would be considered an in-kind contribution. Clearly, that is a frivolous argument. You may not like the fact that the press has the freedom to make endorsements, but this court is not your remedy. Feel free to run for office and change the law, but until you do, I expect you to show a little respect for this court and bring before it only matters that are within its jurisdiction. Do I make myself clear?"

"Yes, Your Honor. Crystal clear."

After the judge left the courtroom, Guy asked Nigel, "Was that it?"

"For today," Nigel said. "It may not have seemed like much, and based on the look on William Mayhew's face, most people would conclude that not much happened here today, but—believe me—this is a big deal. We have been given permission to file discovery requests. They don't know all of what we know, but they know we have a source inside. It's just too risky for them to play games on discovery, so if they have responsive documents, they will have to turn them over. They're going to have to do an internal assessment to determine how much risk they have. When they see what's been going on, I believe they will realize they're in big trouble."

"What do you think they'll do?"

"They won't just roll over. I can guarantee you that. First, they're probably going to fire your man, Sam. His name is now on the public record. Second, they're going to come after you hard. They're going to try to find any dirt they can throw at you. And, last but not least, they're going to figure out their exposure."

"Why wouldn't they do that first?"

"That's going to happen on two separate tracks. They're going to fire Sam and come after you no matter what they find in their risk analysis review. You've done something they don't like, so they're going to try to punish you any way they can."

"I'm sorry for Sam, but I think it will work out in the long run. He's already accepted a job with IAU, and he's taking a look at the keylogging software that Lucinda placed in our servers. I think he's got some ideas about how we can use that against her."

"Now perhaps you can see why I recommended holding off on introducing anything related to that at this point. If we had brought that into the lawsuit, we would have exposed Heather. I think we need to keep it in reserve for now."

"Nigel, you've never steered me wrong before. The courtroom is your area of expertise. I will defer to you."

CHAPTER 6

WHEN WILLIAM MAYHEW BRIEFED MALCOLM Rutherford on the day's events in court, Malcolm issued three simple directives: First, fire the IT employee who had signed the affidavit; second, set up a team to do a deep dive on Guy Pearle; and third, figure out what was in the records that would be turned over during discovery. He knew the newsroom well enough to know that they counted on being able to operate in complete secrecy, with no scrutiny of their emails or records. As a consequence of that shield, they had a habit of being extremely candid in some of their internal discussions—almost to the point of stupidity. Malcolm was certain he had a problem; he just didn't know how big it was.

Within a few days, the scope of his exposure was clear. Not only was Guy Pearle likely to win the defamation lawsuit, there were emails and memos within the scope of the discovery order that would have a catastrophic effect if they ever saw the light of day. He read email after email where the paper's reporters were openly plotting strategies to paint conservatives in a negative light. Any hint of objectivity in the newsroom was gone, and the paper was clearly an open advocate for liberal causes—facts be damned.

Ironically, that was not his greatest concern from the discovery review. Some of his own emails had been unearthed during the process, and these made clear that he had purchased the *Washington Note* to use as a cudgel against his rivals, political and commercial.

William Mayhew, not known for subtlety, had been brutally honest when he briefed the results of the review. "Malcolm, your only option here is to settle. And you need to start with a number that is so mind-boggling to the plaintiff that it is beyond his wildest dreams. You need to get him to agree to a non-disclosure agreement that prevents any of this from ever seeing the light of day."

"It's that bad?" Malcolm asked, knowing it was.

"Let me put it this way," Mayhew continued. "If you don't settle this before we have to produce the responsive documents, this will only be the first of many lawsuits against you and your newspaper. Once this information gets into the public domain, dozens of other companies—all of your competitors—will be able to dig through this crap and file lawsuits against you. And they will have a strong basis in fact for their lawsuits. This will just be the beginning."

"Assume that we manage to get a settlement," Malcolm wondered aloud. "How do we clean this up?"

"Once the lawsuit has been settled, there is nothing to prevent you from getting rid of all of these emails and memos. If you were to do it now, you'd be destroying evidence in a legal proceeding, but if you can get Mr. Pearle to settle, you'll be able to purge all the records. You will need to do it quietly, in a way that prevents any of the reporters from trying to collect a little bit of 'insurance' for their own purposes. We can help you with that, once this is taken care of."

"How do you recommend that we go about it? We're not the only ones involved. The other two defendants would have to agree, wouldn't they?"

"I think we can handle them," Mayhew said, confidently. "David Gordon is, quite frankly, an idiot. He has already blown through all the money he got in his deal with IAU and is already back in debt. There is no doubt that you can buy his silence for a million or two."

"What about Lucinda Hornbuckle?" Malcolm asked.

"She's going to be a little tougher, but I think doable."

"How?"

"She has some money troubles, too, but not enough to make her go along with the settlement. Your recent investment of three million in her business has given her enough of a cushion that she is not feeling any financial pressure. She doesn't know about your exposure, and it wouldn't be good to let her find out, because she will turn on you in a second if she thinks she stands to benefit from it."

"So, how do we handle her?" Malcolm asked. He was accustomed to dealing with fickle and disloyal people, but most could easily be bought. It appeared that Lucinda Hornbuckle had different motivations.

"I think you can get what you need from her with a two-part strategy. She's not completely motivated by money, but she isn't immune to it either. I think you can offer to cover all her costs as part of the settlement."

"You mean bribe her?"

"That's a crude term, but if you want to use it, I won't disagree. However, that's not the most important aspect of the strategy. What you need to do is make her understand that the lawsuit is standing in the way of what she really wants."

Malcolm perked up. "Which is?"

"She wants to destroy Guy Pearle."

"And how is the lawsuit standing in the way of that?"

Mayhew was characteristically blunt. "As a general rule, one does not destroy one's opponents by losing defamation lawsuits and paying them massive damages. She has no idea of what is likely to happen in the courtroom and even if we briefed her on everything, she is so blinded by her obsession with destroying Guy Pearle that she would roll the dice anyway."

Malcolm began to see the picture that Mayhew was painting. "She sees the merger between IAU and CAG as the be-all and end-all of her plan to destroy Guy Pearle. So, if we can persuade her that the lawsuit is a threat to that merger, she might be persuaded to settle?"

"Yes, we need to paint her a picture of what happens to her interests if the lawsuit proceeds, regardless of whether Guy wins or loses. What she needs to understand is that the real risk is in discovery, and whether we win or lose is just a matter of money. Even if he loses, some of the emails that she has written will do great damage to her in the eyes of the IAU board. Those will come out in discovery, and Guy will be able to show them to the board members. Whether the merger takes place or not, she and David will likely get the boot, so she'll be on the outside looking in. We need to persuade her that if she agrees to settle the lawsuit quietly, you will cover her costs and work with her to keep up the pressure on Guy."

"How do I do that?" Malcolm asked.

"I have no doubt that she's got plenty of ideas," Mayhew responded. "We just need to pick the one that offers the best odds of getting her to agree while exposing you the least."

"Okay, set it up," Malcolm directed.

As Mayhew predicted, David Gordon proved more than happy to agree to settle the lawsuit so long as Malcolm Rutherford paid his costs and threw in a little extra for David's trouble. David did, however, make one additional request: that be he allowed to pitch Malcolm as a potential investor on a couple of his ongoing projects. In David's mind, he was operating in the rarified air of the East Coast technical elite, and therefore, Malcolm should be pleased to hear his ideas. When Mayhew passed along the request to Malcolm, however, his response was a more mundane, "Sure, whatever."

Lucinda bounced into Malcolm's office and took a seat on the couch on the far side of the room, well away from his desk. That way, he had to get up and walk over to her.

For his part, Malcolm was unfazed by the control tactic. He grabbed his notepad and the folder with the most damaging of Lucinda's emails, and crossed to sit beside her on the couch. As he had discussed with William Mayhew, his first goal was to show Lucinda that the lawsuit was a threat to her ambitions.

He tried to sound worried for her. "Lucinda, I'm afraid I've got some bad news for you. As you know, William Mayhew of Baker, Mayhew, and Hempstead, is one of the leading First Amendment lawyers in the country. He has done an analysis of the records that would be covered by the potential discovery request in the defamation lawsuit that Guy Pearle has filed, and there are a couple of emails between yourself and Arlene Tann, and others between yourself and David Gordon that were somehow forwarded to Arlene, that raise a real risk for you."

"For me?" Lucinda asked. She knew what was in those emails but suspected he was hiding something. She had no idea of the full scope of what Mayhew had found but thought it odd that Malcolm was trying to pin everything on her. "What about you and the paper?"

"We've got some exposure, because we did publish articles that, in retrospect, appear to be false. This isn't the first time we've made a mistake, and it won't be the last. We can deal with that. We're prepared to issue a correction and offer Guy Pearle a settlement in exchange for dropping the defamation lawsuit."

"I knew it, you son of a bitch!" Lucinda exploded. "You're going to hang me out to dry, and you made the $3 million investment in *Social Tech* just so you'd have the leverage you needed to do it."

Actually, Malcolm had never considered that his investment might give him such leverage. He answered defensively, trying not to betray his real motives. "I'm sorry you feel that way. When I made the investment, I had no intention of using it against you for leverage, and I still don't. When I offered to put up the money, I was investing in the future you described—one that didn't have Guy Pearle at the head of a publicly traded tech company."

"Then why the sudden change of heart?" Lucinda asked, calming down a bit.

"To me, it's pretty simple. I am concerned that the lawsuit might persuade the board to either disapprove of the merger or, at the very least, to put it off. In either case, that puts you on the outside and leaves Guy Pearle on the inside. I don't have any insights into the board, but ask yourself this: Is the board likely to approve a merger where two of the key players, one from each side of the merger, are involved in a major lawsuit against each other?"

Malcolm's logic was unassailable, but Lucinda was not ready to concede. "But we can't let that bastard win!" she fumed.

"Winning is a relative term," he reassured her. "One of the things I've learned along the way is that it doesn't make good sense to press a fight you're likely to lose. I admire your passion. It's one of the things I like most about you, but I think you may lack objectivity when it comes to Guy Pearle."

"So, what do you recommend we do?" she asked, genuinely. How would it be possible, as he was suggesting, to turn what appeared to be a loss into a victory?

"I think we need to button up this lawsuit, and do it quickly," he replied. "I know you don't have deep pockets. To be honest, that's probably why he included the newspaper in the lawsuit, just so he could get to me. Well, as it happens, I do have deep pockets. Deep enough that I think we can make this lawsuit go away pretty easily."

"How?" she asked.

"We're going to offer him twenty million to settle."

"That's absurd!" Lucinda cried. "He doesn't deserve a penny."

"It isn't a question of how much he deserves. We're just looking at a set of numbers that will give us what we want, which is to make this go away, so the board won't have a reason to disapprove of the merger. We offered David Gordon two million if he would agree to let us handle the lawsuit on his behalf and seek a settlement. He agreed."

Lucinda was stunned at the sums that Malcolm was throwing around. She wondered what might be on the table for her but had enough self-control not to ask.

Malcolm relieved her of the need to do so. "We're prepared to offer you five million to let us take care of this."

That would be enough to pay back the three million he had invested in the company and still have a cushion.

"And, we'll draw up paperwork to exit our position in *Social Tech*. In other words, you'll get back complete control of your company, and you'll get five million on top of that."

Lucinda was pleased at the offer and had already made up her mind to accept, but she felt that—given how easily he was piling cash on top of cash—she might as well go for broke.

"I'll be honest," she said, "I am not accustomed to dealing so casually with large sums of money. It must be nice to be able to throw around millions like other people throw dollars at strippers."

Malcolm was amused by the reference but remained focused on learning her real objective. He said, "Being rich does have its advantages, but it's not all fun and games. What matters most to me is being able to have an impact on things that matter."

That provided the opening that Lucinda needed. "Yes, having influence is what matters to me, as well. And that's the main reason that I like and trust you. I believe you and I see the world in much the same way. So, I'll take your very generous offer to settle the lawsuit with Guy. I'm sure you know that I believe we would have eventually prevailed. But I can't deny the logic of your argument about the board not wanting to have two key players duking it out in court, so the settlement makes sense. But I want to make sure that you're not washing your hands of all this. Guy Pearle is still a threat. He's a threat to me, to you, and to what you believe in."

"We're on the same page there," Malcolm reassured her.

"Then I've got just one more request. I'm not going to lay it out here because I think it's premature. It will depend upon what happens with the merger and the IPO. All I am asking is that if I come to you with a future proposition about IAU, you'll at least hear me out. I'm not asking you to commit to a course of action—just to hear me out. Can you do that?"

"Consider it done."

CHAPTER 7

"TWENTY MILLION?" GUY ASKED, INCREDULOUSLY. "Dollars?"

"Yep, that's what they offered." Nigel Winston showed Guy the settlement offer he had received earlier in the afternoon from Malcolm Rutherford's lawyer.

"That's more money than I've earned in my entire life," Guy mused. "Why on earth would they offer that much?"

Nigel explained the potential rationale for the generous offer. "I think they know that the information we've already found is just the tip of the iceberg. What Sam told us about was potentially damaging, but if there are more emails like those—and maybe some that are worse—then they must realize that they need to settle before this gets to discovery. If we get our hands on the evidence and it becomes part of the trial record, all of their dirty laundry will be out in the open.

"Billionaires don't tend to like having their internal deliberations put on display for the rest of the world to see. Because they are billionaires, it's easiest for them to try to solve the problem with money. It's what they know, so it's what they do."

"What do you think they're trying to hide?" Guy wondered. "What could they have in their files that's so bad that they're willing to spend $20 million to cover it up?"

Nigel was candid. "I don't know, and I don't think it would be productive for me to guess. For people like you and me, twenty million is a lot of money, so we naturally assume that he's trying to hide something really serious. But how much does twenty million really mean to Malcolm Rutherford? His net worth has grown by more than $5 billion a year for the past ten years. So, if you do the math on that, twenty million is how much his net worth appreciates every ten days. It would be a fool's errand to try to understand his thinking using our values."

"When you put it that way," Guy admitted, "it doesn't seem like that much. But that's just Malcolm Rutherford. David Gordon and Lucinda Hornbuckle are also covered by this settlement offer. What do you make of that?"

"I think David Gordon was offered some amount of cash. I don't have any idea how much, but I can assume that it was monumental to him and meant nothing to Malcolm Rutherford."

"I was thinking the same thing. But what about Lucinda?"

"There's no doubt that she got some kind of a good deal. She probably got more than what she thought was possible, but a lot less than she could have gotten if she'd played her cards right."

Guy was still unconvinced. "But she's not motivated by money the way that David is. She's got something else planned. I don't know what it is, but I'm reluctant to agree until I have at least some idea of what she's up to."

"Well, this offer is good for twenty-four hours. Whatever you're going to do, you'd better get moving."

"What happens if we don't accept the offer?"

"The case goes to trial."

"And what do you think our odds of winning are?" Guy asked.

"I can't say for sure. The number they put on paper tells me they believe that we're going to win. Either that, or there's something they're trying to protect, and they're willing to find a way settle the lawsuit to protect that, whatever it is."

Nigel could see that Guy was struggling to put things in context, so he did what he did best—he walked Guy through the legal possibilities one step at a time.

“Let’s go back to square one,” Nigel suggested. “We need to recall the desired outcome.”

“We filed the lawsuit to prevent the merger with CAG,” Guy said. “That’s the bottom line. It was our only way to stop the merger from happening.”

“How would accepting this settlement impact that decision?” Nigel asked, knowing that Guy wasn’t in a position to give a meaningful answer.

Guy immediately realized the need to poll the board to see how they might react to a settlement like the one he was being offered. Although the lawsuit was filed in Guy’s personal capacity, any legal matters affecting the CEO would be relevant to the board. A favorable settlement would clearly prove that Guy had a case against Malcolm, but it didn’t prove that Lucinda had been up to no good. He thought the settlement would turn the board against the merger, but he didn’t want to rely solely on his instincts. “I’ll call each member of the board and get a read from them. What am I allowed to tell them? Are there any restrictions in the settlement agreement on what I can say about it?”

“Well, it’s a good thing you asked. It appears that some of my good sense is rubbing off on you. The offer says you’re not allowed to say anything other than that you reached a settlement and consequently dropped your lawsuit. If you say anything before you accept the agreement, the offer is null and void. And if you accept the agreement, you are also accepting a non-disclosure agreement that prevents you from saying anything about the lawsuit.”

"That's not very helpful. With those limitations, I won't have the ability to persuade anyone on the board that the merger is not a good idea."

"Well, then, it's a good thing you hired a smart lawyer who told you not to include the evidence from Heather Alston in your defamation lawsuit," Nigel boasted.

"Before you break your arm trying to pat yourself on the back," Guy said, smirking, "why don't you walk me through what you have in mind?"

Nigel explained how Guy could use the information about the keylogging software that Lucinda had planted on the IAU servers to persuade the members of the board that she didn't have IAU's best interests in mind. The defamation lawsuit that Guy had filed contained no mention of this information, only the affidavit from Sam about the emails he had seen on Arlene's computer. The info about the keylogging software was purely an internal matter and was therefore fair game to bring to the attention of the board. Doing so would not interfere in any way with the proposed terms of the settlement.

"But you know that as soon as I start talking about Lucinda," Guy said flatly, "they're going to ask about the status of the lawsuit. How can I answer when they ask me about that?"

Nigel did a quick scan of the paperwork he had received from William Mayhew. "It says here that while settlement talks are pending you are not allowed to say anything about the status of the lawsuit."

"What happens if I say something?"

"Then the settlement offer is withdrawn immediately."

"So, I can either accept a settlement agreement within the next twenty-four hours, not knowing what Lucinda is up to, or I can try to find out what the board might think about accepting the settlement and nullify the agreement in the process."

"That's a pretty good summary of the situation," Nigel said, in a voice he hoped would dissuade Guy from doing anything rash. "Let me remind you, however, that $20 million is a lot of money. As you pointed out not long ago, you've got my law firm on retainer, so when I say it's a lot of money, you know that I don't have dollar signs in my eyes. That's a big pile of money, so you should think carefully before you do whatever it is that you're going to do."

CHAPTER 8

NIGEL WINSTON WAS NOT THE LEAST BIT SURprised when he learned that Guy Pearle had decided to reject the settlement offer. He was only mildly surprised when he learned that the IAU board had, after being briefed individually by Guy, formally rejected the idea of merging with CAG. And he was delighted when he got a call from Susan Cole asking him to prepare a letter of termination for David Gordon.

When he got Guy on the phone, Nigel said, "I don't know what you said, but I wish I could have been on the call to hear it. You got the entire board on your side."

"It's a bit early to go popping champagne corks," Guy reminded him.

"You'll get no argument from me on that, but when we go to court against Malcolm Rutherford and his stable of high-priced lawyers, I hope you'll be willing to share some of your secrets to success. I might need them."

"Actually, Nigel, there were no secrets. This stuff is a lot easier when you've got facts and principle on your side. Thousand-dollar-an-hour lawyers aren't all that useful when their client did exactly what was alleged."

"You just keep telling yourself that. I'd be a lot happier, and prouder, to be a lawyer if I thought what you are saying was true. But I've seen too many cases where the guy with the most money wins, regardless of facts or principles."

"I'll tell you what," Guy said, trying to buck up Nigel's confidence. "I want you to draw up a modification to our representation agreement. You can bring in up to five lawyers for your team, and you can take a contingency fee of 30 percent on top of your billable hours."

"What's that all about?" Nigel asked, defensively, fearing Guy suspected him of gold digging. He couldn't see any relationship between warning Guy about the risks of proceeding to trial and Guy's sudden response.

"I know you feel like David up against Goliath . . ." Guy started but cut himself off at the same time that Nigel interrupted.

"I'd have to say," Nigel said, "that things haven't gone so well lately for the David you and I know."

"Right," Guy admitted. "Sorry. That wasn't the best analogy. But here's my point. I know you're feeling outmatched, like I'm asking you to do an awful lot with very little."

"That I can agree with," Nigel said, softly.

"But you know as well as I do, they made their settlement offer so large because they know they're wrong. They're trying to shut this down before any real damage is done."

"Actually, I don't know that, and neither do you. We've surmised as much. But sometimes good poker players fold even with a strong hand, knowing they can set you up for later. How do you know they're not doing that now? If you're wrong, and you end up losing this case, you're going to have some pretty big legal bills when you could've had $20 million instead."

"Nigel, you know I'm not wealthy, but I am comfortable. I'm perfectly happy with where I am financially, and I wouldn't know how to spend $20 million if I had it. But that's beside the point. The reason I want to continue fighting this lawsuit is because, if we settle, Lucinda gets away with everything she's done. She has to face some consequences, as does the newspaper that helped her carry out her agenda. We can't let them get away with it."

Nigel thought Guy was starting to sound a bit too much like Lucinda but wasn't about to point that out. He took Guy's meaning. The next few days would decide the fate of a lot of people, including Guy Pearle.

At the second hearing, both sides were surprised to see Judge Samuel Kincaid presiding once more. They had supposed a full-time judge would manage the case now that it had been assigned to the appropriate track.

But Judge Kincaid wasted no time getting down to business. "Mr. Mayhew, I've read your motion to file all of your discovery under seal until the case is decided. I will take that under advisement, but I will not rule until I have seen the material in question. Alternatively, if you believe you can persuade me that the material is so sensitive as to be prejudicial to your client in ways that go beyond this case, you may file a motion explaining your reasons."

He turned to Nigel. "Mr. Winston, I see that you've had the good sense to amend your filing to exclude the claim of an in-kind contribution on the part of the *Washington Note*. I'm going to ask you a question. You are not obligated to answer since you've amended your complaint, but I'm interested in the legal theory that brought you to your first filing. How on earth could you claim an in-kind expenditure against your client when, by your own accounting, your client has never even considered running for the US Senate?"

"Your Honor," Nigel said, plaintively, "we have no answer to that question, and we are grateful that the court has allowed us to remove that element from our filing."

A week later, the parties returned to court. This time, Judge Kincaid seemed to focus his initial interests on the plaintiff. "Mr. Winston, I've read all of your filings, and I'd like to review them as I understand them in the context of a defamation trial.

"As to the first element, all that is required is for the defendant, in this case the *Washington Note*, to make a false and defamatory statement. The defendant has already admitted that the articles in question were both false and defamatory, so that element has been met, as has the second element which merely requires these statements to be about your client, the plaintiff.

"The third element is contested by the defendants. The statutes require that the statements be published without privilege, to a third party. In this case, attorneys for the defendant have argued that they enjoy a First Amendment right to make such claims because they are a newspaper, but Mr. Mayhew is too good a lawyer, and too much of a bona fide First Amendment expert, to expect me to accept that argument.

"Which leads us to the fourth element, which is that the defendant published the information with fault, at least of negligence. As initial proof of negligence and in order to reach the discovery stage, you submitted an affidavit from a now-former employee of the newspaper, which you offered as proof that the author of the news article, Ms. Arlene Tann, acted negligently when she published the articles, because she had evidence that the major claims of the articles were false.

"And hereupon we arrive at the fifth necessary element of a defamation claim, that the information was defamatory, per se, or that the publication caused special harm to the plaintiff, Mr. Pearle."

"Yes, Your Honor, that's a fair reading of our pleading," Nigel volunteered.

"That wasn't a question, Mr. Winston," the judge chided. "It was merely the predicate for my recitation of the second—and to be frank with you, more questionable—part of your lawsuit, in which you argue that the defamation was performed in furtherance of a plot to commit tortious interference in a business relationship, namely the plaintiff's ability to run his company."

Nigel remained silent and the judge turned to counsel for the defense. "Mr. Mayhew, your filings are quite thorough, with one exception. You have cited just about every precedent about freedom of the press except the one that is most relevant."

William Mayhew knew better than to take the bait, and simply shuffled his papers, waiting for the judge to continue.

"The precedent that is most relevant from the standpoint of your client—and I say this after having reviewed some of the discovery that you submitted under seal—is the 1944 case of Associated Press vs. United States, in which the Supreme Court held that news is commerce and is therefore subject to the Sherman Act, which prohibits unfair trade practices.

"Your client is in the very unfortunate position of having to produce information for discovery in one case that could conceivably result in a whole string of lawsuits against you from other parties who happen to be mentioned in the materials you would have to produce.

"It is clear to me why you have requested to keep this material under seal. Any reasonable person would see the potentially explosive consequences of some of this information getting into the public domain. I must tell you, however, that I have very little sympathy for you, and I am duty-bound to ensure that the plaintiff has available all the necessary information to make his case. I have studied the material quite carefully, and I do not see a way that it can be redacted that would both protect your collateral interests and give the plaintiff his due. If I am forced to rule on this matter, I am afraid to tell you that I would be forced to rule against you."

Guy whispered in Nigel's ear, "What does that mean?"

Before he could answer, William Mayhew said, "Your Honor, if it pleases the court, we'd like to request a brief recess to see if we might be able to re-engage the plaintiff in settlement talks."

Judge Samuel Kincaid gaveled the hearing to a close. As soon as the judge exited the courtroom, William Mayhew walked directly to Nigel Winston and handed him a new proposed settlement agreement. "Your client may be the luckiest son of a bitch alive. He can walk out of here with $100 million in his pocket, or he can continue fighting a legal battle that he might win, but at great cost. You know me, and you know exactly what I mean when I say this. Do the smart thing and get your client to accept this offer. It's good for one hour."

Guy and Nigel made their way to the courthouse parking lot and climbed into Nigel's car.

Guy was first to speak. "Jesus, Nigel, what have we stumbled into?"

"I have no idea," Nigel replied, "and if Malcolm Rutherford is willing to spend $100 million to keep it quiet, I'm not sure I want to know. This has gotten well beyond Lucinda and David. Whatever is going on here, it's about Malcolm Rutherford."

"I would feel a lot better about taking the settlement if we didn't just have all those discussions about the importance of doing things on principle," Guy said. "There's a point at which the amount of money is just obscene, and I feel like I'm doing something wrong if I take it."

"Don't be a martyr, Guy. You may be right. Maybe Malcolm Rutherford is the worst person on earth. But nobody elected you sheriff. If he's done something criminal, let the legal system sort it out. You filed a lawsuit about defamation. You've won. They're offering to give you $100 million and publish a retraction. Sometimes, you just need to learn how to take the win and leave it at that."

CHAPTER 9

THE LAST SEVERAL DAYS HAD BEEN TROUBLEsome for Lucinda Hornbuckle. The IAU board had formally rejected the merger with the CAG. Now, with the merger off the table, her best chance at real financial stability was gone. On top of that, her key source of information on the inside, David Gordon, had been fired. All the work she had done to get David back on the board had just been undone in an instant, and once again she was blind and powerless.

Not everything was bleak, however. The defamation lawsuit that Guy Pearle had filed was settled. Although she'd never really considered it a threat, she was glad to see it resolved. To top it off, Malcolm Rutherford had given her five million in cash and relinquished his shares in *Social Tech*. That was the equivalent of giving her an additional $3 million. If there was such a thing as a silver lining, the way the lawsuit was resolved had to fit into that category. But she couldn't help feeling that the silver lining was tarnished by the knowledge that Guy Pearle had received more than a dozen times what she had been given.

But Lucinda still faced a long-term problem. She desperately needed to find a way to generate cash, and lots of it, if she wanted to keep *Social Tech* afloat. Moreover, with all the trouble and stress she had been through, what she really wanted was "walk away" money—enough that she could dabble in politics and media without having to spend all her time fundraising. With the money she received from Malcolm, she could operate for a couple more years, at most, but it was clear that her business model was no longer viable. The companies she reached out to were quite bluntly refusing to even meet with her. She was occasionally able to get real interviews with solid technical experts, but those made *Social Tech* just another blog. And everyone watching the industry knew that tech blogs were not going to be around much longer.

That left her with only IAU as a potential solution to her money problems. She still had her keylogging software in place, and she was getting useful information. And she still had Heather Alston, who, despite the oddness of a few months ago, seemed to have settled down. Heather was producing good work, strong articles that brought in a lot of readers. And she was still spying on IAU, as requested.

As the IAU IPO loomed on the horizon, Lucinda spent a great deal of time running financial forecasts, trying to project what might happen if she invested the $5 million she received from the settlement. None of the scenarios looked promising. If the stock came out at twenty dollars a share, which was a normal price for tech IPOs, it would have to triple or quadruple in value to give her the kind of financial return she craved. She studied the histories of similar companies and none had experienced that kind of pop right after the IPO. Some had even gone down in value, so that an investment right out of the gate would have negative returns for some period of time. Most had just trundled along, gaining a few percent here and there, but nothing dramatic.

After hours of research and analysis, Lucinda returned to the notion that she had entertained when IAU first planned to go public—to orchestrate a massive short. This time, however, her objective was different, and much simpler. She wanted financial independence that would enable her to tackle Guy Pearle head-on in the political arena. No matter what happened, the IPO was going to make Guy Pearle rich—on top of the money he already had from the settlement. She knew that she could never match him, but she was confident that if she could put together a $25 million war chest, she could do battle with him.

The math was fairly simple. If she invested $25 million by shorting the stock at fifteen dollars per share, she could double her money if the stock plunged to $7.50 per share. Doubling her money would allow her to pay back the money she'd borrowed to invest, and she'd still have $25 million left over. Ordinarily, that would be highly unlikely, but Lucinda had a plan, and she had a promise from Malcolm Rutherford to hear her pitch.

"Malcolm," she said, when he answered her call, "do you remember the promise you made to me when I agreed to let you settle the lawsuit with Guy?"

"Yes, why?" he replied.

"Well, I am calling in that marker."

"All right, let's hear your pitch. As you recall, I promised to hear you out. I didn't promise to agree to anything."

"I know, but I think you'll want to. Based on what you were willing to pay to settle the lawsuit with Guy, I know the numbers

I'm bringing up are really in the noise level for you, but I want you to keep in mind that he's still the same threat he was when I first came to you several months ago. The difference now is that he has your hundred million in his pocket, and he's about to get a lot more when IAU goes public."

Malcolm agreed as noncommittally as he could.

She continued, walking him through the math of her plan, which Malcolm readily understood. What he couldn't understand was why she was so confident that the stock would fall rapidly enough to make her model work. He had learned that the only way to deal with Lucinda was to pin her down with direct questions.

"The only way this works," he observed, "is if something comes out almost immediately after the IPO that devastates the company. And it has to come out in a big way, not just through the rumor mill. So, I'm assuming you've got a story you want the *Washington Note* to publish right after the IPO. Is that correct?"

"You hit the nail on the head."

"As I recall, the last time I published something I got from you that wasn't properly vetted, it cost me $100 million. Why on earth would I want to run another story like that?"

Lucinda was prepared for this. "Do you recall what it was that turned the tide in that case?"

"Yes," Malcolm replied, somewhat pained at the thought. "It was an affidavit from one of my IT guys about a couple of emails he saw."

"And that was considered proof positive, was it not?"

"It was enough to put us back on our heels. But I heard that your inside guy, David Gordon, got fired, so what could you have that's in the same league as an inside source?"

"What if I could give you proof, in the form of internal memos, that IAU has made material misrepresentations in their SEC filing?"

"Like what?"

"I don't want to get into too much detail at this point, but let me put it this way: I've been told that the filing with the SEC will say that they are going to raise $500 million to support investments in new technologies. They're planning to do that based on a book value of five billion, which means they are offering 10 percent of the company in the IPO. But I have reason to believe—very good reason—to believe that their book value is a lot less than what they are claiming."

"Why?"

"Because they have a lot of undisclosed liability left over from what happened in Africa. They have massive exposure, and they underreported it in their SEC filing."

Malcolm began to see the picture she was drawing. "So, you're suggesting the *Washington Note* perform a public service by exposing fraud in an IPO. In your view, we'd be doing the investing public a favor by running an article that highlights the differences between what IAU is saying publicly and what they're saying internally. Is that about right?"

"Exactly."

"If we're going to go down this road, I've got to have a lot better proof than what you came to us with last time. I'm not going to get burned again. But even if we do this, I don't see how you're in a position to get a windfall. By your own calculations, you'd need at least $25 million to invest. When we were talking a few weeks ago about the settlement, you said you needed three million to keep *Social Tech* running for a year. You got that, plus an additional five million out of the settlement, so even if you put all of that together, you're nowhere near $25 million."

"Right, and that's a good segue to the second part of this conversation. It's got to be worth something to you to have a guaranteed path to doubling your money. I mean, if you put in a $100 million of your own, you can get back everything you paid out in the lawsuit."

"Well, first of all, I doubt that any single investor is going to be able to take 20 percent of the offering, so the idea of me investing $100 million is off the table right from the start. On top of that, how do you think it would look if the owner of the paper that ran the story that crashed the IPO also did a short on the stock? I'll answer that for you—I don't think so.

"But I do agree with you that Guy Pearle is a threat, and a successful IPO will only make him a bigger threat. Here's what I'll commit to: I will loan you twenty million in exchange for 75 percent ownership interest in *Social Tech*, but I won't exercise that until at least two weeks after the IPO. The way I see it, if you really believe in what you're telling me, you'll be willing to put up the eight million or so that you already have on top of the twenty million I'm going to loan you. With that money, you can buy as much stock as you like, at whatever price you want. If things go the way you predict, you'll be able to settle within a few days of the IPO, and you can pay me back the twenty million and keep full ownership of your company. Anything else is upside for you."

"So, you'll run the story if I get you solid proof?"

Malcolm responded with a question of his own. "Do you think I would put in $20 million if I didn't think I would get it back?"

CHAPTER 10

"ARE YOU SURE SHE SAW IT?" GUY ASKED.

Sam Fischel and Brandon Leather nodded in unison, then Sam detailed the extent of their knowledge. "We know that the file was accessed several times over the past two weeks from the same IP address at the public library in downtown DC. We can't be sure who actually saw the file, but we're pretty sure it's either Lucinda or someone working for her. Heather Alston has told us that Lucinda sometimes makes her go to the library to gather information by looking at files on our servers. Heather says she saw this file and reported it to Lucinda. Heather has been working with us for some time now and she's been keeping us in the loop on what Lucinda is up to, but she has not been able to determine if Lucinda has personally viewed this specific file."

The file in question was an analysis, done by a summer intern from Georgetown University who had given himself the impressive-sounding title of "senior strategic operations analyst." Anyone reading the file quickly, without a detailed review of the footnotes, would conclude that the terrorist attack on ARP had done significant damage to IAU's financial standing. It would also be easy, after reading the file, to jump to the conclusion that there was a major discrepancy between IAU's SEC filing for the IPO and its own internal analysis.

After consultation with Nigel Winston and the legal team at Advanced Capital Placement, Guy had decided to lay a trap for Lucinda. There was nothing that prohibited IAU from war-gaming scenarios. The only requirement was that their public filing not differ in any material way from their own internal analysis.

The mandate given to the intern was to do a worst-case analysis of what would happen to the book value of IAU if everything that the company had put in place at ARP had been destroyed and the insurance claims were denied. The intern had worked hard on the project, giving it his full attention for more than two weeks. The end result was not surprising—it predicted an end-of-days scenario for the company. The ARP investment had been massive, and if everything there truly had been destroyed with no insurance to cover the losses, it would have been catastrophic for the company. The intern predicted that such a scenario would call into question IAU's ability to continue as a going concern, which was tantamount to saying that the company would collapse.

In reality, Guy had spoken to Salim Hadithi multiple times since the TAN attack on ARP and he knew from those conversations that none of the equipment there had been seriously damaged. Salim also reported that the Solar Powered Plastic Processing Plant was still in operation and bales of plastic were still being created. In short, everything was fine.

For good measure, Guy had instructed Salim to report all external inquiries about the attacks on ARP to him, and to wait for written guidance before responding. With the IPO coming, Guy had explained, it wouldn't do to have information getting into the public domain that wasn't properly vetted.

Salim reported that he'd received an email from Brenda Bullock asking how he was and wondering how things were after the attacks. Guy told him to hold off on responding until after the IPO, and Salim was more than happy to comply. After Brenda's meltdown on the trip to Agadir, he was in no mood to become pen pals with her.

To meet the requirement that internal analysis not deviate too far from the SEC filing, the intern's analysis was accompanied by a series of strong disclaimers making clear that the report was only a worst-case scenario, that the equipment in Tarfaya was fine, and that there was no reason to believe the insurance company would not pay claims. However, these caveats were contained on a slide that flashed across the screen only momentarily.

Sam Fischel had observed that whoever was accessing files had only been viewing them, not downloading them. He suggested that if the information were included in a presentation that was pre-configured to open in presentation mode, the viewer would see everything, but the caveats would be onscreen for only a short amount of time.

"But what happens if she downloads the file this time?" Guy asked. "She'll see all the caveats and figure out that we're setting a trap for her."

"We've got a plan for that," Brandon answered. "We had Heather tell her that the file contains tracking software that sends a message back to our servers if it's opened on any domain other than ours. The cover story is that it's a security measure that's being added to all of the files associated with the IPO so that nothing gets into the public domain outside of channels."

"Do you think she bought it?" Guy mused.

Across the Potomac, in Lucinda's seventh-floor office, it was becoming clear that the cover story was having the desired effect. Lucinda had summoned Heather Alston and Brenda Bullock for a late evening meeting. Even though Brenda had formally terminated her employment with *Social Tech* shortly after returning from Africa, she wanted to maintain good relations with Lucinda and readily agreed to attend.

"This analysis has been sitting there for the last ten days," Lucinda said, looking directly at Heather. "Why are you just now telling me that it's protected by some sort of tracking software?"

Heather could smell the panic on Lucinda. "I can't say for sure that it is," Heather replied. "Brandon was just telling me about the new system they're putting in place to make sure that nothing leaks out before the IPO. It's part of their compliance program for the quiet period. I couldn't ask about this specific file or he'd know that we have access to their servers. I'm just assuming."

Lucinda turned to Brenda. "This analysis is describing what would happen if everything at ARP were destroyed. You were there. Did you get the impression that everything was destroyed?"

Brenda was disappointed that she could not be more helpful. "I'm sorry, Lucinda, I just can't say. There was a lot of shooting and explosions all over the place, but I don't know what happened to the IAU equipment. Most of it was located in warehouses outside the main compound, and I never went there after the attack started. I just headed for the rally point and got evacuated straight from there."

"But don't you have someone you can ask?" Lucinda pressed.

"I reached out to one of the guys I worked with, but he hasn't answered my email, and I can't get in touch with him by phone or on Skype."

Lucinda knew that she couldn't reveal any more to Heather and Brenda. There was no safe path ahead. She didn't have all the information she needed, but she was out of time. For a brief moment, Lucinda wondered if she was so intent on getting the better of Guy Pearle that it was clouding her vision. Unfortunately, she was too close to the problem to understand how reckless she had truly become, and she persuaded herself that her actions now were more about reaping a financial reward than about destroying Guy.

Lucinda laid down a cover story of her own, hoping to establish deniability in the event that she was able to get the file and the resulting story caused the IAU IPO to go sideways. "Well, I first heard rumors about this from a reporter at the *Washington Note*. You may have heard of Arlene Tann. She's the one who wrote all of the stories about IAU and what happened in Africa. She seems to have an inside source of her own, and she'll either run with this or she won't. I was just hoping that we could act as a second source for her, so she'd feel more comfortable running the article. But, if we can't, we can't. Thanks to both of you for trying to be helpful."

Brenda had no reason to doubt Lucinda and accepted the story without question. Heather knew exactly what was going on but needed to persuade Lucinda that she had bought the cover story, too. "I read those stories. I hope that she does keep digging and gets to the truth behind all of this. Something is fishy. I can't put my finger on it, but there's something going on with IAU and this IPO. If the *Note* needs a second source, I hope they're able to find it."

Based on Malcolm's last warning, Lucinda knew that she would need to provide physical proof of the analysis. Up till now, she'd been relying on Heather to access the IAU servers from the public library, but that was no longer an option. There was only one course of action left. Lucinda had to make a trip to the library and take screenshots of the presentation to share with the newspaper. They were never going to run the story without solid proof, and she couldn't trust this assignment to anyone else. Lucinda had to do it herself.

When Lucinda showed the screenshots of the memo to Malcolm Rutherford, he viewed them without comment. Arlene Tann took notes on the main points laid out therein. "This is very interesting," she said. "I think we can do something with this."

After Lucinda left, Malcolm called Arlene over to his desk. He showed her a social media profile of a student from Georgetown University, whose profile matched the name of the "senior strategic operations analyst" who had written the report, and it even noted that the young man was doing a summer internship at IAU.

Malcolm said, "This tells us everything we need to know."

"So, do you want me to kill the story?" Arlene asked.

"No, I want you to publish an online teaser around noon on the day after the IPO. Use a headline that says something like,

'Mystery, Intrigue, and Deception Behind a Major Tech IPO.' Then write the full story, the real story of what's been happening—how Lucinda Hornbuckle tried to use this paper to engage in a personal vendetta against her former lover. Publish that late the following day."

Suddenly, it all came together for Arlene. As she started to leave, she couldn't help herself. She reached out and shook Malcolm Rutherford's hand.

When the IAU IPO happened, it was much larger than Lucinda anticipated. The company's valuation was still five billion, but the IPO covered 40 percent of the value, or $2 billion. If Lucinda had thought carefully about that that meant, she would have realized that the internal documents she had seen—suggesting that the total value of the shares sold in the IPO was going to be closer to $500 million—were wildly off the mark. If she had thought it through all the way, she would have realized that short selling twenty million against a five hundred million IPO might create some short momentum, but against a $2 billion IPO, that twenty million couldn't move the needle anywhere. Instead, she simply hoped that she could find someone who was willing to buy $20 million worth of shares at fifteen dollars a share.

When she saw the online teaser from the *Washington Note*, she thought everything was moving in the right direction, so she pulled the trigger.

She was somewhat surprised that the teaser did not have a more significant impact on the price of the stock. She had hoped to get in and get out quickly, but she knew she had three days to clear her short sale, so she decided to wait until after the full story hit the street. She was confident that Arlene's story would drive the price of the stock low enough that she could buy the shares to cover what she had already sold.

When Arlene's story went live the next day, Lucinda couldn't believe her eyes. Instead of crashing the IAU IPO, the article was a five-thousand-word expose of everything Lucinda had been up to for the past eight months. All the tricks, all the lies—everything she had done was laid out in gory detail.

Lucinda realized she was practically ruined. The stock was now trading at around twenty-two dollars a share, and she still had to buy enough shares to cover her short selling. Her only saving grace was that she had not done a short sale for the entire $28 million. She had used just the twenty million that Malcolm had given her after their last meeting and had held rest in reserve. She would need every penny of it now to cover her position.

When Lucinda called Malcolm, she was almost surprised that he picked up.

"I thought we had a deal," she pleaded. "What did you do? More importantly, why?"

"I wasn't able to recover all of the losses that you have caused me, but I was able to at least partially recover. Who do you think took your short sale at fifteen? It was me. As soon as you cleared the transaction, I turned around and sold all of those shares at twenty-three bucks a share and made a nice little profit."

"But," she stammered, "you told me that you were going to go short. If you had done that, it would have made a difference. The price might have dropped enough that I could have bought at fifteen and at least broke even. Now I'm ruined, all because you didn't go short."

"But I did go short—on you," he shot back. "I've never seen someone so completely obsessed with destroying another human being. It's clouded your judgment and made you do destructive things. Instead of destroying IAU, you've destroyed yourself and *Social Tech*, in which I now own a controlling interest. In light of what has been reported in the *Washington Note*, I don't see how I can keep you in place there, so as of now, you're fired. I've got a security team on the way to escort you out of the building."

Lucinda was shocked beyond belief. "Why would you do this to me?" she wailed.

"How do you think I got to be a billionaire?" he replied, coldly.

EPILOGUE

IN THE WEEKS AND MONTHS THAT FOLLOWED THE IPO, Guy Pearle learned to enjoy being the CEO of a publicly traded company. The pace was fast, and the work was intense, but it was enormously rewarding. And the value of his ownership stake in the company, when coupled with what he had left of the defamation lawsuit settlement after he gave 30 percent to Nigel Winston and paid all of his other bills, left him more than financially comfortable. So comfortable, in fact, that he briefly toyed with the idea of actually running for the US Senate seat from Maryland. But a conversation with Sam Fischel, who reminded Guy that Maryland was still a very liberal state—one in which Guy stood almost no chance of getting elected—persuaded him to steer clear of politics.

But that didn't mean that Guy gave up on having influence. The funds the company raised by going public made it possible to finance a whole raft of new projects, and IAU had never really given up on its groundbreaking work at Tarfaya. There were two major challenges that had to be addressed, but they didn't seem insurmountable. First, Guy had to come to terms with the Chinese–American Green group's participation in ARP. Following the terrorist attacks, the CAG essentially took over the operation.

They were doing it under the guise of providing security, but, with nearly all of the Westerners long gone, there was no doubt that they were running the whole place—and with a stern hand.

Even if Guy could sort out something with the Chinese, and he felt sure that he could, there remained the issue of security. TAN had been defeated somewhat handily in their first attempt at flexing their muscles, but it would be a mistake to think they had learned nothing from their encounter with the Marines. Guy was sure that, if and when TAN decided to strike again, they would not be pushovers. Whatever lay ahead for IAU in Africa, Guy would need to give careful thought to the growing influence of Islamic extremists in the region.

And Guy remained puzzled by his brief encounter with the billionaire owner of the *Washington Note*. He couldn't escape the nagging feeling that if Malcolm Rutherford did have a secret he was willing to pay $100 million to keep hidden, it was probably something that needed to be exposed. He didn't have a specific plan of action, and every time he brought it up, Nigel Winston warned him to let sleeping dogs lie.

One thing Guy didn't waste much time thinking about was Lucinda Hornbuckle. Her downfall had been remarkably far, and astronomically fast, but Guy felt there was some genuine karma in the way it had all gone down.

As summer turned to fall, Guy began to think about how best to commemorate the first anniversary of Janet's passing. He had been to her graveside many times and often took Peanut with him. Janet and Peanut would have gotten along well, and Guy wished they could have known each other.

When the anniversary came, Guy put on an outfit Janet had loved. He had purchased a special coat for Peanut and dressed her up as well. They walked through the cemetery together, following a path that both had come to know well. When they reached Janet's headstone, Peanut seemed to recognize it. She sniffed at the lettering and lay down with her tiny body pressed against the cold marble. She seemed to sense that this place was special to Guy, and she lay there quietly while Guy draped the leash over the headstone and knelt beside her, shifting aside just enough so he could place fresh flowers on the grave.

It took only a few minutes for Guy to update Janet on the drama that had unfolded over the past year, and it wasn't more than fifteen minutes before Guy knew he had accomplished what he came for. Plus, Peanut would get too cold if they stayed much longer, so Guy said his goodbyes and stood up to leave.

Just as he was about to turn away from Janet's grave, he looked out toward the fence that marked the cemetery edge. A small chickadee was sitting there. While he stared, a second, smaller bird flew down and took its place on the fence next to the first. Guy did his best to see if one of them had a larger black bib that would identify it as a male, but they were too far away for him to be sure. He reached down to pick up Peanut and the motion seemed to startle the birds, which flew away together.

ABOUT THE AUTHOR

DOBIE MCARTHUR IS A PRIOR-ENLISTED MARINE who later attended the Naval Academy and was commissioned in the Marine Corps in 1982. He attended Oxford University on a Marshall Scholarship, obtaining a master's degree in Middle Eastern studies, and continued his Marine Corps service as an artillery officer and Foreign Area Officer specializing in the Middle East. After his active duty military service, he split his time between politics—serving on the staff of two Republican senators and as a political appointee at the Pentagon in the George W. Bush Administration—and industry. He currently lives in Southport, NC.

Made in the USA
Columbia, SC
01 May 2022